ORIN: THE UTOPIA

Austin McClelland

Orin: The Utopia

ISBN: 978-1-7337559-0-0

Cover art created by Roger Creus Dorico

"What the caterpillar calls the end of the world the master calls a butterfly."

- Richard Bach, from *Illusions: The Adventures of a Reluctant Messiah*

This book is dedicated to my family.

Thank you for your support of my work and inspirations.

Table of Contents

CHAPTER 1: BROTHERS

The haunting wind hammered Orin's bones piercing the veil of ghost-silence in the snowy night. Taking a swig from his flask, he shifted his weight as he stood peering into the darkness of the wasteland. The air was crisp, the sky clouded, and howling noises floated over the nearest ridge. Orin stood facing the hill and let the crisp flurry blow through his stringy, coarse ash-brown hair waving below his shoulders. He directed his gaze toward Liam, watching the campfire dancing light across his face.

Liam caught his eye and groaned, "You've been doing that a lot more these days."

Orin gave a telling smirk and pretended not to understand. He thought he hid his flask from his brother rather well. "The drinking," Liam continued, "you've been drinking more often these days. I haven't seen you drink this heavy since mother died."

Orin figured Liam was correct in his assessment. It was true, he was drinking more often these days. Orin would wake up with a flask filled to the brim of booze and fall asleep each night with it emptied for several weeks. The alcohol comforted him throughout his day. He found the liquor made even the most mundane of tasks a little brighter.

Orin noticed the fire casting its radiant glow across Liam's face. His dark brunette hair was blowing over his shoulders in the wind. In this light, Liam reminded Orin of their mother. Liam had the same light green eyes and a jaw that protruded slightly outward from his gaunt cheekbones. Liam's flashing smile could brighten the mood of those around him.

Orin's rough leathery skin and long prominent nose with full flushed cheeks bore more of their father. His thick canopy of bushy eyebrows enshrouded his deep rust-colored eyes, with patchy stubble scattered about his plump jawline. Orin was tall, like his father. The years of helping various settlements with their farming gave him callouses on his rough-textured hands and feet. Orin shot his brother a striking glance and saw his olive-colored skin reflecting a rosy golden hue as firelight swayed behind the men.

"You sound more like mother each day," Orin retorted while maintaining his reserved gaze.

"I just don't want to have to bury you because of the drinking," Liam replied between mighty gusts coming down from the ridgeline.

"Well, don't forget that you didn't bury her." Orin snapped back. Liam winced and looked away from Orin back toward the ridgeline. When their mom died, Liam was out with Squad members, foraging for plants and berries. When Orin found their mother, she was clutching a bottle of gin in her right hand. She died in a shanty shed on the outskirts of a modest farming settlement they established some time ago. Orin found her while patrolling the encampment. With the Squad members' help, he decided that rather than allowing his younger brother to experience the pain of seeing their mother in such a fateful state, he would bury her a short distance from the shed. Orin made the fateful decision to bury his mother without his brother two years ago to this day.

Orin could see Liam's eyes tear up and placed his hand on his shoulder. "Look, brother, I fully know what I am drinking. Malted rye, and it's delicious. Hah! You shouldn't concern yourself with it. Perhaps it's an, what do they say, oh! An acquired taste!" Orin finished with a sizeable smug grin and took a light, playful jab at his brother's arm attempting to change his brother's mood.

Liam looked back, grunting while shaking his head, "if you didn't have me watching you, who would?"

Orin took another swig of the drink. The liquid burned as it flowed down his throat. He felt the soothing warming sensation enter his stomach, and a warm hazy feeling coursed through his body.

Shortly before their mother's death, Orin and Liam worked with the Squad of Liberty, helping pockets of people establish farms and other communities along the foothills. The Squad accepted the brothers while supporting groups of settlers, including their mother, grow corn, among other essentials. The Squad of Liberty was a humble group when the brothers joined. The group was now at over twenty members and climbing with each settlement they helped. For the Squad's service to these communities, they would accept any food or extra seeds from the harvest to pass along to additional hamlets. Their goal was to re-establish civil harmony across the Rocky Mountain front range.

"How are you holding up?" Orin asked desperate to change the subject. The howling gusts sent a simultaneous shiver through both the men.

"I've been thinking about what Atticus was discussed earlier this evening," Liam answered.

Atticus, a lanky man who appeared to tower over most other persons in the wasteland, was the Squad leader. He earned his right to lead the Squad after successfully defending off attacks from the Righteous Warheads during one exchange. There were many bands of mercenaries who sought to conquer for their own personal greed, with the Righteous Warheads being one of the more dominant forces. The way Atticus saw it, the Squad's mission was to ensure civility existed during these perilous times.

Orin raised an eyebrow maintaining his gaze on Liam. "You don't believe the nonsense about a utopia, do you?"

Orin pulled his dull brown leather coat closer to his body, letting go of a shiver as it swept over his shoulders down to his arms. The small thin hairs raised along both arms underneath his flannel as he adjusted the zipper on the front. The brothers both wore the same faded leather coats for years now. Good quality clothing was becoming increasingly difficult to find in this wasteland. Down in these settlements, which were far south of any significant community and many miles from the nearest large settlement, Ádyto. The ruins dotting the steppes were picked bare years ago by scavengers.

"What if there is something to it?" Liam inquired.

"I find it hard to believe such a place exists. I have never seen such in all my life. Probably stems from the rehashed stories, like those told by men of the old days before the war," Orin replied.

Liam was ever the optimist, entertaining stories of old. When rivers flowed elegantly over turquoise, and bellies filled with ale, Orin recalled.

Orin reflected momentarily on the stories Atticus told the brothers of the "war to end all wars." The bombs rained down from the sky with chaotic scorching fury. Many people instantly lost their lives, others within minutes, and most from sickness and disease brought about by the fallout. Atticus told the brothers of how ash covered the ground for decades after the war. Crops rarely yielded, and the pockets of survivors lived off canned goods and whatever soups they conjured. As a result, most storage facilities, processing plants, grocery markets, and other places to buy foods were subject to looting and pillaging by scavengers. Eventually, the ash cleared from the wind and thunderstorms over the decades. Life sprang forth from the ground covered in slag, soot, and dust after years of tilling and spreading what seeds they found.

"The Earth can provide what we need but cannot contend with man's greed," Atticus often said. It was now five decades since the last bombs fell on humanity's creations.

A gentle smile formed at the corner of Liam's lips as he looked over his brother's face. "It fills me with genuine hope that there may be a better tomorrow. A tomorrow where the world does not have a stranglehold on us. Where crops grow taller than my knees, where acid rainstorms do not cause boiling blisters, and where the meat goes untainted by the fowl of tumors."

Orin leaned his head back, raised the flask, and took two long gulps. The booze tasted earthy with a hint of malt. That was how he liked it, and he smacked his lips with satisfaction. Orin held the flask up and pointed it to Liam.

"All that dreaming must have you thirsty," Orin squinted his eyes and looked at his brother, "I suppose you want to quench."

Liam took the flask and knew it was a gracious gesture coming from his brother. Liam did not drink often. The excitement of thinking about this utopia left his mouth dry, and Liam was eager to subdue this with liquid. Liam took a couple swigs and handed the flask back to Orin.

"Thanks."

Orin clicked his tongue against the roof of his mouth while scanning the ridge. The fire crackled behind them and cast the men's shadows out before them. The watch rotated among the Squad each night. Tonight, the brothers were on the lookout.

There were dangers out in the wasteland, and many of these dangers wandered about during the night. It was not uncommon for a pack of coyotes or even wolves to walk close to the camp at night. An occasional bear did not strike fear in the men. However, some of these animals were feral from radiation exposure. These creatures were widely feared by settlers. Feral animals were aggressive, territorial, and often had an insatiable hunger. Often these animals had multiple diseases, and one bite ripping flesh could kill a man in days if not hours.

The last encounter the Squad had with a feral creature was still fresh in Orin's mind. These days, it was not uncommon for a pack of vicious coyotes to cross paths with settlers along the foothills. One feral coyote could turn the whole group rabid in a matter of days.

Orin reflected for a moment on feral coyotes that entered the campsite of the last settlement four months prior. The confrontation took place late in the evening with Orin awakening to shouts from the men on watch-duty. By instinct, Orin picked up his rifle and bolted toward the center of camp. Orin saw ten or eleven coyotes.

After a quick skirmish, the sounds of their yelps from defeat emanated across the foothills that evening. By morning, the settlement had not seen or heard the feral coyotes again. Orin counted himself lucky in that incident, and he understood that a single bite from a vicious creature could mark the end of his own life. They easily won the victory over the ferocious coyotes with no loss of human life, at least that time. Orin recounted encounters in which members of the Squad were not so fortunate. He knew that particular experience of victory without loss with the feral coyotes was not the norm.

As he reflected, Orin continued peering into the darkness while squinting his eyes and scanning the ridgeline. The brothers stood there in silence for a moment. The camp was darkened except for the campfire, which was burning to a smolder. They heard another howl over the nearest ridge. The bitter scent of campfire smoke lingered. A rabbit peeked its head out of a hole, its eyes producing a deep red glow from the firelight reflection. Orin watched the rabbit as it sniffed the air, searching for potential predators. The rabbit lifted its body out of the opening showing its matted lustrous fur and briskly hopped toward a nearby juniper bush. Orin noticed a third lingering howl coming from the ridgeline looming toward the west.

Orin cocked his head to the left, trying to identify if he could hear the yipping of coyotes between the howls.

"Wolves," Orin muttered casually as his heartbeat quickened while scanning the parameter.

Liam widened his stance and shifted his gaze steadily on the ridge from which the howling sounds originated. If wolves were to threaten the safety of those in the camp, it was the brothers' responsibility to ensure they alerted their fellow members. The Squad currently resided in a protected valley sheltered from the west and south by large fountain formation ridges. They were nestled on the outskirts of a local farming settlement. The settlement mud huts and tarped ruins were located a short walk to the east of the Squad's campfire and tents.

The wind produced a dust tornado swirling in a counterclockwise motion, passing over juniper bush where the rabbit concealed itself. The dirt plume dissipated almost as quickly as it began. Orin watched as the red-eyed rabbit scurried away from the juniper bush toward a fallen log up the hill out of sight.

Above the log, on the ridgeline, an obscuration appeared. Orin caught sight of it and squinted his eyes to sharpen his focus. He had difficulty discerning what the distant shadow represented and gave his brother a soft punch in the arm while pitching his head toward the ridge. Liam met Orin's line of sight and saw the shadow.

"You think wolves?" Liam inquired in a nervous voice. Liam was not much for confrontation, especially with the possibility of a feral pack of wolves within a short run's distance.

Orin tilted his head forward, "Aye, they are hungry."

He stole a glance over his shoulder and looked back at the camp. The only sounds heard were faint snores being carried along by the icy wind. Orin looked in the direction of the hanging food and noted they were in the air hanging eight to ten feet. At that height, the food should be out of the reach, but that wouldn't stop the wolves should they smell the fresh rabbits from the hunt earlier that day. Squad members stripped the rabbit meat from the bone and pressed with a layer of salts and a small pinch of grounded cicer to keep the insects and disease from contaminating the meat. After hanging the food in the dark, one could keep the dry-cured meat edible for upwards of several weeks. However, cicer and salts' curing process produced an overpowering stench, which created a honey trap for predators.

Several new shadows appeared in a line formation along the ridge's top edge. The brothers kept their eyes trained on these adumbrations. Orin could feel the steady thuds of his heart pounding through his chest and the icy rush of adrenaline coursing through his veins. The obscurations disappeared from the dark ridge's edge, almost as soon as they appeared. Orin cast his eyes to the jagged precipice left of where they saw the shadows and squinted hard. The light of the smoldered fire was fading quickly.

"Brother, we will need light if those wolves get closer," Orin whispered without removing his gaze from the ridgeline. Dense clouds matted the moonlight on this chilly evening. Orin had to rely on his acute sense of sound paired with his limited visibility. He dared not take his eyes from the last known position of the beasts. Liam agreed and said a curse as he ran toward the woodpile a few meters away before placing massive logs on the embers. Liam created a teepee with the wood over the smoldering charcoals before poking the embers with a stick to reignite the flames. The fire grew with ease, cackling while dancing as it consumed wood fibers.

The shadows moved down the precipice to the left of their previous location. Orin counted nine obscurations moving in a zig-zagging line down the narrow rocky crag. Orin thought the wolves appeared to be in a hunting formation and were searching for an evening meal.

Orin picked up his rifle, leaning on a stump and checked to make sure he loaded it with a full magazine. Satisfied upon seeing eight cartridges, Orin hoisted the gun and rested the stock against his inside shoulder. Orin peered down the rifle's iron sights and trained his aim toward the approaching targets, holding with the movement of the first few shadows.

Standing firmly with his barrel trained on the wolves descending in the camp's direction, he heard Liam return panting from the run.

"You think they will head this way?" Liam inquired between heaving breaths. Small clouds of moisture hovered in front of his face as he spoke.

Orin raised his bushy eyebrows and strained his eyes to see further into the darkness. The campfire cast shadows of juniper bush out toward the precipice. "They might," Orin said as he kept his sights on the moving obscurations, "but based on their formation, they do not appear feral."

"Should we alert the others?"

"No, alerting the camp may cause undue attention from the wolves and unnecessarily attract other threats. I think it's best we wait longer and see what they do."

The last thing Orin wanted to do was cause a stir among the Squad camp for naught; they would not let the brothers live it down. They may even put Orin on latrine detail, which he despised as a monthly chore. *Commotion may also attract other threats far more significant than hunting wolves*, Orin reasoned.

The shadows continued to come closer, enough so that the brothers made out the reflection of light bouncing from their beady eyes. The long muzzles of the first few obscurations took shape out of the darkness. The wolves continued marching forward with their noses pointed at the camp and tails lashing as they strolled down the ridgeline. Sounds from the occasional wild yelp floated over the muffling draft. The silvery-sand color of their coarse fur reminded Orin of the concrete on the dilapidated ruins strewn across the plains and steppes.

The wolves broke into two formations with five silhouettes moving toward the south and the other four moving toward the north. *They may head around the camp, or the wolves could try to flank us and feast on the rabbit,* Orin thought as he glanced toward his brother. The latter kept his gaze steady on the wolves heading north with his palm gripping the back strap of his 9mm handgun.

"Keep to the ones on the right and do not lose sight of them!" Orin directed.

Liam stammered a short word of acknowledgment. The wolves moved faster in two smaller formations, keeping a nearly straight line as they headed around the camp's sides. Orin felt his heart pound through his flannel as he turned to face the wolves heading southbound around the field.

He tussled to alert the camp. But if the wolves went around the encampment and avoided it altogether, he would inform the Squad to an unwarranted threat. Orin's pride would not let him make a hasty decision. Orin concluded it was best to continue watching the wolves.

The four northbound creatures disappeared beneath the sagebrush twenty yards from the camp. Their bodies' contours did not reach higher than the top of the brush, and they quickly faded into the darkness.

"I can't see them," Liam blurted out while pointing his gun in their last known direction.

"Find them quickly!" Orin insisted between gritted teeth with spittle flying out. Gun in hand, Liam jolted to the north edge of the camp, positioning himself in what he thought was between the wolves and the hanging bags of salted meat. Short yipping bursts of excitement echoed through the air above the relentless gusts. Orin watched

Liam crouch down into his position and waited until they made direct eye contact before turning back toward the southbound wolves' area.

The southbound wolves slowed their speed and moved further out of range from Orin's rifle as they moved around the camp's outskirts. Orin set his gun with the stock resting on the dirt while he clasped the muzzle with his right hand. With hands shivering, he took his flask out of his back pocket and, without removing his eyes from the creatures looming in the distance, took a long gulp. After replacing the cap, he hoisted his gun back up and pitched the stock against his shoulder while taking aim. The alcohol provided a soothing burn as it warmed his throat.

Orin studied the wolves pacing slowly downrange. The wolves would walk a few steps in one direction before pivoting in the opposite direction. The behavior of the wolves implied that they were waiting or watching for their next move. Sounds of excited yaps emanated above the bush as wolves stuck their noses toward the clouded moonlit sky. Orin kept his rifle trained on this peculiar pack and slowed his breathing. The light from the fire shone off their eyes and provided a sparkle to the hollow darkness.

These wolves better get on to where they are going. Otherwise, I will put a bullet in their mangy heads.

Branches from a neighboring juniper tree came crashing to the ground behind Orin. Orin whirled around to find three wolves fighting over the bag of salted meat now on the ground. The wolves appeared famished with mangled silvery fur clinging to their bodies like lichen to a rock. From ten yards away, Orin could count the ribs on these creatures. Teeth snapped as the wolves lurched forward toward the meat spilling onto the soil.

"Wolves!" Orin shouted.

Orin picked up his gun, pointed it at the nearest of the wolves, and shot the wolf in the face. The wolf immediately dropped to the ground with a crimson blood trail leaking out of a hole in its dense mane. Orin began hearing the Squad waking up by the sound of shouts rising over the howling wind.

Liam ran toward the two remaining wolves discharging his pistol in rapid succession. One wolf was hit twice and staggered toward Liam. The second wolf lunged forward and caught Liam's calf muscle in a terrifying gnash of its fangs. Liam's pant leg ripped from the canines' strength, and Orin could see Liam wince under the excruciating agony. Training his rifle on the wolf clinging to his brother's leg, he could not find a clear shot amidst the contest. Liam panicked and flailed his arms as he fought to kick off the wolf. Crying out, Liam gasped from the pain through clenched teeth. He twisted his body helplessly, trying to remove his calf from the clenched hungry jaws of the predator.

Orin aimed his rifle at the limp wolf and finished it with a shot to the sternum. Every member of the Squad was awake and readying the camp for a defense. Atticus dashed with his shotgun in hand and two of his loyal men, Gaspar and Marlow, by his sides toward Liam wrestling with the wolf. Once Atticus reached the beast, he immediately slammed the butt plate down hard onto the top of the wolf's skull. The wolf immediately unclenched its jaw and shook its head, trying to bear the sudden injury. Before the wolf could recover, Liam pointed the muzzle of his pistol at the top of the wolf's skull and pulled it. The wolf was dead upon the impact of the blast.

The sudden cracking of tree branches from juniper shrubs not far behind Orin caused him to turn his head. Orin puffed and squealed out in surprise. Five wolves were speeding toward him! By the time Orin could place himself taking aim with his rifle, the wolves were lurching at him with snapping jaws. Orin let off a shot just as two of the beasts came crashing down. The bullet did not meet its target, and Orin lost his balance, dropping his rifle and falling swiftly to the dirt. The two wolves stood above Orin, snapping their jowls, trying to strike at his throat. Orin used his arms to help fend off the wolves' relentless attacks.

Orin thrust his heels at the wolves biting his legs and clawing at his arms. He heard a creature yelp loudly in distress and glimpsed Marlow crushing his steel pipe into the ribs of a wolf near his feet. Marlow beat the wolf back several paces through the air with a resounding thud. Orin saw Marlow exert an overhead swing at another wolf, contacting the wolf's left eye, which ground its teeth into Orin's right arm. The wolf recoiled from the force and jumped away, sneezing and shaking its snout vigorously. The wolf yelped as it tried rubbing its nose with a gnarled paw.

Orin seized his opportunity and punched the second wolf attacking his arms and connected with a stiff right hook to the mandible. The wolf lashed again at Orin, narrowly missing his neck with its canines. Marlow lumbered over to the wolf and finished the job sending an audible clunk to the wolf's head. A mineral taste entered Orin's esophagus as he clenched his teeth to recover his strength.

Upon seeing the battle lost and their comrades dead, the two remaining wolves turned and fled toward the western crag. Atticus ordered the Squad to fire upon the fleeing wolves. Bullets did not connect as the wolves' silhouettes became more distant. Orin watched as they sprinted through the bushes toward the ridge.

Orin shook the remaining wolf off as it regained its composure from the punch to its jaw. Orin quickly picked up his rifle and surged toward the wolf, hitting it repeatedly with the gun's stock in a blind rage. Orin hit the wolf until blood splattered in tiny squirts covering the rifle and Orin's legs. Orin looked down at the wolf with its skull bashed open, fluids dripping from its holes, and grunted.

Satisfied with his kill, Orin acknowledged Marlow and saw Liam sitting and mending his leg with a bandage. Atticus made his way over to Orin and Marlow. Orin nodded at their leader as he walked over and firmly placed a hand on Orin's right arm. The pressure made Orin flinch somewhat, but he regained his composure promptly.

"Glad to see you came out of that one, Orin," Atticus said with a small bow of his solemn face, "but I have to wonder how a pack of wolves made it into our camp." His voice trailed off with a trace of disappointment.

"Apologies, Atticus. Liam and I were watching the wolves from the ridgeline, and we lost sight when they diverted amongst the brush."

Deep wrinkles formed horizontally across the leader's forehead, a sign of his concern. "You and your brother were on watch tonight. The responsibilities of those on watch-duty are to report any possible threat before the camp is attacked," Atticus pounded his fist to emphasize his last words before continuing, "how did these wolves enter the camp and tear the sacks of meat from the trees?"

"I told Liam to watch one set of wolves while I watched the other once they broke from the main formation," Orin replied after a slight hesitation. He was not accustomed to being in situations where his judgment was questioned. "The ones that entered the brush were hardly visible and snuck by my brother to make their way to the meat." He continued.

Marlow grunted, shook his head, and scolded. "Yer brother and ya need ta do better than ta let 'er wolves int'er our camp."

Orin caught Liam's eye as he sat by the tree, treating his injuries. Liam looked to be suffering from his pain as he winced while covering his leg.

"Thanks, Marlow, for getting them off me," Orin placated.

Marlow sneered and uttered something hardly audible before sauntering toward the campfire.

"Why did you not alert the camp before trying to fend off two packs of wolves between the two of you?" Atticus inquired, looking back at Orin. His eyes seemed to have a way of seeing right through a person's psyche to find the answers.

Orin shivered from a flurry as he shrugged his shoulders and sighed. "I thought they may continue on."

"The Squad does not wait until they are in the middle of a dangerous situation before taking action!" Atticus scolded, "by your hesitation, you risked not only yourself and your brother but also the entire settlement!"

Orin did not return an explanation to that statement but instead stared into their leader's cryptic eyes. He knew he should have alerted the camp of the wolves' dangers when they had noticed the creatures making their way down the ridgeline. Failure to warn the Squad had, in fact, created a dangerous situation and caused the rabbit meat to become tainted.

"It's that pride of yours, Orin," Atticus continued after a minute, "that pride of yours wouldn't allow you to make a call to the camp."

Atticus was right, and Orin knew it. "It was his arrogance!" Liam shouted over from where he sat. Orin shot Liam a penetrating look.

"Well, if you would have been watching your pack of wolves more closely!" Orin started in on his brother as he took a step in his direction.

Atticus held up his hand to silence them before directing Gaspar to provide Liam with Fern-leaf Lousewort to ease the leg pain. Gaspar tromped off toward the tents in search of the purplish native flowers.

The fire grew as it consumed massive logs placed in the pit by Marlow. Orin watched as the light danced and, after a moment, looked over to Atticus and nodded, "yes, Atticus, you are right. I will not let this happen again."

"Good!" Atticus proclaimed, pointing his shotgun toward the night sky. "Bless that those were not feral! Or it could have been much worse with the Squad having two dead bodies to contend with. It may be best if you and your brother take the evening to rest. We will need you both to resume work in the morning."

"With your leave." Orin picked up his rifle and shuffled toward his brother. He held out his hand and helped Liam to his feet. Liam took his brother's hand, wincing as he stood and hobbled a few steps. Even with the bandage wrapped tightly around Liam's leg, Orin noticed the spotting of blood underneath the cloth. Liam slung his arm around Orin's shoulder and limped with his brother toward their tarped tent. Gaspar met the brothers' several yards from the entrance and handed them the purplish flowers and a few pinnately divided leaves.

"That helps with the pain," Gaspar said as he tossed Liam a bag of the flowery mixture.

"Thanks," Liam responded. Orin clasped his shoulder, and the brothers headed into the tent. They sat on their quilts on the frozen solid ground and attended to the remainder of their injuries.

"What was that about?" Orin inquired of Liam as he took out his flask and raised it to his lips.

"I think your arrogance resulted in the wolves getting into the camp," Liam replied curtly.

"Perhaps it was, but you shouldn't have let a pack of wolves sneak past you either," Orin shot back.

The brothers looked at each other for a period before chuckling. Their laughter began in spurts and rapidly ascended into roaring maniac cackles as they sat staring at each other.

"I am glad to have you around Orin. That was a hell of a shot you made on the wolf tearing at my leg." Liam gave a slight smirk toward his brother.

"You held your own," Orin flashed a warm grin toward Liam, "now, let's get sleep." Orin tossed the empty flask to his feet near the rifle.

"Agreed," Liam said with a sigh, "I agree." He repeated softly.

The brothers laid down and listened to the gusts pulling their tarp strings from the juniper trees while the Squad's voices grew fainter.

CHAPTER 2: RIGHTEOUS ONSLAUGHT

The daylight pierced through tiny needles protruding from brittle branches of the weathered pine trees. Orin laid on the ground and moved carefully to avoid startling his prey. He winced from the injuries to his arms the previous evening as he deliberately progressed through the woods. The pressure from propping himself fingerbreadths from the ground made his limbs feel worse than the cuts and bruises he sustained. Twenty paces from the fawn, Orin needed to move a few more to trust his aim.

The sounds of petite twigs and pine cones crunched. Orin used his arms for leverage crouching low over the dead needles underneath to avoid detection. Orin cursed the fragile underbrush he contended with to reach his prey. Atticus once told Orin before the war, bushes, and trees were much sturdier. The remaining forage often succumbed to diseases and harsh weather, including periodic acidic rainfalls. It was common to find vast forests of dead greyed branches protruding from the Earth along the foothills, remnants of their former glories.

The trees in this area returned to a cyclical lifespan. Orin enjoyed the sight of life returning after so many years of poor survival. He had known death his short life, and the view of these pines helped brighten his mood. A smile formed in the corner of his lips as he thought of his brother.

Perhaps Liam was onto something with his hope for knee-high crops.

CRACK! Orin's knee landed on a hollow stick, causing it to disintegrate while producing the obnoxious noise. The fawn looked up from its grassy meal toward Orin. Orin stopped moving, staring back at the fawn while slowing his breathing.

Please do not run, please do not run, he muttered under his breath. The fawn's glossy charcoal eyes gleamed in Orin's direction as it deliberately chewed its meal. After a moment, the fawn turned its back to Orin and resumed its meal.

Orin whispered another obscenity, before reaching with his hand around his rifle to remove his flask. The flask was sentimental to Orin, gifted to him by Atticus during his eighteenth name-day. Orin slowly raised the container to his lips and gulped down a long sip while attending to the fawn. Carefully, he placed the flask back into his rear jean pocket. He wanted to avoid any sudden movements.

Orin reflected on the previous evening with the wolves. He could not believe he let the Squad down. Orin counted his blessings to come away unscathed during the fight. If they had been feral, he might not be crawling toward the fawn or even breathing. He took a moment to thank the Gods; his injury wasn't severe as he watched the fawn eat its meal.

Orin felt a tinge of liability and shame when he thought about how he lost trust with Atticus. The brothers looked up to their leader, admired him, even saw Atticus as a sort-of fatherly figure toward them. Orin vowed to not only replace the meat lost but also obtain double the quantity as a token of gratitude toward Atticus and the others for helping fend off the wolf attack.

Atticus ordered Liam to help the settlement with the final stages of growing the barley and corn. Orin despised fieldwork and would rather be out on his own hunting prey. Hunting provided Orin with time to clear his mind. Working in the fields, they gave him orders to complete sequential tasks. Orin didn't take kindly to authority as he didn't have much of a father figure in his life. Atticus was the one man he respected and would follow until the end.

Orin knew he had to take responsibility for his lack of communication during the previous evening. Providing food for the camp was the best way to do it. After all, who can complain when they have full stomachs? Orin did not mind the prickling needles that seemed to stick right through the inside jacket into his chest as he scraped along the terrain.

The sun descended over the mountain peaks looming on the western horizon, providing a myriad of colors as it retired behind a jagged edge. Orin hunted in a patch of groves on the ridgeline from which they saw the wolves the previous evening. He believed this to be one of this best hunting spots around because of the surrounding grasslands. From the wooded area, Orin watched across the grassy field for signs of movement amongst the patches of magenta-colored flowers dotting the landscape. The wooded area provided protection from constant buzzing and stinging of the enlarged wasps, which naturally hovered above sweet-scented flowers. Too many stings from the giant wasps in a short amount of time could make a person delirious.

When Orin was in a comfortable range from his target, muscles in his shoulders twitched, and his mouth went dry, so he paused to remove his flask from his back pocket. After taking a long gulp of the burning liquid, he loosened the strap holding his rifle. Taking a final swig to still his racing heart, Orin proceeded to screw back the cap before placing it back into his rear pocket. Orin reached for his rifle strap and hoisted it around his shoulder onto the dirt in front of him. He then pointed the barrel in the fawn's direction while peering down the iron sight.

Orin lined up the shot, ensuring that the three notches were horizontal. With the fawn in the sights and finger on the trigger, he was ready for his kill. He steadied his heart palpitations and took slow breaths to qualm the tremors in his hands.

A buzzing sound reverberated through the woods. The vibrating murmur sent an instantaneous wave of icy sweat coursing through his veins, and the world around him spun. The fawn eating grass made a squeaking noise as it hopped in the opposite direction into the trees and undergrowth. Orin heard the tone again, and another wave of chilling fear swept through him. He looked down to see his flannel thumping rhythmically away from his chest. He knew the source of the buzzing noise. They were horns. Orin remembered hearing them the day his father disappeared many years ago. Atticus once told the brothers to run the opposite direction should they ever hear those horns again as it meant certain death.

The trumpet blasts originated from a group known as the Righteous Warheads. Although Orin never saw their leader Kraken, he was familiar with the whispers around the campfire, speaking of his brutish stature and sadistically violent temperament. Kraken ruled by force, and his legion of mercenaries respected his authority. People knew the Righteous Warheads as one of the most tremendous savage troops across the front range. They swept over the foothills destroying settlements while looting supplies they contained. Once satiated, the Righteous Warheads would venture deep into the mountains. Orin was not sure where they lived. In this manner of pillaging and retreating, the Righteous Warheads have established a dominating force. It was common knowledge the Righteous Warheads allowed murderers, thieves, and extortionists to seek refuge among their ranks.

Orin stood up and felt a wave of fatigue wash over him as the Earth spun around him. Slinging the rifle over his shoulder, Orin tightened the strap, before running full sprint toward the Squad's camp. His attention turned to Liam. *How will Liam hold up against the Righteous Warheads? He is not a fighter! Those savages are ruthless and will kill him. I must get back to the Squad quickly!* Sprinting across the grasslands, Orin suppressed these negative thoughts as he darted toward the ridgeline overlooking the campsite.

When Orin made it to the ridge's edge, he looked out toward the settlement noticing a greyed haze rising. Settlement shelters were ablaze and gloomy columns of smoke plumed toward the sky. Orin saw flames bouncing across the landscape and tens of people running in all directions through the fields and campsites. He heard the deep vibrating tone once again, much louder than before coming from the eastern plains.

Orin stood for a moment on the edge of the ridge and listened to the commotion. From the Squad's defensive position, it was apparent Righteous Warheads were attacking the colony. Orin identified tiny shadowy figures running around the outskirts of the distant settlement. Gunshots pierced through the sporadic shouts and cries across the scene. Orin couldn't see much further than the fields because of the smoke debris. The ensuing chaos echoed across the settlement.

Orin raced over to the precipice and made his descent toward the camp. He ran down the ridge, conscious of his footing to prevent himself from falling. He stumbled over a small stone but retained his balance as his thoughts raced. *Is Liam, alright? What is happening? Is the Squad ready? What about the settlers? Is Liam with them?* Orin hoped that he would reach the camp in time before infliction befell his brother or comrades. He kept darting his eyes to the settlement and back to the rocks at his feet as he swiftly descended toward the Squad camp.

Upon reaching the edge of the camp, Orin scanned the site for signs of Atticus. He spotted Atticus barking orders at Gaspar and several other men by the campfire. Gaspar nodded and quickly ran over to the northern section of the establishment.

Deafening snaps and crackles of bullets soared above his head, shattering the air as they ripped through space, caused his ears to ring. Orin crawled toward the stone wall where Atticus and a couple Squad members were taking cover and exchanging shots with shrouded figures behind plumes of smoke. He slammed his back into the wall next to Atticus and took his rifle from his shoulder, firing a few shots at the intruders. The smoke was dense, and it was difficult to see more than several paces from their position. Orin coughed as the smoke seeped into his airways, and tears formed in the ducts of his eyes as he fired blindly over the wall.

"Where is Liam?" Orin shouted above the chaos.

Atticus peered over the wall before firing two shots with his own rifle. Orin could see the sweat and soot clinging to Atticus's face. Atticus tilted his head toward the barley fields and shouted, "Liam was in the fields when the fighting began. The thick of it is to the east of those fields. I have not seen Liam, but I am sure he is holding his own," several cartridges ricochet off the stone wall and into the soil, "your brother has a fight in him, Orin. Don't worry. Help me hold this position!"

"I have to find my brother!" Orin demanded.

Atticus shook his head, discouragingly, "your brother can hold his own!" Atticus waved his hand in a downward motion.

Orin ignored his command and followed the low stone wall along the western side's outskirts where the barley met the cornfields. Bullets continued ricocheting from the wall above his head as he crouched low and made his way toward the fields.

"Liam!" Orin shouted above the snapping gunfire, crouching low as he crept his way along the stone wall. After a dozen paces, Orin peeked above the stone while scanning the perimeter. He didn't see anything through the dense clouds of smoke from strewed fires.

Gaps in the wall allowed him to stop and listen for the sound of his brother's voice. Shouts from people commanding others and the occasional scream or groan as bullets met their targets echoed above the cracks and booms.

No sight of Liam, Orin thought as he leared against the wall. Pressing on, he tried to block out thoughts of Liam's possible demise while creeping his way south along the boundaries of fields.

Orin heard a loud BOOM and CRASH vibrating through his body as he leaned against the stone wall. Orin stole a look in the Squad's direction. He noticed tents flying in the air over the camp, scattering debris into the sky with tarps disintegrating from the fire. The raucous sound sent another chilling wave of perspiration through his body. His flannel clung to his skin as he sweated profusely. The constant shrill ringing in his ears dulled the shouts and cries from those around him.

If I go back now, I may not find my brother; he's got to be in the fields, Orin considered while placing his fingers against his temple and feeling wetness. He looked down at his hands and saw blood unsure if it were his as he felt no pain. A sickening feeling crept in his gut, and he felt nauseous as he held himself up against the wall. The stinging stench of rotten eggs floated in from the direction of the Squad camp. *Could it have been a bomb like those used in the war?* Orin remembered Atticus telling a story about weapons of destruction as if they were a legend long past.

Orin slapped his face as the world blended around him before resuming his crawl along the wall. Debris of pebbles and foreign objects flew through the sky, raining down everywhere. He methodically made his way searching for his brother. Gunfire shot across the cornfield directly behind the wall toward his position. He could hear the whirls and thuds as cartridges slamming into the other side of the rock wall. Orin's palms were moist, and his hands trembled as he crawled over stones. He felt his stomach tighten into knots high in his chest as he raised his arms to keep moving.

Orin crept toward a break in the wall and peeked over the edge at the cornfields covered in plumes of greyed smoke. Marlow swung his steel pipe at a few Righteous Warhead mercenaries, quickly dispatching them as the blunt object crashed against their skulls. A short and stout member of the Righteous Warhead charged Marlow, shooting toward the burly man with a small hand cannon. Orin watched as Marlow swung the steel pipe in a full circular motion resembling a windmill in high winds. The tube connected with the attacker's right arm, knocking the man's gun to the soil. Marlow stood over his attacker, making eye contact and sent the steel pipe smashing into the man's forehead. The Righteous Warhead mercenary twitched several times before he laid facing Orin flat on the ground. Orin could see the whites in the man's eyes and his tongue touching the Earth as the savage went limp.

The dense smoke around Marlow cleared as he swung his steel pipe around his massive body. Scanning the field, Orin saw his brother. Stumbling to his feet, Liam tried to stable himself before falling swiftly back to the Earth. Liam was hardly recognizable as mud-covered his entire body, and his hair matted down over his face.

"LIAM!" Orin shouted at the top of his lungs while cupping his hands over his mouth.

"LIAM! I AM HERE!" Orin continued to shout over the sporadic gunshot cracks.

Liam stumbled back into the mud again as he clambered to try to regain his balance. Marlow continued swinging his steel pipe toward additional members of the Righteous Warheads in the vicinity and did not appear to pay Liam any attention. Orin stood to get to his brother's recognition as a passing bullet flew inches from his neck. Orin instinctively ducked back behind the stonewall, his sweat dripping from his forehead and stinging his eyes. He used the sleeve of his leather coat, trying to clear his vision as rocky debris fell onto Orin's head from the top of the wall.

"LIAM!" Orin shouted again. Using the gap in the wall for shelter, Orin spotted his brother trying to regain his balance in the fields.

"LIAM GET DOWN!" Orin screamed with seemingly no avail as his brother repeated his attempt to walk.

Why is he trying to stand with bullets flying by him? Orin wondered as he tried glancing his head around the corner of the break.

The bangs and pops from the gunfire overwhelmed Orin's senses. He saw a few skirmishes irregularly, but this was different. The encounter with the Righteous Warheads terrified Orin as he continued calling toward his brother. Orin fixated his eyes on Liam and watched with horror as a bullet met its target in his brother's right shoulder.

Liam's body twisted, and his face contorted from the impact. Orin watched as his brother reached for the wound with his left arm before falling face-forward into the soft ground.

"NO!" Orin cried and climbed over the stonewall toward his brother. As he lifted his leg over the wall, he heard a tumultuous BOOM and felt his body flying. Orin landed on the firm soil with his head slamming against a slab. Orin saw a flash of brightness and felt solid stones covering his body as he sank into the mud. Sounds around him dulled away and soon became a distant hollow echo. Orin relaxed and thought this was all a dream as his world waned to black.

CHAPTER 3: WANDERER

Frigid heavy droplets of rain fell upon the side of Orin's face. He awoke, sputtering saliva into the pool of water collecting near his mouth. Exerting himself up with one arm, he arched his neck to look around, feeling a wave of exhaustion sweep him back to the ground with dizzying force. Orin laid in the mud, staring up at the sky for several moments, breathing laboriously. He swallowed droplets landing in the back of his throat and blinked profusely. The air stung with the smell of gunpowder and wood-burning with a tinge of crisp-sweet metallic odor, which Orin knew to be blood.

Silvery clouds hovered overhead with dense droplets of rain splashing down as far as Orin could see. The sun was not out today as the sky cried onto the fields. Rolling thunder clapped every few minutes lingering in the distance.

Orin's head pulsated blood abundantly into his temples. The rainwater splashed refreshingly on his face, neck, and hands. The rain dampened his coat to his chest and sagging toward the ground, weighing him down. Orin's legs itched and throbbed underneath his soaked jeans. The woolen socks on Orin's feet seemed to be moist but not yet soaked. Lifting a leg from the ground, he felt water pour from his boot splashing mud onto his face and hands.

Orin lifted his head up again and pushed through the brief flash of white light rhythmically coinciding with his throbbing headache. A slight persistent ringing in his right ear like that of a continuous high-pitched whistle left him half-deaf as he shook his head. It was enough to drive a man mad, assuming he wasn't already, he thought as he winced from the pain. A tinge of nausea swept through his stomach. Orin relieved himself, tasting the lingering sour bile as the acids spilled into a puddle.

Sitting up with his hands, propping himself behind him, Orin gazed around. He soon noticed the large chunks of charred stone gathered around him. One giant rock near his hands appeared stained like dark red wine. Puddles of dirt dotted the terrain every several yards for as far as he could see toward the foothills. Orin brought one hand up to his forehead and rubbed his face with a thumb and forefinger until the throbbing receded.

His hands violently trembled as he took the top off his flask. Rye dripped around the corners of his mouth and down his chin as he fumbled with the container. The vial fell toward the Earth as Orin watched drink spill onto the moist soil. He quickly brought the vessel back to his lips for another sip. As the warm sensation dulled the ringing in his ears, he used his hand to wipe his stinging eyes. His headache was subsiding with each pulsating thud.

Orin stood up, pushing off the ground with his hands and using his upper body for support. His legs were aching, and his knees popped as he stood to his feet. Scanning the field where he last saw Liam and Marlow, Orin spotted a dark shadow lying on the ground but could not distinguish distinctive features. Judging by its size, Orin assumed it was Marlow.

There were no sounds other than rain falling to the Earth with slapping thuds and occasional rolling of thunder. Orin loudly groaned as he shook his head to prevent the intense ringing. Every step ached and made his movement difficult. His legs felt as if they were dragging heavy chains behind him, and his back burned as though someone was poking a hot iron through his lower spine. Each step took a conscious effort as Orin focused on moving toward the field.

Orin picked up his rifle from the ground near the blasted wall and used a fingernail to scrape muck from its cavities. Water poured from the muzzle as he tipped it toward the dirt and attempted to brush off the miry rifle. He removed dirt from the strap before slinging the gun over his shoulder and limped toward the dark shadow.

Each step sent a throbbing ache from his knees to his lower spine. His arms hurt and were hard to lift as if he were carrying massive weights in both hands. Orin continued to press forward toward the lump on the ground. The fires extinguished their flames as they provided short hisses, pops, and gasps from the downpour of rain. Thick, pale haze clung heavily to the air in a fog that parted as Orin moved through.

Sauntering over to Marlow's body, Orin recognized the scraggily profuse beard. Marlow laid lifeless on the ground, and Orin paused to take a long look at him. Large rips were strewn across the dead man's clothing, telling of a melee struggle during the battle. Orin spotted pools of dried matted blood dotting the fields around Marlow along with bodies of several men he didn't recognize. Orin patted Marlow's pockets to check if he had any additional items of value he could use.

Upon closer inspection of Marlow's face, Orin noticed a dark hole in his forehead with a thin trail of dried gore that ran down the center of the man's scalp toward the ground. Other than the rips in his clothing, there were no cuts or bruises anywhere on his body. *To think such a brute of a man, taken out by a single cheap bullet*, Orin reflected as he sighed and placed a hand over the dead man's eyelids. "Sleep well," Orin whispered.

Not finding anything of value, Orin pushed himself up with his hand on Marlow's chest and looked around for Liam. Orin was preparing himself for the worst. Liam did not appear to be lying anywhere in the vicinity. Orin started toward the spot where he last saw his brother.

"LIAM!" Orin shouted.

Listening for any signs of a response, but there were no reciprocating calls, nor any acknowledgment that Squad members survived the battle. A crow cawed from a neighboring pine tree.

"LIAM!" he called again.

After a moment of gazing around in solitude, he walked through the cornfield back toward the Squad camp. Every so often, Orin stepped over a lifeless body of one of his former Squad members or a farming settler.

"Hello?! Anyone here?" he shouted with a crackling parched voice. His hands trembled as he reached for his flask and took a drink while walking around the field. His eyes burned and began tearing up as he stumbled over dead bodies and burned vegetation. Occasionally, he noticed a member of the Righteous Warhead group motionless on the ground. Orin would glance twice and even kicked a couple in the head to ensure they were dead as he walked toward the Squad camp.

When Orin return to the Squad camp, he noticed Gaspar and several other men dead on the ground. Rainwater continued to fall from the sky, pooling near their bodies. Orin made his way toward the stone wall where he last saw Atticus.

Atticus's body contorted in a pose a dozen feet from where Orin last saw him with one leg missing and a bloody charred mess sticking out from his pants' stump. Atticus looked at peace and more relaxed than Orin could ever remember seeing the man.

His eyes were slightly closed, and his mouth gnarled into a thin smile. *Death has a way of making peace of the living*, he thought as tears fell from his face toward the ground.

He knew Atticus most of his life, raising his brother and himself. Atticus gave selflessly to others and wished for humans to regain their once-prosperous nature. He always put other's needs before his, especially the Squad. Orin felt a twisting pain seize his heart as he stared down at his mentor. Atticus laid silently in a pool of rainwater covered in his blood and missing a limb.

Orin wasn't sure how much time passed as he knelt over Atticus. Standing up, he shifted the load of the rifle on his shoulder. Taking several moments to gaze around the battle-torn settlement, he let out a long sigh rubbing a thick hand across his dirt-covered face. *Where is Liam? Surely, he was right next to Marlow before the explosion. But where was his body? Perhaps Liam had survived after all!* Orin thought as he stood scanning the parameter.

The thought of his brother surviving sent a momentary sense of relief throughout Orin. *But if Liam is alive, did he escape the Righteous Warheads? No, it is unlikely, considering they shot Liam.* The dreaded thought hit Orin suddenly, gnawing through his core and sending his stomach-turning upside down. *They've captured him! They must have my brother as a captive!* A chill of terror coursed down Orin's spine, and his heartbeat palpitated quickly. He felt nauseous and placed both hands on his stomach while breathing deeply and focusing on a nearby boulder.

I must find Liam! Orin resolved when he collected himself. The rain relented, and the last of the smoke was dissipating from the air. The storm provided a pleasant refreshing smell across the Earth, replacing the stinging stench of gunpowder blasts. Orin stumbled around toward the lifeless bodies scattered about and searched each person for useful items. *The dead have no use for the living's treasures.* Orin looted several packs of ammunition, rabbit jerky, salted veal, and a shiny black semi-automatic handgun from his fallen comrades within the camp.

Walking the parameter of the settlement, Orin attempted to identify any survivors or additional items of use. Settlers scattered about lifeless in the mud on the outskirts of the field. From their contorted poses, Orin figured many of them fled the chaos and ensuing carnage to meet their demise on the camp's outskirts. The settlers had nothing of value to Orin on their bodies, and so he turned his sights toward the north. *Kraken and his men would have likely continued along the foothills.* Orin intended to follow the Righteous Warheads until he found his brother. He wasn't sure, but he believed that they would head northbound along with the front range based on their attack direction.

Determined to find Liam and avenge his Squad comrades, Orin stumbled across the remains and through the Squad's camp. He searched the area where his tent was pitched in vain, looking for any personal items or his back-up bottle of booze. He couldn't find any of their items as the tents were strewn about in tattered pieces, and the remaining elements of clothing were found in a charred clump. As Orin walked toward the center of the camp, a dark leather wineskin caught the corner of his eye. *That's strange, I remember none of the Squad members having this container for alcohol,* he reflected curiously.

The wineskin seemed heavy enough with liquid, and he removed the cap from the container to smell the contents. His sinuses cleared up as the sour mash wafted through his nostrils into his lungs. Orin replaced the lid and tied the wineskin to his waist using shreds of leather hanging from the bottom of his belt. The leather pouch hung and

flopped around until Orin tightened the straps snuggly against his thigh. A warm,

pleasant feeling swept through Orin as he thought about his fortune of finding a full

wineskin. Embers lightly popped as the fires in the camp gradually smoldered. The

stinging tinge of burning clothing and flesh filled the air as the rain subsided, and the

flames extinguished, releasing gasping trails of smoke.

Orin wiped his eyes with his arm and looked around for any final items of value.

He noticed several small cans of unopened food items on the ground around the central

campfire. He searched for a container to carry them. Orin identified a nearby tent that still

stood despite being burned on one side.

Orin walked over to the charred tent and lifted the flap to look inside. *Nothing but

an old cup and a dusty book.* These useless items wouldn't serve a purpose for finding his

brother. Orin dropped the flap and looked around the campsite.

Orin glanced toward another tent across the smoldering campfire. This tent was

not burnt but appeared trampled, with its contents bulging from under the tarp. Orin

walked around to the shelter and lifted the broken sticks, which propped the tent upright,

moving them to the side. Fumbling around in the mess of scattered pieces, Orin heard a

familiar crunching noise of a plastic bag. The plastic was caked in mud, and Orin flung

off the excess dirt with quick swiping motions. The container did not appear to have any

tears in it, and so he headed back over to the cans of food around the central campfire.

After placing several cans of food items into his plastic bag, he twisted it up to

eliminate the excess air. He then tied it to his belt buckle on his jeans, opposite of his

wineskin. Pleased momentarily with his craftiness, Orin stumbled toward the main cracked gravel road due north along the foothills. After several paces, Orin stopped and looked back over his shoulder at the campsite. Shaking his head solemnly and feeling a tinge of guilt seize his chest, he removed his flask and drank the remaining contents. As the spirits flowed down his throat, he welcomed the familiar lightness of his body and took a side step. Orin smacked his lips, tossed the container onto the cracked, and blackened asphalt, before turning to walk northbound up the winding road.

CHAPTER 4: PEOPLE. ARE. STRANGE.

Orin hiked for miles up the rough north road. Mounds of rubble heaps and rebar jolting out from concrete slabs lined the street. The amber-colored rebar tips looked corroded from generations of exposure to the sun, radiation, and heat. A brisk wind whistled through the cold evening air. Orin occasionally inspected hollowed-out vehicles representing immobile grave markers on the abandoned road for supplies. He found nothing.

His pace was sluggish as Orin sauntered along the winding route. The yammering howls of coyotes echoed in the distance. Rabbits scurried in the bushes when Orin walked within the vicinity. Orin kept alert for any sights and sounds of interest that would signify danger. From his years guarding settlements, Orin knew the major menaces along the road came from either enlarged insect hordes or thieves looking for an easy target. Sometimes it was both.

His hair flew across his shoulders in matted clusters as the mountain breeze rushed from the foothills. Orin was thankful this evening, at least, was not unduly cold as it were previously. Stars glimmered across the sky as Orin made his way along the route toward Ádyto. His intuition kept any uncertainties creeping into his mind, aligned with his mission of finding Liam.

Orin's moved his hand around to his back pocket, feeling for his flask. *It's gone! Where is it?!* Orin stopped walking and stood for a moment gazing out into the heavens while lost in his thoughts. *Where did I last drink? Was I drunk when I awoke?* Icy sweats crept over Orin's forehead, and his hands trembled.

I need alcohol! Orin looked down at the darkened wineskin and untied the straps from around the stalk. Uncorking the wineskin, Orin took a sniff of the contents. *Fermented barley and sour mash spirits.* The stench made Orin's nose crinkle, but he lifted the rim to his lips and took a large swig.

Floating in the liquid were small grains providing a grinding, abrasive texture making it difficult to swallow the drink. Orin found the taste rather satisfying and, after a few swallows, felt his trembles wane. Orin screwed the top on the wineskin and pondered going back to look for liquor or, better yet, his flask. After a moment, he decided to press forward, and so he continued walking along the beaten asphalt road.

When he heard another creature, he would crouch for a moment beside the nearest object until he decided there was no immediate threat. After wandering countless miles, he paused to eat the contents from one of the unmarked tin cans in his plastic bag. Orin took his knife from its sheath and stabbed the top of the can repeatedly to create a series of rounded perforation points. He used the blade's handle to break the seal inward and carefully peeled the lid off the can to expose the contents—pickled potatoes. Orin didn't blame the owner of the container for removing the label. *No person in their mind should seek to eat the contents of this container.* Orin's stomach turned, and he held in a tinge of queasiness while the pickled potatoes slid down his throat.

He felt dizzy and sat by the stump of a dead tree beside the road to choke down his tart potatoes, one pale oval clump at a time. Afterward, he lifted the container to his lips and sipped the liquid. The sour taste accompanied a wretched odor. *Leave nothing to waste* as Atticus would tell the young men. Orin tossed the can to the side and sat up sipping from the wineskin. After dusting himself off and collecting his items, he proceeded on his journey alongside the road meandering through the rest of the uneventful night.

* * *

The western foothills were bathed in ambient auburn lights across the rolling terrain. Sunlight spilled over juniper bushes, and Orin could see the silvery branches and the green hues of the thistles. To the east towards the plains, concrete ruins dotted the landscape of former dwellings. Navigating the winding roads north, Orin noticed the rubble heaps of concrete ruins becoming denser.

Relics from glory days of humanity, Orin reminisced. He never ventured this far north. Walking among the fields, ruins, and juniper trees created a sense of nervous bewilderment. A peculiar sense of calmness coursed through him as Orin sensed he was on the correct path to find his brother.

Ravens cawed atop decaying wood poles comprising metal spirals sticking out the tops. Orin heard the loud buzzing sounds to the east. His blood went cold as he saw monstrous wasps in the distance hovering above towering golden grasses. These wasps were territorial creatures and became vicious contenders if an unfortunate soul wandered too closely near them.

Orin edged along the pavement remaining hidden from the wasps and came across a vast yellow vehicle. The rubber wheel treads blew out long ago with serrated alloy poles in their place, and rust corroded the mainframe up to the dashboard window. Empty space replaced the opening where doors existed, allowing Orin to glance aboard. A wet, mildewed fragrance wafted from deep inside, lined with rows of coffee-colored leather seats. Dust floated effortlessly in the musty air while Orin paused to look longingly at the row of seats. He imagined people talking with each other inside this vehicle as it traveled along its route toward a destination.

What would these people be doing? Where would they be heading? Are they farmers? Orin lost himself in his fantasy before twisting his neck, snapping back to conscious awareness.

The vehicle was vacated, and Orin sifted through the first seat nearest the door for anything of value. Unique knobs and dials caught his attention on the dashboard, and he tried touching a few of the buttons with no effect. Scavengers made their mark by gutting the vehicle. Atticus taught the brothers to *never underestimate a scavenger leaving their own loot for other treasures.* Orin decided to take a closer look and slowly walked the aisle, checking each of the seats. Two rows of chairs lined toward the back of the vehicle, leading Orin to believe it was a large transport vessel. He wasn't sure how it operated as he never saw a car that wasn't rusted out and destroyed.

"What do yah propose we do with 'em, Jenks?" a man's voice cracked the silence of the morning.

Orin instinctively crouched low, remaining still. His heart started thumping rhythmically through his flannel. The palms of his hands perspired, and he cleaned them on his washed-out jeans.

"Take his belong' uns and leave 'em ter tha dogs," roared another raspy voice.

Orin's head pulsated from blood, rushing toward his temples. He leaned forward toward the floor to appear less visible while cursing the small windows dotting the vehicle.

"I say we have fun with the curious fella, Jenks. Hah!"

Orin lifted his head somewhat, enough to peek out of the nearest window toward the voices. Orin saw two men overlooking a pasty, hairless meager man wearing a tattered drab brownish robe. The man looked feeble as he crouched beneath the crooked pine tree with his hands folded out. Orin watched as the robed man's hands shook uncontrollably, and a pool formed near his feet.

"What type o' fun was yer think'n?" asked the raspy-voiced man while slapping the end of a metal bat in his palm.

He had a stocky nature with massive shoulders and several flaps of neck matted in wheat-colored hair. *This man hadn't missed a meal a day in his life*, Orin mused. In contrast, his companion was tall and lean with narrow shoulders supporting a sword hanging from his hips. Both men wore black ball caps shielding their heads and looked severely sunburned with patches of dried skin hanging from their cheeks.

Orin silently watched as the heavyset man lifted his foot back and kicked it hard into the pathetic man's ribs. The bandit lifted his foot and struck their victim repeatedly as the lean man giggled maniacally. The victim squirmed out of range from the approaching strikes.

The powerless brown-robed man curled into a fetal position and sobbed vehemently, "pl-please don't hurt me. I-I-I have nothing of value! I am just passing by. Pl-lease!" He fended off incoming kicks by putting his hands out.

The slender man shrieked shrilly, "o-oh, but we saw you rummaging among the ruins, didn't we Jenks?"

"Aye, that'er we did. 'Nd we ain't no fools! No," the man with the bat bellowed.

Jenks enlarged his chest, his long stringy hair clinging to the back of his ruff. Raising the bat into the air, the stout man wildly swung his arms while squawking like a feral creature.

"That's right, Jenks! And those are *our* plunder. Right, Jenks!?"

Orin's breath escaped him, and he realized he had been holding it upon first listening to the thieves. The two bandits had not discovered his presence in the vehicle. Orin wanted to help this miserable fool from being persecuted. Still, he likewise didn't know how well-armed they were or if they brought comrades. He remained inside the transport, watching the commotion through a narrow slot.

"You! What d'ya find?" The emaciated bandit asked, pointing a skeletal finger at the huddled person.

"I-I found no-nothing! I swear it! Please!"

Jenks tilted his head down toward the robed man as if examining him for a moment. The heavy man extended his arm, swinging the bat sideways to beat the robed man. The robed man clutched his arm and snorted.

"Please! I pray to you, please! I have nothing! I am no one," screeched the veiled fellow.

"I expect he's lying to us, Jenks!" shouted the lean man, "let's shake 'em down and see what he gots!"

The husky man complied and whirled the bat again, connecting the metal to the man's femur. Orin heard a resounding thud as the weapon struck its mark. The slender bandit continued his merry behavior while removing his sword from its sheath.

"Owww! Please, no more! I-I-I am speaking the truth, I swear it!"

The gaunt bandit pointed his gleaming sword toward the sufferer, "well, we'll just see that, now won't we?"

He used the weapon to tear the bottom of the man's garments, stabbing inward nearly missing his limbs by inches while swiping downwards. The blade struck against rocks between the hairless man's feet. The missed strike sent the bandit stumbling for a moment, causing his stringy hair to fall forward from his ballcap. The bandit staggered backward and, with a swift motion, swept the hair aside from his eyes while leveling the sword point toward his victim's torso.

Orin felt a knot form in his gut as he stared at the vulnerable man being struck. *I can't just stand by and watch this man get butchered,* he conceived. Placing one hand on top of the nearest seat's headrest, he reached toward his side and untucked the handgun he held in his waist.

Lifting the handgun gradually so as not to alert attention, he pointed it out the window, straight at the large man with the bat.

This gun weighs as much as Marlow, Orin reminisced. He steadied his aim as the thin bandit pointed the sword toward the robed man. Orin cocked the semi-automatic handgun's hammer and readied his aim on the more significant target with the bat.

The bandits heard Orin cocking the gun and spun toward his position. Orin watched as the lean bandit's eyes widen. Orin's knees and fists shook as he raised his arm to the portly man's center mass. His blood ran chill as he stared back at the bandits who sneered at him. Their gaping black smiles sent a shiver cascading through Orin's spine.

"What have we here?"

The stocky man grunted and said, "looks like we got us 'nuther 'un!"

43

Orin shot his pistol, missing both bandits and hitting the dirt several paces away. He muttered a curse as he trained his aim on the target. Orin squeezed the trigger, releasing a successful strike to Jenks' abdomen.

The thin bandit roared before sprinting toward the vehicle stooping his head while shaking his sword. Jenks dropped his bat, clutching his stomach before stumbling a few feet back and falling. The stocky bandit released audible gasps while hurling with each exhalation.

Orin kept his handgun trained on the thin bandit as he dashed toward the side of the vehicle. He fired another shot at the small man shattering glass in the window but again missing his target. As a result, the bandit flung his body against the transport and bent low to remain out of Orin's sight.

"JENKS! You a'ight?"

Orin glimpsed over to see Jenks contorting on the dirt while seizing his abdomen with both fists. He rotated his body while propelling his legs in the air with each cry of agony. The man choked and lifted his hands, revealing a deep red puddle forming in the front of his tunic.

"I'm shot," Jenks cried, "that 'un shot me."

Orin moved away from the window as the bandit darted around the back of the vehicle. The thief was soon out of sight as he made his way around the side. Orin aimed his handgun out the busted opening toward the stocky man on the ground and fired again. Direct hit. The man jerked before slowly twitching his limbs. Orin watched as he twisted his head to face the vehicle with his mouth hanging open in a bewildered grimace.

"You'll pay for that," the thin robber shouted while sprinting, "I'll get 'em, Jenks. I swear it! I will kill 'em!"

Orin listened to the bandit's feet, kicking up pebbles while rushing toward the vehicle entrance. Orin kept low in the center, training his handgun toward the vehicle's door. His hands shook, and sweat fell from his forehead, stinging his eyes. Orin briefly lost his balance, and his knee slammed into the floorboard as his wineskin weighed him down. He shifted the weight of his rifle across his shoulders while snubbing the tingling sensation in his calves as circulation cut off from his crouched position.

Thunderous pounding noises echoed through the vehicle as the thin bandit made his way up the entryway steps. Orin tilted his barrel to meet the top of the man's head above the front seats. Glass splintered into numerous shards as a bullet sailed through the cracked front windshield. Orin's ears began a symphony of ringing from the shot. He placed a hand toward his temple to try silencing the sudden burst of light.

"Is that all ya got? Heh," the bandit paused and coughed, remaining behind the front seat, "I'm gonna enjoy skinning you alive."

Orin saw him waving his sword above the seat. He kept his handgun trained down the aisle toward the bandit while using his other arm to wipe sweat from his eyebrow. Time slowed as Orin felt the measured thud of his heartbeat. He became lightheaded and trembled more.

I need a drink, he thought as he ran his tongue across his dry, cracked lips.

Orin saw as the bandit moved his hand to grip the top of the seat, turning his sunburned red fingers a milky pale. The forceful thrusts with his sword, stabbed toward the roof of the vehicle. The man's howls reverberated through the automobile as he raced down the middle aisle toward Orin. Orin squeezed the trigger. A bullet soared over the bandit's shoulder and out the front windshield.

Orin swore while steadying his trembling hand, squeezing the trigger again. The bandit contorted his body as the cartridge punctured the bone in his arm carrying the sword.

"Ouch!" The bandit blurted as he looked at the hole in his arm. The bandit glanced back at Orin and snarled while lurching forward and using his free hand to guide his sword. Orin fired his weapon a third time and heard an exhausted clicking noise. *Out of ammo*. Scanning quickly, Orin tossed the handgun at the thief, knocking him in the eye.

The bandit closed the distance toward Orin. Orin knocked the blade swiftly to his side while simultaneously hitting the bandit's hand into the nearest seat. Orin quickly thrust his right elbow toward the bandit's head, knocking him into a forward, bending position. Kicking at the weapon with his leg, Orin sent an uppercut, sending the slender man staggering. The sword clattered to the floor while the robber fell to his knees, sputtering out chipped teeth, phlegm, and blood.

The bandit spat blood drool toward Orin's feet before gradually shifting to match his gaze. Orin thought the man wretched as he knelt before him with an imploring gaze. Orin smelled the stench of ammonia waft through the confined hollowed vehicle.

"Please don't kill me," the bandit whispered as he spits more blood onto the floor, "please, don't." The man pleaded, shaking his hands and swaying on his toes.

Orin stood for a moment staring at the bandit. He put his boot onto the sword and swung his foot backward to bring the hilt closer to his reach. Orin lowered his torso toward the ground and stretched for the sword.

The sunlight gleamed from the sturdy sword as Orin gripped the crossguard. Orin pointed the acquired weapon toward the bandit and produced a broad grin showing his yellowed teeth. A burst of adrenaline surged through Orin as he realized his power over the supplicating bandit.

"Please," the bandit susurrated while shaking profusely.

Orin breathed deeply and held it in as he heaved ahead with a firm thrust. The sword's tip punctured the bandit sliding through his skin like butter. Orin heard a crunch as he pushed the weapon into the man's abdomen.

The bandit recoiled, wheezing in wide-eyed horror as he fell face-forward in the aisle. Orin kept the weapon in the bandit and watched as blood dribbled from the wound pooling onto the floorboard, near the man's face. He sighed, releasing his breath while looking back out the window toward the hairless man.

A loud groan arose from the man nestled beneath the tree. The miserable fool spun and moved his legs out before him as if trying to stand. Not far away, the stocky robber lay flat on his back with his fists unclenched. Orin watched for any movement, but the bandit laid still.

Stepping over the bleeding thief in the vehicle, Orin left the pistol and stepped outside. He walked over to the fellow gathered beneath the rotten tree while rubbing his moistened palms on his dirty jeans. The brown-robed man puffed and grimaced as he held his ribcage.

"Don't move," Orin said.

He glanced toward the corpulent bandit while picking up the bat and using it as a cane. Orin stared at the big bandit with his scraggly beard and sad expression while picking his tongue. He poked the large man with the end of the bat. The bandit appeared drained and exuded with his tongue stretching to the dirt. A dark crimson stain formed in the center of his shirt, and a mass swelled from the man's wound.

"Th-th-thank yo-ou!" the robed man gasped.

This guy needs help, Orin mused as he glanced over the wretched robed man. He reeked of sour milk and musk. Orin knelt near the robed man and grimaced to keep from inhaling the foul redolence. He extended his hand toward the feeble haggard man.

"Orin. What is your name?"

"Libiditus," the man gasped, shifting his weight and taking Orin's outstretched hand, "that was some decent shooting. Oh-oh, yes!"

Orin held Libiditus firmly while lifting him to his feet and using the bat for stability. Libiditus clutched his ribs with his left hand and dusted himself off with the other. Libiditus next wiped dirt from his robe sleeves hastily.

"Not my finest, but it got the job done."

The hairless man brought a heavily matted sleeve up to his eyebrow to remove a droplet of sweat. The man's pasty skin clung tight to his face, and Orin noticed his emaciated frame. Libiditus wore deep wrinkles sprouting from the ridges of his cerulean eyes. His skin flayed away from the top of his head in thin sheets, separating to float in the breeze.

The beefy man on the ground seized. Orin looked down toward the bandit clutching his abdomen and tossing his arms uncontrollably above his head. The bandit heaved and audibly groaned numerous times.

"Yo-o-ou," the hoarse voice called, pointing toward Orin.

Orin swung his bat in a powerful arch and connected with the bandit's skull. *Clunk*. The man's eyes circled back, and his head rotated to face the hollowed tree—a deep purplish swell formed from the impact of the bat on his head. Deep gurgling sounds erupted from within the bandit's throat as he choked on his final breaths.

Libiditus turned and plucked up a leather handbag, tucking it beneath his robes. He glanced up at Orin, cracking a brief smile and winking slyly. Libiditus dusted off the bottom of his robes, wincing as he tightened his cloth sash.

"Where are you off to?" Libiditus raised a hairless eyebrow.

"Searching for my brother."

"Oh, and where might your brother be?" Libiditus prodded.

"I am not certain; I suspect he headed in this direction."

Libiditus bowed his head and tilted his face. Orin kept his responses short as he did not want to provide the stranger with too many details. There was something about the fellow that seemed unpredictable. Atticus repeatedly said, "*be wary of other's intentions while expecting the good.*" It was a philosophy Orin tried his best to follow. He missed the Squad, and his brother as a tinge of grief stabbed his chest.

Orin shifted the bat and used it as a cane again. He had never seen a man as fair as Libiditus and was perplexed. Even his lips appeared a pale shade of rose. Orin thought the man seemed to have never been in the sunlight. *Perhaps he lives in a cave along the foothills*, Orin conceived.

"What about you?" Orin asked, breaking the abrupt silence.

Libiditus did not promptly reply. Instead, he reached into his leather pouch hanging at his backside to remove a large chunk of hard bread crust. He broke the bread into two sections and offered one to Orin, who accepted without hesitation. Orin squeezed the food in his hand, trying to soften it.

"Figured you might be hungry after saving my life. Let's break bread," Libiditus said.

Orin tilted his head and devoured the bread taking many large bites in rapid succession. The sustenance was hard and crunchy, hurting Orin's teeth as he bit through the stale crust. There was no taste, and Orin relied on his saliva to finish moistening the bread to choke down a swallow. He removed the top from his wineskin and chased the dry mouthful with grainy spirits.

Orin thought it odd this peculiar robed man would be out here alone. The chances of surviving these harsh elements alone were no easy feat, and Orin held suspicion for lone wanderers. Often, they were scavengers and not thieves or beggars. Choosing to forage for survival rather than stealing possessions or relying on the generosity of others. Most were harmless vagabonds trying to scrape by an existence. Besides, he didn't see this frail man posing much of any threat.

Both men stood staring at the concrete ruins while gorging their bread chunks. The sun burned hot on the Earth as it approached midday. Wasps noisily buzzed while hovering above wild golden wheat fields in the distance. They were too far away to notice the men standing under the rotting tree, eating their lunch.

Flies swooped in over the dead man humming a low hum. Orin waved a few off as they tried to descend on his bread. These flies were small, but Orin once saw a fly as large as his wineskin.

"So, what brings you around here?" Orin asked.

"Exploring for items of value in these abandoned structures," Libiditus said, waving his arm at the adjacent landscape.

"Are you a lone wanderer?"

"Nay. I have a group just west of here away," Libiditus gestured with his hand toward the area of the foothills, "aye, but oh yes, yes! You should come with me! Yes! We have shelter and food! Come with me and rest a while!"

Orin stood, examining the hairless man. He reflected on his current situation. *Earlier I was alone in my search for Liam. But I may eventually run out of food and drink. A resourceful companion may prove useful in finding my brother.*

"And what exactly do you people do?"

"Ah, good question! It is! Well, we have created what I like to call a utopia of sorts. We have no illnesses, diseases, or poisonings. We have a private shelter near here. Penumbra is praised, we keep to ourselves while foraging food and other items to survive these wastelands." As he spoke, the bald man waved his loaf around in exaggerated motions.

Orin stood watching the man and finished the last of his meal, wiping his hands together afterward. The talk of utopia brought back memories of his conversation with his brother the night the wolves attacked the Squad. Orin's gut reaction told him following this curious man was his best course of action. *It couldn't hurt to see what these people are about. They promise food and shelter for the night.* After he finished his meal, he slightly angled his head and put his hand on the robed man's shoulder.

"You had me at utopia. Let's be off before sundown," Orin stated resolutely.

Libiditus clapped his hands together in agreement while rocking on his heels. He made short shrieks of excitement as he looked toward the foothills behind them. The buzzing of flies grew louder as more joined the fray over the lifeless man.

"We should head back toward the shelter. They will expect us."

"Us?" Orin inquired.

The bald man chuckled before equivocating, "oh, uh us? No, I meant me! heh."

Orin shrugged off this utterance and gestured for Libiditus to lead the way. The sun continued westward toward the mountains while bathing the landscape in glimmering gold. Rabbits darted among the grain fields while the wasps floated toward the north. Orin and Libiditus turned west onto the damaged road to the foothills and followed the hot midday sun.

CHAPTER 5: PENUMBRA

The men walked for hours along the cracked pavement in silence, interrupted periodically with occasional remarks. Juniper trees and sagebrush dotted the region. The breeze blew billows of dust tornadoes every so often twisting around wildly until dissipating into the gust. The air became colder as dusk crept gradually over the eastern plains turning the skies a deep shade of indigo.

Coyotes broke the silence in the distance as the men walked toward a set of concrete ruins several paces away from the road. Chunks of debris blasted from the original structures laid covered among the towering grasses. The light became faint, and it was tough to identify the concrete masses to avoid stumbling. Furniture silhouettes appeared along a crumpled wall of the ruin. A mineral smell hung heavy in the air reminding Orin of the stench of dried blood. The breeze picked up, rushing down the foothills, sending Orin's brown oily hair floating in the air. A few flies lingered in the area, wavering in the wind.

Libiditus led them to a square hatch door protruding from the center of these ruins. Pulling the handle firmly, Libiditus led them to an underground bunker. A rusted set of stairs hung to the side of the opening. The door produced an audible screech sounding like a dying fawn.

Surely, any bandits around here would now know our position, Orin thought.

"I'll go first and let the group know we are here," Libiditus stated with a chuckle, "wouldn't want them taking you as common rabble or bandits, now would we? Oh, oh!"

Orin shivered and maintained a watch. The hairless man clambered down the stairs and disappeared below the structure within seconds. Orin noticed a faint flickering of fire deep within the cavity and listened to murmuring voices. He stood there, surveilling the landscape, seeing the decayed cement ruins around him. Massive slabs dotted the proximity as if these ruins were separated during a blast demolishing the area.

The wind blew gently, and he could hear the whoosh of the sagebrush. Condensation from his breathing appeared as he exhaled warm air. He vigorously rubbed his palms to maintain the warmth while the muffled voices discussed something inaudible over the breeze.

"All right, Orin!" Libiditus called while slapping the surface of the metal container twice.

Orin shifted the weight of his rifle to make it straight before clutching the ladder rails while progressing downwards. He descended enough to swing the hatch opening shut and continued down the stairs. It was slower going than Libiditus, who seemed to slide down the ladder rungs with familiar ease.

Once at the bottom, Orin saw Libiditus and several others dressed in similar tattered brown garments, each with clean, shaven scalps. Orin looked the crowd over swiftly as he stood before them. There was nothing too surprising about these people other than slightly different facial features. One of them was a female with her head shaved and characteristic feminine traits, including her slender jawline with a sharp nose and chin. The other two were males, one of them exposed a long scruffy black goatee with round plump cheeks and the other clean-shaven with a five-fingered forehead. Orin shivered as dull brown eyes stared back at him while the female stepped forward with her palms clasped together in a prayer formation.

"I am Zara," the woman announced with a slight tilt of her head followed by a bow, "allow me to welcome you to our sanctuary. We are the Children of Penumbra."

"Praise Penumbra," the group responded.

"To my right is Perikles," Zara turned her head toward a gaunt, pale man.

Perikles placed his palms together in a prayer formation while maintaining eye contact as he nodded. Firelight in an adjacent room reflected off the sweat from his head.

"And to my left is Elliot. He is our wonderful chef," Zara gestured her left arm toward the man standing somewhat behind her.

Elliot put his chubby fingers together while providing a modest acknowledgment. As he bowed, his long goatee clung to his gown cincture, which protruded awkwardly from his barrel-shaped chest. Orin examined each of the four robed characters.

What have I gotten myself into? He marveled as he breathed the pungent, sour milk, and musk odor. The stench was robust, and Orin tried keeping composure while accepting their receptions. A recurring drip echoed throughout the chamber beyond the narrow hall. His mouth became dry as a cotton pad, and he clicked his tongue on the roof of his mouth to help generate saliva.

"Praise you for the pleasant welcome," Orin paused and managed his yellowed grin, "I am Orin."

"Penumbra welcomes Orin," the group chanted with matching expressions.

"It is absolutely our pleasure," Zara's deep eyes peered through Orin, "Libiditus told us of your heroic feat. Why don't you stick around a while and share details with us over tea and stew?"

"With pleasure," Orin responded.

Libiditus placed his hand on Orin's back between his shoulder blades, grinned, and waved him toward the next room. Orin followed the four robed persons into the adjacent area with the bright blaze. It was a sizeable windowless chamber composed of massive concrete cinder blocks. In the center of the room, two men stoked a campfire enough to heat several rooms. A hole in the middle of the ceiling guided the cloudy smoke trail away into the twilight sky. A ring of several heavy stones foraged from the foothills restrained the flames.

A collection of metal shields and weaponry hung along the surfaces of the room. Orin noticed specks of dried blood splattered across many of the guards and weapons. Mud-tattered fabric draped loosely over the shields. Dark green soot lined the walls below the weaponry. Orin noticed in one corner; a corridor led to additional dimly lit rooms. The chamber gave an overwhelming pungent odor of musk, pinewood, spoiled milk, and roses.

The men in the heart of the room rested on wooden stumps. There was nothing exceptional regarding these additional robed figures. One was a muscular and clean-shaven black man with a long neck. The other wore a long beard hanging to the concrete floor covering his sun-burnt skin. Orin could not help noticing a large gnashing scar running across the unshaven man's face.

Perhaps he grew the beard to cover the injury, Orin thought while examining the two persons.

"These two are Fasile," Zara said as she pointed to the clean-shaven man.

The dark-skinned man stood up to face Orin before placing his palms together in a prayer formation. The fire crackled and danced a light around the room.

"And, Denk," Zara continued as she gestured over to the unshaven man.

Denk provided a hoarse grunt before asking, "and you are?"

"Orin.," he said firmly, "it's a pleasure. Thank you all for allowing me to join you for the evening meal."

"Penumbra welcomes Orin," the group echoed.

There was something about the manner with which the group intoned the word simultaneously that made Orin suspicious. He was not used to group members acting in unison. In the Squad, there were several diverse personalities with differing mannerisms that happen to operate efficiently enough to protect vulnerable settlers.

Zara gestured toward various vacant seats around the fire. Orin walked over to a log nearest Denk while the others sat next to him. Elliot leaned against a wall expressionlessly, gazing into the light. Orin rested his rifle and plastic sack on the floor near his boots. He fumbled with the wineskin cork and took a long whiff of the stinging fermented aroma. As the booze poured down his parched throat, Orin took a moment to appreciate this fantastic find.

I don't know what I'd do without it, he thought as the warm buzz filled his brain.

A continuous drip from an adjoining room and the crackle and pop of the fire broke the silence. Orin studied the faces of these people as he wriggled on his log. Each person appeared absorbed in thought, unaware at least for the moment, Orin was with them.

Denk stared into the fire, occasionally stroking his long goatee falling over his potbelly. Orin offered the wineskin to Denk, who shook his beard forcibly without removing his eyes from the fire. Libiditus also refused when offered the drink.

"Thank you, Orin, oh yes," Libiditus said, "but kindly, we do not drink devil's swill, no, no! No offense! We cannot accept such an offer; it would be sacrilegious!"

Orin saw the fire dancing across Libiditus' dull eyes. *Libiditus seemed to be in a relatively happy mood despite being beaten a few hours ago.* He leaned backward with his wineskin while having another long drink. He realized he wouldn't be able to stay here too long if these cultists didn't drink. *Perhaps just for tonight to get some much-needed rest in a shelter and then head out at first light,* he considered.

"Orin, why don't you describe yourself?" Zara asked, "the proper thing for a guest to do would be to provide us with insight. A backstory, perhaps? Hmm?"

"I don't have much of a story to tell."

"Everybody has a story of consequence to others. We are ready to listen to yours."

Orin took a swig out of the wineskin. He glanced at the others who were keenly observing him, waiting for his response. He choked down the grains, feeling them scratch at his esophagus as they went down.

"I lived not too far from here," Orin began after a short interval, "my early years as a settler, supporting mother and father establish a plot of land. One day, a group of mercenaries who needed able-body people took my father. I've never seen him again."

"Who were these 'mercenaries?'" Perikles asked.

"Kraken's Righteous Warheads," Orin whispered.

"We have heard their drums beating into the distant foothills on many nights," Zara returned, "they have the numbers and are a force to reckon with. It is unfortunate to hear about your father. I fear your story is a narrative most common around here. Please continue."

"When they took my father, my brother Liam and I helped our mother work in the fields. Our mother drank often," Orin paused as he stared down at his wineskin, "she passed away from drowning in the booze."

"I buried her near the field," he continued somberly, "my brother Liam and I tried growing crops, but it was overwhelming work managing the food while also keeping wild beasts and the mercenaries away. After that, we encountered a group of people who protected settlers along the foothills," Orin said, "Squad of Liberty led by a man, Atticus, my mentor and friend. Liam and I joined the Squad, and Atticus took us under his wing upon our first encounter."

"Ah, the Squad!" Perikles proclaimed, raising a hairless eyebrow, "I heard of the Squad's valiant deeds. Many settlers thrived because of the Squad."

"Sadly, the Squad is no more."

"Penumbra bless the Squad," Perikles sighed.

"Penumbra blesses the Squad," the group resounded.

In the ensuing silence, Elliot left his position against the wall walking down the corridor. He returned with slabs of preserved venison, a bag of potatoes, and a plastic pouch containing herbs.

"We will have venison with potatoes if you want to stay Orin," Zara announced, extending her arm toward the fire.

Orin graciously accepted as Elliot placed the meat onto a cast-iron skillet watching it crackle and seethe on the fire. The chef shook the skillet using short forward movements. The fats and oils mixed in the pan created waxy, sulfurous, and sweet scents mixing pleasantly with the smells of burning pinewood, rose petals, and musk.

"Something knocked me out during a blast," Orin resumed, "when I woke, it was too late. The battle was over. A smoke so thick you could cut it with a knife."

"And what of your brother?" Perikles asked.

"When I awoke, Liam was nowhere in sight. I do not know how long I was out. What I know is that Liam is missing, and I intend to find him."

The fire crackled, and the venison provided a sizzling howl with an occasional pop from a grease bubble. The aroma of the meat hung heavy in the air, making Orin's mouth water. He watched Elliot placing halved potatoes into the pan alongside the meat. The chubby cultist sprinkled a few herbs from the plastic bag into the pan. He then took another pot of water, placing it beside the fire. Orin's eyes darted up toward the round hole in the room's ceiling and quietly watched as the smoke trailed through the opening.

"You speak of a noble purpose. You appear to be a man in search of the truth," Zara stated.

"Thanks for the compliment."

Orin corked his wineskin and set it down on the ground. *I am not confident if I can trust these cultists. But they seem rather congenial. And the meat smells delicious.* Orin's stomach tumbled in the core of his abdomen as he shifted his load on his log.

"Dinners about ready," Elliot said, shifting the pan in his hand.

The venison noisily crackled. Elliot made a sudden motion that sent the meat slab flipping in the pan, exposing its cooked side. Denk grunted and stomped his foot deliberately on the ground. Libiditus giggled as a burst of grease flew toward his robes.

"We eat in a moment," Elliot repeated.

Zara made eye contact with Orin providing a cheery smile. He saw dark lines around the corners of her mouth, reflecting from the firelight.

"Thank you for sharing your story," Zara said, "it is good to learn the lives of others in the wasteland. It gives us hope for a better tomorrow to see the struggle and how our species flourishes. Praise Penumbra."

"Praise Penumbra."

"Let us eat this meal, Elliot has prepared," Zara continued, "Libiditus, I would prefer to hear more of how you met our wonderful new friend."

Elliot handed out wooden plates and cups to those around the fire. Orin took a plate and held it in his hands as Elliot tore shreds of venison while pushing potatoes onto the dishes. Using his hands, Orin shoveled the hot food into his mouth as soon as it touched his plate.

The potatoes melted in a piping abyss with oils and herbs soaking into his taste buds, satiating his watery mouth. It's been days since Orin had a hot meal. And the venison was delicate, supple, and exploded with flavors upon each bite. Orin closed his eyes, savoring the last of his morsels.

Elliot poured a watery herbal concoction into the cups and gave them to everyone. Most appeared absorbed in thought while they deliberately chewed their food. The smoke thickened across the ceiling, and Orin brought a fist over his lips as he choked. He took a large gulp from the wooden cup and tossed it toward a growing pile of dishes.

When they finished their meal, Elliot collected the plates. Venison gristle and other food particles clung to his overgrown goatee spilling over the tops of the plates. The chef headed down the hall, out of sight from the group. Orin heard the clatter of cookware in an adjacent room.

"I suppose I can start with how I came to meet Orin," Libiditus said, "Oh yes! A fun tale it shall be! Fun!"

"Take us from the beginning," Zara requested, "what were the events leading up to your meeting with Orin? You mentioned earlier of him saving you, explain. For there is a way, Penumbra provides all blessings."

Denk cleared his larynx, hocking a spitball onto the concrete. The fire sparked and crackled as Fasile stoked the logs with a gnarled staff. Orin glanced toward Perikles, who appeared lost in his own thoughts, casually wiped his mouth using his forefinger and thumb.

"Well, you see! Where to begin? Hmm. Oh, oh! I was scavenging ruins, oh, oh yes! I kept my eye out, too, and came across what I believed to be a lone traveler. I wanted to share the story of Penumbra with the lonesome traveler, see?"

"Praise Penumbra."

"Yes, yes, praise Penumbra," Libiditus continued, "I watched a traveler explore ruins, was I! I got canned goods in my ruins. I crept over to the lonely traveler's ruins to peek, see? Just as I was sneaking over to the traveler to share our good graces with him.

Oh! I was!" Libiditus paused for a moment, holding his palms up and away before him, fingers extended in a peculiar expression.

"BAM! A bigger one calls out from behind me. I got away, I did. But I was too slow and these robbers. They cornered me against a tree near the highway, they did! Oh, oh! Not my proudest moment, true. Fooled by the bastards."

Libiditus sighed and dropped his fists to his lap and faced his thighs. He spat on the ground near his feet as the firelight shone from his glistening head. Orin almost felt sorry for the guy.

"Orin, see, he shot the fatter one from inside the bus on the eastbound road. He did! He shot him, and the big man fell. The other one he rushes to the vehicle and Orin kills him too, he does! Oh, oh, praise Penumbra."

The group parroted the chant. Orin smiled as he lifted his wineskin, taking another gulp of the grainy beverage. Zara flashed a crinkled grin as she raised a hand toward the roof. Dense smog whirled around her palms as she gestured toward Orin. Libiditus rubbed his ribs while grinning at Orin.

"So, you saved Libiditus from rebirth."

Orin raised his eyebrows, taking another drink before wiping his cheek. He wasn't certain Zara's point regarding a 'rebirth.' Orin wasn't acquainted with the phrase, and he didn't want to provoke these cultists while accepting their generosity.

"It was nothing," Orin replied, "I did what I felt was appropriate. I saw someone in need, and I wished to teach those thieves a lesson."

"I assume you want to find out more concerning us. I am sure our fashion may appear unusual to an outsider."

"Perhaps," Orin smiled.

But then again, who am I to judge, he reflected. For as long as Orin could remember, he would wear what garment scrapes he discovered among the spoils or plucked from the deceased.

"Perikles, would you please explain to Orin the concept of Penumbra?" Zara asked.

"Yes Zara," Perikles stated, placing his hands in a prayer formation, "Penumbra willing, I will bring Orin understanding as to who we are and what we represent."

"As is obvious, the Terrible War left the Earth in a pit of despair," Perikles began, "people struggle for survival. Many others do not survive. Our order formed decades ago, shortly after the Terrible War. Though merely a few members, we believe our message transcends this life into the next. The line dividing good and evil cuts through the heart of every human."

"Some being bad more than good, oh, oh!" Libiditus interjected.

"We praise Penumbra as we believe there is life after death," Perikles continued, "harmony in the universe, even with all the devastation on our planet. A shared consciousness exists in which each person provides their understanding of the universe's teachings. This collective consciousness already knows everything there is to know. Still, the unconscious mind cannot make sense of this information without our mindful awareness. Children of Penumbra seeks to balance this input by practicing not only virtues but also recognizing the value of exhibiting our vices. A balance to the order."

"Why not practice being virtuous and eliminate the vices from the world entirely?" Orin asked.

"One completely overlooks that people are carried away entirely and miserably, not merely by virtue but also by a vice."

"There are virtues committed for self-interests entailing as much injustice and violence as a vice," Zara interjected.

"We live through, and we worship our shadow," Perikles continued waving his arms in a sweeping gesturing movement, "and these rocks were here before us and will remain here long after us. We must bring balance to the surrounding energies. Some aim to live virtuously, even in the wastelands, and our order seeks to provide a purpose for the implicit. And also the unacknowledged part of our human condition."

"How do you practice these vices?"

"Sacrifices," Fasile whispered.

"We sacrifice to Penumbra appreciating vices of the human experience," Perikles divulged, "in this way, Penumbra allows us to prosper and continue our service. We provide the essential balance required for our species to thrive."

"Praise Penumbra," the group echoed.

The shields with hanging tattered bloody rags on the walls hinted that these sacrifices were human. *None of the group members aside from Denk and Elliot looked strong enough to wield both sword and shield,* Orin conceived. He stole a glance toward his rifle near his feet.

"The hour is late," Zara said, holding up her palm, "it is time we retire for the evening. Libiditus, will you kindly show our guest to his sleeping quarters?"

"Certainly, Zara! Oh, oh, yes!"

The members of the cult stood up and stretched their legs. Orin stood up and heard his joints release an audible pop. He picked up his rifle and hoisted the strap across his chest while tying the wineskin to his belt. Orin thanked Perikles, who leaned inward with hands pressed together, making eye-contact with Orin.

"Have a good evening," he replied, looking toward the fire.

Orin followed Libiditus down the hallway containing several open doors, two on the right, and two on the left. The first opened door they passed on the right included a huge wash bin along the distant wall and candles dotting the tiles and ledges. Elliot stood scrubbing something within the wash bin. Soapy suds clung up to his elbows.

As they went, their footsteps echoed on the solid floor. The surfaces of the corridor were barren and cream-colored. Orin glanced into the next passage on the right, dimly lit via candles. A massive slab of concrete resembling a table jutted from the center of the room. On the far wall hung a pentagram made of rose stems with large thorns protruding from the sides. A goat's head hanging on the wall in the center of the pentagram sent a chill through Orin.

A darkened stained fabric hung over the table onto the floor. The dim lighting from the candles made it difficult to identify other silhouettes within the room. Orin's hairs on his neck stood up. Libiditus casually walked toward the door on their left.

Stopping outside the entrance, Libiditus turned toward Orin. He gave a yellowed grin as he gestured inside the room. Orin heard muffled voices speaking from the main chamber.

"This is where we will sleep for the evening, oh, oh!"

"I appreciate it."

Removing a tiny burning candle from a holder along the wall, Libiditus bent down to light the candles. Orin noticed there were no windows in this room, and the walls were bare. A thin layer of straw covered the floor below tattered blankets. A black and green residue clung to the concrete cinder blocks a foot above the straw.

"That'll be your, uh, sleeping area, Orin."

Orin cleared his throat, stealing a glimpse down the hallway. He saw the other's obscurations bouncing along the walls in the central room. He heard Elliot banging various objects against the wash bin. A sweet metallic smell wafted through the air from the room across the hall.

Something is not right with this place. I have a feeling I know what type of sacrifices these cultists perform, he thought.

"Blow the candles out, yes, once you settle in! I know my way around, and I wouldn't want the straw the catch fire, no, oh, oh!"

"Will do," Orin said, "I believe these furnishings will do just fine."

"Glad to hear it, yes!"

Orin listened to the cultists' whispers while watching the wax drip slowly down the candle on the post. He sighed, leaning his rifle against the wall near his bedding in the corner. He set his gun within reaching distance.

Just in case, he thought.

Orin sat on his bedding, unlacing his tattered boots. The dry leather sent a plume of dust into the air as he placed each boot on the ground. Untying the wineskin and plastic bag from his belt, he put these items next to his shoes.

His thoughts changed to Liam, assuming he was alive and, at the least, surviving through captivity. Finally, Orin's thoughts roamed to the conversations he had with the cultists earlier. The way the group appeared to be holding back information about their rituals. Orin wished he would have pressed further into the 'sacrifices' these cultists made to Penumbra. He had a feeling he knew the type of sacrifices made in that room.

Perhaps there were things better left unsaid. Orin shivered as a vision of the thorny pentagram swept through his mind.

Orin wrapped the blanket around him as he laid on the straw bedding. Placing his hand around the base of his rifle, he took deep breaths while closing his eyes. The murmurs of the other cultists faded into the background. Blackness engulfed Orin, and he drifted into a light slumber.

CHAPTER 6: NOT TODAY!

Orin opened his eyes and sat squinting for a brief moment. Libiditus slept in the center of the room. Orin watched the man curled up in a fetal position as his back expanded with his breaths. A more massive irregular shadow laid against the distant wall toward the entrance, appearing to be Elliot. Orin noticed a dim light flickering down the hall and heard the whispers of voices from another chamber.

Orin stretched his arms, throwing the blanket against the wall near his rifle. He blinked his eyes and reeled off the sleep. Carefully, he crawled across Libiditus, heaving from his whispering snores. Orin was cautious not to touch him or place too much pressure on the ground.

I need to see what these cultists do at this hour, he thought.

Orin made his way to the doorway, peeking down the hall. The main chamber where they ate was pitch black. Utterances murmured from across the room. A sliver of candlelight flickered through the crack in the doorway.

"But he's too much of a liability, Zara... He is not bought into the concept of Penumbra. He will not side with our cause," Fasile whispered.

Orin shifted closer toward the door to eavesdrop on the conversation. While pressing his eye in the doorway's break, he saw various shadows bobbing on the surface. Concealing himself in the hallway's shadow, he overheard the cultist's discussion.

"He could be reliable, and if we give him an ultimatum, perhaps we can get him to see why he is better off with us," Zara murmured.

"Oh, nonsense! He wants to find his brother, he has no interest in joining our cause," Fasile hissed.

"Then we'll use that to our advantage," Zara responded, "we will string him along with promises of finding his brother until he commits to helping us with our rituals. I don't expect it would take long to convince him."

"If he knew of our rituals," Fasile's voice shook, "he would kill us."

"Not necessarily," Perikles elucidated, "he is a mercenary. He knows the cost of spilling blood in the line of duty. He may very well side with our faith."

So, they want me to join their cause, Orin thought, *they may never let me leave here without pledging to their Penumbra.*

"You've seen him chugging down his booze tonight, it is doubtful he would give that up to join us," Fasile raised his voice, "I don't want him here!"

"The choice is not entirely yours in the matter," Zara refuted, "he may prove to be an asset. He saved Libiditus's life when he could have continued on searching for his brother. Surely Penumbra led this man to encounter our organization for a divine purpose. The drinking we can manage at another time, it is not a priority."

"Yer don't increase the numbers by shunnin' others Fasile," Denk grunted.

"Fine," Fasile remarked, "so we present him an ultimatum. Either he pledges to Penumbra and joins our order, or..."

"Or we kill 'em," Denk's scruffy bark finished for him. Orin shuddered as Denk uttered those words.

So much for the hospitality here.

"Denk, I need you at the entrance until dawn," Zara commanded, "we'll deliver the ultimatum to him once daybreaks. If he accepts, we will perform the oath sacrament. If he refuses, kill him."

"Yer got it!"

Orin heard heavy footsteps shuffling toward the door. He quickly scurried back through the opening of his quarters. He saw candlelight sweep across the corridor floor as the door swung open, revealing a towering shadow. Orin slipped behind the wall and looked back at Libiditus, still curled in a fetal position. He carefully crawled over him as Denk plodded down the hallway toward the main room.

Sitting on his bedding in the darkroom, Orin stared at the hall. His heartbeat pounded after the close encounter. He resolved to leave before sunrise. Orin listened as Denk dragged a wood stump across the basement and released a belch. He couldn't hear what the cultists were discussing across the room.

Perikles left the ritual room, followed by Fasile. They walked together, whispering as they entered the room neighboring Orin's quarters. Zara broke the ensuing silence by droning in a strange dialect from across the corridor. Zara's tone fluctuated as she continued her chant. When she stopped chorusing, Orin heard her blow out the candles before her silhouette walked into the adjacent room. Orin strained his eyes toward the hallway as he tried listening to what they were whispering in the nearby room.

Time passed, and Orin watched candlelight flicker in the corridor from the central chamber. Occasionally, he heard Denk grunt or shift his load on his stool. When Orin overheard snores coming from the neighboring room, he felt assured he could creep to the hallway without alerting the others.

Orin kept low as he made his way deliberately down the corridor. The radiance from candlelight provided Orin with clues about Denk's whereabouts in the room. Orin glanced toward the neighboring doorway as he carefully stepped along the corridor. He could not see far inside the darkroom but noticed shadows lying on the ground and heard snores from within. Convinced he went unnoticed, he crawled toward the edge of the hall while peaking his head around the corner toward Denk.

Denk perched on a log seat, blocking the entrance to the basement. He idly carved a wooden staff into a point, sending tiny chips of wood curling toward the floor. Orin watched as the large man beamed while staring keenly at his work.

Wouldn't wish to be on the receiving side of that one, Orin surmised.

Glowing candles perched on logs near Denk with tiny flickers barely lapping the air. Denk didn't notice Orin as he sat with the wooden stick between his legs, whittling a sharp tip. Orin glanced at the cloths draped over the shields hanging on the walls of the central room. Although weapons were hanging on the walls behind the shields, Orin didn't think it was possible to retrieve one without alerting all of the cultists. He knew he had to find a way out of this musky cellar.

Orin watched the large man blocking the entrance for a moment. He needed to identify a suitable plan without being detected, and so he crawled meticulously back toward his room. Curled in the fetal position, Orin gingerly inched over the gaunt, hairless man. Once on his bedding, he poked around for his plastic bag of food items. The bag made a crinkling racket as Orin ruffled through it. Orin found his wineskin and had a quick drink, listening for signs of the others awakening. Inhaling the sour juice from within, he took a long gulp from the container.

I could try to charge him, Orin imagined, *but that might not work successfully against Denk. I could also try shooting him from the hallway, but a .22 bullet or two may not take him down. I could try to throw something into the wash bin in the room down the hall to distract Denk. Although the cultists might hear the clatter and investigate.*

Orin wanted little commotion to successfully run for the stairs, climb them, and lift the hatch door to freedom. Preferably doing so without alerting the cultists.

What if I ask Denk to use the lavatory outdoors? Orin wondered. *I could probably escape from him if only I were outside the hatch door. That's it! I will come up with an excuse to leave and then make a run for it.*

Determined to escape, Orin collected his food items and tied the wineskin around his belt. He picked up the rifle and slung the strap across his shoulders to distribute it evenly across his back. Orin rose to his knees and planned his exit route over Libiditus' body.

What a strange man, he reflected as he looked down at his body.

One of his shins rubbed against Libiditus's thigh, which caused Orin to pause. Libiditus snorted and murmured something while smacking his lips. Orin's heart was pulsating through his chest, and he heard the rhythmic thuds against his ear canal. Convinced Libiditus would remain sleeping, he crept over his body toward the entrance of the room.

Orin kept his eyes forward while sneaking down the hallway toward the main chamber. He tried to calm his nerves as he inched his way along the corridor, passing the snoring sounds and occasional grunts. Crossing the room next to his sleeping area, Orin stole a glance inside to identify if Zara and the others were asleep. Satisfied upon hearing silence broken by wheezing, he proceeded down the corridor keeping near the washing room.

Stealing a glimpse around the corner of the hall, Orin observed Denk, who examined the spear tip he created. Orin took two heavy breaths before walking out into the candlelit room. Denk looked up from reviewing the spear tip, locking Orin's eyes as a look of confusion swept across his face.

"What wakes yer up this evenin'?"

"Need to use the latrine," Orin replied curtly.

"Hah!" Denk grunted, "Yer don't haft ta go outside ta relieve y' rselves. Yer can go in that den there washing area and use'r ta sink!"

"I'd rather go outside," Orin said, shaking his head, "and get fresh air anyway."

Taking a few steps forward to move past Denk, Orin found himself promptly confronted with the point of his spear. Denk grasped the middle of the bayonet tightly with his knuckles becoming white and the butt of the spear resting on his meaty thigh. He lowered the tip directly centered with Orin's chest.

"No! Yer can't go out there, it'd be too dangerous to open ta hatch at night. Now git and use the washroom and go 'er sleep."

Denk clenched the spear tighter while gritting his teeth into a snarl as Orin took a step closer. Orin saw Denk's forehead perspire and drip toward his barrel gut. Orin raised his open palms before him as he took another step.

"I need fresh air. I won't go very far."

"You will not go outside before break o'er day."

"If you'll just move slightly over, I can squeeze by."

He nudged Denk's heavy leg in one direction with his knee as he came closer. He could smell his musk as if he hadn't bathed in months. Denk's bare head glistened from the candlelight with sweat. His knuckles were ghost-white as he clasped the spear toward Orin.

I wouldn't have time to reach for the rifle, let alone shoot it if he were to attack. I could perhaps take him by surprise if I swiftly pound his face. Would I have time to make it out before the others arrive?

"Last time, I'll warn ya," Denk's voice raised as he swayed his head, "get back in-er' room 'fore I call de others."

Denk's leg moved as he uttered his threat. Orin stood in place, staring down the stout man tilting his spear toward his face. Making it this far, Orin was determined not to back down from this confrontation.

Besides, at this point, Denk may inform the others, he contemplated.

Denk swayed forward with his spear while grumbling in a low gurgling resonance. Orin snatched the spear reflexively as it thrust toward his face and brought his knee up hard, connecting with the stick's midpoint. The spear snapped from the force of Orin's knee with a loud *CRACK!* Orin held the spear tip in his hand and instantly twirled it around with the tip facing Denk.

Orin watched as Denk's eyes widened with fear, and his face flushed from beet red to colorless. Orin slammed down with all his might toward Denk. The spear tip met Denk's groin and pushed through to the wooden stump with a commanding plop.

Denk wailed in pain and looked at the spear tip, now between his legs, impaled from the wooden stump. Pinned in place by the spear, his groin appeared stuck through like a shish-kebob. Orin heard a commotion in the backrooms and swung his fist, rushing to meet Denk's nose. He felt a crunch as his fist united and watched momentarily stunned as blood spurted and gushed out the bottom of Denk's nostrils. Blood poured down his shirt to meet the red stain pooling on the wooden seat. Orin then pushed the stout man to the side, causing his log chair to clatter to the ground with the man crying in pain.

"I'll get you, oww! For that. I'm' ma kill you, you, uh! Oww!"

Orin glimpsed back to see movement in the corridor while Denk clutched his nose suffering on the dirty floor. Orin scrambled up the rusted stairs and slipped on a run, sending his shin bone racing to connect with a step. The pain was intense, but Orin tried to disregard it for the moment to finish climbing the remaining runs. He could hear yells, screams, and other disturbances from the cultists below.

Orin unlocked the lock and flung the squared door open, revealing the frigid night air. Orin used his strength to lift himself out of the basement.

"Get him! Kill him! Bring him back quickly!" Zara roared.

The gusts slapped at Orin as he raised his legs out of the opening and settled onto the dirt. Orin slammed the hatch door closed and noticed a giant slab a pace away. Orin immediately clambered over to the rock and heaved it swiftly with arms wrapped in an embrace. Orin tottered back over to the hatch door and dropped the hefty boulder. It seemed to remain in place with a flat base that would provide resistance when they came through the door in pursuit.

Orin arranged the rifle strap from burrowing into his shoulder and stood up fully erect. His knees popped as his bones accustomed themselves to the elements. There was a throbbing feeling in the joint which connected with Denk's makeshift spear. His shin also stung from where he slammed it against the stairs on his way out of the basement. He quickly rubbed his leg and winced as he took a few steps to get his blood moving.

I must move on before that boulder comes loose, which it likely will once Elliot pushes on the door, Orin considered.

The wind was a steady force from the foothills moving toward the plains. A blast would whip Orin a few feet forward as he made his way northbound. He floundered past the ruins as he ran through the steppes. He could hear uproarious noises behind him as the cultists clattered on the metallic door attempting to escape the basement in pursuit.

Orin pushed through the nagging injury from his shin and a bruised knee using the shadow of sagebrush and trees to help navigate northbound. He tripped over a pine tree root, sending him flying toward the Earth with his hands outstretched. As Orin laid in the gravel, he heard faint voices and cries above the slapping wind. The cultists had escaped the basement and were trying to catch him.

I won't let that happen; Orin determined standing up.

Orin pressed onward following the edges of the foothills. He knew of the giant stadium where settlers converged somewhere to the north. As he ran, Orin thought about the stories Atticus and the other Squad members shared of their visits to this settlement. Even though Orin never been to this stadium, with the stories shared by settlers on the front range, he was familiar with it. Atticus referred to it as a "sanctuary" with locals possessing little thought toward survival like those in the wasteland. People felt protected behind the stadium walls with its own well-trained and well-armed militia safeguarding the borders. This stadium, known as Ádyto, was located approximately thirty miles north of his current position.

If I keep a steady pace for two days, I'll reach Ádyto by tomorrow night.

The periodic shouts of the cultists grew more distant with each stride. Several times the wind gusts would push Orin into the sagebrush, but he would recover and press onward. His shin pulsated, and every step, Orin grit his teeth attempting to manage it. Spittle flew out from his clenched teeth as he continued flailing his arms around to provide support.

Orin pushed forward, stealing occasional glances behind him. He saw torchlight in the distance from the direction of the cultists. They were chasing him into the night.

How long might they pursue? I am sure they may try to kill me for what I did to Denk. But I didn't have a choice. It was that or possibly being killed down in that basement.

Snow flurries settled onto Orin as he progressed through the night. The air was becoming more frigid, and Orin billowed puffs of condensation from every breath. The soft desert sand of the steppes became hard as pavement. Snowflakes stung his face and numbed his fingers, making them rigid. Orin braced his leg with his hand to help keep it steady and to apply pressure to the soreness.

Ádyto would be my best chance to find the whereabouts of Liam.

The moon was barely visible through the clouds above the foothills, and it was challenging to see ten paces ahead. Orin kept moving swiftly, fearful of the vengeance he would face from the cultists should they catch up. His face and hands stung from the biting wintry wind. Teardrops formed in the ducts of his eyes, and he used his arm to wipe them before they froze.

I wonder if the cultists will follow my tracks through the night? I haven't bothered covering them up. The snow will help cover the divots of my footprints.

Orin needed to find shelter before the fervent wind froze him to death. He couldn't keep this pace through the evening. There were threats out in the wilderness, he knew, far more dangerous than cultists.

As Orin ran, he noted the various decaying concrete ruins he crossed along the way. Orin was imagined the way people once lived. Peacefully in houses, having lawns to upkeep, retrieving food from a local store. Orin never experienced these conditions, at least not simultaneously. But it was warming to fabricate comfortable living from stories told around a campfire. Most of the ruins were barren and empty, a relic from bygone glory days of civilization. A few contained broken furniture or miscellaneous items such as faded books, children's toys, cooking utensils, and some provided tattered clothing, which was strewn about.

Orin continued stumbling through the remains, without stopping to inspect them. He wanted to create a sizable amount of separation between the cultists and himself. After a period of keeping his steady pace among the flurries of snow and zephyrs, Orin came across a concrete structure with a partial roof for shelter.

He paused and peered south to determine if the cultists were still trying to track him down. After examining and listening intently for several moments, he saw no torches burning or detected any voices. Relieving himself on a nearby tree, he scanned the panorama, watching the moon ease from behind a vast cloud. He could see into the great distance the obscurity of ruined structures and sagebrush across the steppe. The sky turned a light cerulean across the horizon, and the stars punched through the void above.

Watching the scenery, he listened to crickets playing their piercing melodies. There were no signs of wolves, coyotes, or cultists near the ruin. As the wind pierced through to his bones, Orin decided it was best to try to rest for the evening.

Crawling over a low disintegrated wall, he squatted inside and surveyed the structure. It was desolate aside from a few old wooden shelves. Black smudges ran along the interior walls and ceiling, reminding Orin of fire damage. He walked across the ruin and entered a short, narrow corridor leading toward a small opening near the back.

Walking into this room, he noticed the outer concrete walls decayed away from the ceiling. Several abundant bird nests sat unopposed along the top of the wall, each appearing abandoned. In the moonlight spilling through the opening, Orin noticed white stains dropping from the nests onto the floor. In the opposite corner, Orin saw crumpled textiles with luminous frost glazed over them.

Orin walked toward the cloth on the ground, crouching over while collecting a handful. The coarse fabric hardened from the freeze and would not make suitable bedding. Orin tossed the textiles back to the floor and slung his rifle from his shoulder to lean against a nearby wall. Untying his food bag and wineskin, he sat these items near his gun. Sitting down on the cold ground, he removed his boots, placing these next to his pieces. Orin laid on his back and listened to the crickets beyond the crumbled wall. He tucked the frozen fabric behind his head to use as a cushion.

Thoughts raced through Orin's mind as he reflected on his experience with the cultists. He figured they would pursue him for some time after injuring Denk. Orin chortled alone in the darkness and allowed a smile to crack his lips as he felt pleased. Using his foot, he nudged his wineskin within grasping distance. After uncorking the wineskin, Orin drew a deep swig and swished it around his mouth. He didn't mind the grains cutting at his gums as he felt the alcohol warm his blood. Smacking his lips, he recorked the pouch and dropped the wineskin near his face. Closing his eyes, Orin chased his galloping thoughts into a deep slumber.

CHAPTER 7: TWO-BIT'S OUTLANDISH CREATURES

Orin awoke at daybreak from the chirping of songbirds in nearby trees. The sun pierced rays of light through the break in the wall above his head. As he sat up, shaking off his sleep, his limbs popped. Bracing his hand against his forehead, he shook the lingering impression of his dream.

A loud gurgling in the abyss of his stomach sent a brief twinge of agony into his gut. In the daylight, he saw scorch marks along the surfaces. The substantial amount of beak bird feces fell from the abandoned nests toward the soot-covered tiles. Orin felt queasy as he stared at the clumps of silvery and rust-colored fecal matter interspersed inches from where he slept.

That's almost enough to satiate the appetite, he deemed.

Examining his food items in the plastic bag, Orin glanced over several aluminum cans without labels. The rays of sunlight gleaned from the items as he held each up and rattled them to ascertain the contents. Orin sighed and looked up toward the nests on the wall.

There might be eggs. But I don't have a way to spark a fire.

Orin shivered as he stretched his tattered boots over his thick woolen socks. He was thankful to have warm socks covering his feet as he stood up, hearing his knees pop again. One knee that broke Denk's spear was sore, but he found that he could fully extend his limb with a little stretching.

Orin took a broad step over the bird droppings to reach the nests on the wall. The hole was just above his head but within reach of his extended arms. He felt around inside the nearest nesting and touched a piece of fabric in his fingers. In the adjacent nest, he found broken twigs and several acorns. In the last nest, he found a little bluish egg. Lifting the egg carefully from the nest, he took a whiff and winced from the foul odor. Shaking the egg, he felt an oscillation as something bounced against the interior shell. As he tapped the egg on the stable stone wall, it surprised him the egg split in half, leaving a watery yellow yolk seeping from the crack.

Orin put his lips to the rift and squeezed the egg lightly to expand the tear. A translucent liquid discharged into his mouth before running down his throat to his stomach. He didn't want to taste the egg, and so he kept his tongue pressed against his bottom teeth. The sour taste of the thick yolk was as foul as the stench. Juicing the egg, he finished the remaining yolk before tossing the shell on the ground. As he stepped on it, he listened to the gentle crunch of the eggshell pulverized under his boot.

With the rumbling in the cavity of his abdomen subsiding, he gathered his belongings and hoisted his rifle. He examined the remaining decayed rooms within the structure and saw they were mostly barren with a few scattered books. Convinced he wouldn't find anything of value within the edifice, he surmounted over the low broken wall from which he entered during the evening.

The sun blazed vividly across the landscape. Looking through the pine trees surrounding the ruin, Orin noticed patches of disintegrating structures across the fields into the remote horizon. Sagebrush sprouted from the soil among waving meadows and rotting tree stumps. The foothills rose directly toward the west. Looking south, he listened as a raven cawed out on a wood post protruding from the Earth. Satisfied the cultists lost his trail, he looked toward the north in the area he needed to travel.

Decomposed ruins grew densely crowded the further north he gazed toward the central concrete jungle.

Ádyto must be around there. By the looks of it, I should reach Ádyto by tomorrow evening. Let's hope Liam is there or someone knows his whereabouts.

His ashy brownish hair lifted from his shoulders as the draft swept from the ridgeline above. Tilting his head, Orin rubbed his thumbs across his thick eyebrows to try matting them closer to his forehead.

Walking toward the north, he felt a pulse in his shin, and his knee burned with each stride. Orin gritted his teeth and exhaled slowly, focusing on objects in front of him. As he walked, the soreness receded, and he eventually forgot about his injury. Orin took heed around the concrete structures he walked past, scanning these for potential threats, particularly bandits or perhaps a pack of dogs.

Orin managed a measured pace. He followed along the foothills, pausing only to swig from the wineskin and listen for the cultists' sounds. As Orin exclusively heard the occasional call from the ravens, a broad grin ran across his face.

The scorching sun edged overhead as Orin happened upon a deteriorated asphalt road. Bleached white and golden markings were painted on the begrimed asphalt. Snaking lines of gravel jutted from the road. To his left, he saw the pavement zigzag its way into the foothills resembling a river. The path led from the foothills far to the plains in the east across rolling hills separating grasses and ruins of ancient dwellings.

Orin turned his face toward the sunshine welcoming its warmth. His skin was dehydrated and fractured as it peeled from exposure. Vapor rose from the pavement. The grumbling feeling from earlier resumed, and Orin decided it favorable to stop and open a tin of food. Orin tripped over a piece of gravel and recovered his balance before wandering toward a nearby tree. His desert eyes teared up with the breeze blowing directly at his face.

The shade under the pine needles dropped the heat as Orin placed his rifle against the tree. He plopped down, bracing his back firmly against the supporting tree trunk. Orin instantly felt relief from the strain in his muscles. Rubbing his hand over the chap of his neck, he browsed the parameter toward the northeast in the stadium's direction.

I wonder who I should seek once I arrive at Ádyto? Perhaps a bookkeeper. Liam always had a love of old dusty books.

Reaching into his bag, he removed another can without a label. Orin picked up a nearby rock with a sharp edge and tapped the tin until breaking the seal. Once he poked the holes around the can, Orin pared back the cover to expose its contents.

Pickled potatoes, Orin observed repugnantly, *just my luck.*

Orin gagged down the tart pickled potatoes until he cleared its contents before swallowing the vinegar syrup. The gnarling pit in his stomach subsided as he rested under the tree. After a deep belch, Orin noticed the buzzing of insects. As he sat under the tree, he recollected his encounter with Libiditus.

I saved that feeble runty man from death, and he tries to enslave me in his cult. What a peculiar, detached world this is. I will find Liam. I will find Kraken and kill every one of the Righteous Warheads, too. They will pay for what they've done to the Squad, those innocent settlers, and Liam.

He wiped away a tear, realizing he was sobbing and took an abundant drink from the wineskin. The quivering in his hands subsided, and his dry lips were wetted. Smacking his lips, he took another sip and closed his eyes.

A whistling noise wafted above the breeze, growing louder in a musical tone. Orin turned toward the foothills to identify its origin. A dark blue wagon led by two mules rounded the western bend, alongside the cart a short, stout potbelly figure with a tall hat and long black coat continued his tune. The man's clothes swept the rocks as he walked adjacent to the wagon, kicking up a tuft of dust behind them.

Orin watched the man make his way along the broken road. The animals snorted the flies off from their snouts. The man in the top hat raised his hand and waved. Daylight gleaned from his jewels dangling from his wrists and over his button-down shirt. Shiny gemstones sparkled from rings on his plump fingers as he smiled from ear to ear. Orin observed as they made their way down the way from the foothill pass. The man inserted one hand back into his overcoat pocket, jiggling a golden bracelet.

The man halted his mules with a tick of his tongue. Their bulky harnesses draping below their bellies came to a creaking standstill. The stranger called toward Orin as he lifted his hat and sifted it.

"What a lovely morning it is, partner. Relishing much of it?"

Orin noticed the way this man spoke in a crisp tone as though he were a trained orator. He had an unusual manner about him by how he languidly waved his hands around as he conversed. The man appeared well-traveled and relaxed, talking to strangers.

"Best I can," Orin affirmed, studying the freckled sun-tanned face, "and I'm not much for conversation at the moment."

"Oh, my pardons, sir," the man said, "But I simply mean to break up the dullness of my tour. Oh, it can be such a bore walking for miles with no one for conversation. Well, now, I mean no mischief, for I am a nomad myself. You see, I manage a freak show caravan. The name's Two-Bit," his chains jingled as his physique bounced when he spoke.

"Orin," he replied curtly, "and what is a 'freak show' without freaks?"

"Ah, a keen one, are you?"

Two-Bit motioned for Orin to follow him to the back of his cart. Orin shrugged and took a drink before corking the wineskin and standing up. He felt a dizzying buzz from the booze, and he began to smirk. Tying his food and drink sack to his belt, he slung his rifle over his shoulder and followed the odd visitor.

"A tall fellow, aren't you?" Two-Bit asked with a wide toothy grin, "I venture you can hold your own in a fight, undoubtedly well, can't you?"

Two-Bit tilted back on the heels of his polished black boots, fixing his leather suspenders. The sunshine shimmered from his chains as Orin raised a high eyebrow watching the man with suspicion. Two-Bit giggled while directing toward the back of his wagon.

Orin paused before accompanying the round man around the corner of his extended carriage. Painted lettering on the side of the wagon read, "Two-Bit's Outlandish Creatures." A golden dragon wearing a top hat followed the last word in the freak shows' name.

The carriage was reasonably broad, overlooking Orin as he strolled along the side. Long wooden wheels afforded ample clearance from the road. A fastened hatch door painted in matching blue and gold was hardly visible until Orin walked toward the back.

Two-Bit swung the wagon doors open, revealing the contents within. Two youthful and slight, twin ladies sat on a side seat wearing identical outfits. Both had long black hair and ghost-white appearances nictitating with vacant expressions on their angular faces. Slanted beady eyes cast high in their faces were spaced evenly apart on either side of their distinctive noses.

The carriage appeared crowded as Orin noticed the young women sat next to a sizeable dome-shaped metal birdcage. Inside the enclosure, a hen nestled up inside itself with its beak tucked into its wings. The chicken was unphased by Two-Bit's display, and it jerked its head to peck a small bug from inside its wing.

Boxes of all shapes enclosed the twins and hen. The adolescent ladies sat in their golden chiffon gowns with their hands folded, not seeming to notice these stifling conditions.

"Good day, ladies. How d'you do?" Orin asked.

The young woman furthest inside the wagon, tilted her head, squinting while maintaining her thoughtless stare at Orin. Both remained quiet and peeked with hollow black eyes. The daylight stung hot as Orin reviewed Two-Bit's wares.

"Well, what do you think?" Two-Bit questioned, smacking his lips, "they don't talk, mutes or something of that nature, I presume. But they belong in the show and do an exceptional performance. Although the chicken might talk if you feed it enough seeds."

Two-Bit cackled at his own joke as Orin gazed at the twins. Feeble limbs stuck out of their dresses like brittle stems. Orin wondered why these two young women would join Two-Bit's show.

"You seem to have a fine caravan traveling with you. Where were you performing next?"

"Oh, just headed to Ádyto, same as you, I presume?"

Two-Bit waved his hand gently toward the northeast as a tumbleweed bounced across the road. The breeze picked up, cooling them off as they stood in the sweltering sun.

"How did you figure I was going to Ádyto?"

"Same reason as I, for supplies," Two-Bit cracked a grin and pointed to the shrinking food bag clinging to Orin's side, "you don't seem to have much food left, and you look like you've been journeying for days, if not weeks!"

"You're right. I need supplies. I would imagine Ádyto is a day to the north."

"Yes, a day or perhaps slightly less," Two-Bit affirmed, "say, would you like to keep each other company on the rest of this journey? I could use help to guard the wagon against degenerates. The mercenary I enlisted in Fire Water succumbed to an infection after a vicious wolf bite. I can hold my own, of course, heh, but a little help could be nice."

"I travel alone."

"Oh, come now! We are heading to the same place. I will make it worth your while. Tell you what," Two-Bit leaned into the wagon, removing a lid from a box, "you help me reach Ádyto safely, and I'll give you a clean bottle of distilled whiskey."

Sunlight glistened from the clear glass of the caramel-colored bottle. A sizeable striped label read, "Turnerburg's *Distilled Whiskey*." The precious brown liquid inside sloshed as Two-Bit tilted the bottle for Orin to see clearer.

Pristine whiskey.

Orin salivated as he imagined tasting the whiskey. His hand strayed down toward his own wineskin filled with his grain alcohol. The leather pouch swayed easily from his touch, revealing it was becoming empty.

It might be nice to have someone watch my back after what happened with the cultists last evening.

"Oh, all right," Orin said hesitantly, "we'll head to Ádyto. But no shady business along the way! And you pay me on the outskirts of Ádyto."

"Deal," Two-Bit said, "and you'll need this for our journey by its looks."

Two-Bit reached under the bench inside the wagon, unstrapping a piece of Velcro while fumbling for an object. He pulled out a revolver with a long barrel and cherry-wood grip. Turning it over in his hand, Two-Bit caught the sun's rays across the chamber. He popped the barrel and readied the chamber. Two-Bit held the gun out toward Orin and gestured.

"Nice gun!"

A silvery floral etching ran across the cylinder down the barrel of the revolver. The gun was heavy as Orin lifted it, aiming down the road toward the foothills. The iron sights were dipped in a neon dye, which made the two tips glow. Aligning a target in the views was a quick and easy process with this enhancement. Orin thought the cherry-wood handle was beautifully crafted, providing flairs of reds and woodgrain undertones. It was apparent this double-action revolver was well-maintained.

"She's a real beauty," Two-Bit agreed, "hold on to it while we travel as you don't seem to have a handgun. Also, you'll need ammunition. Just in case."

Two-Bit reached into his pocket and flung a carton of ammunition toward Orin. He popped the cylinder open to see six cartridges in the chamber. Satisfied, he slapped the barrel back into place, holstering the revolver in his waistband. Orin slipped the ammunition into his leather coat pocket.

Two-Bit removed two packages of cracker from his overcoat before halving each pack and tossing two toward the young women. Two-Bit tossed another sling of wafers toward Orin and removed the wrap from his remaining portion. Orin unwrapped his bundle and hungrily ate his crackers.

"Thank you," Orin said, pointing to the twins, "how did you come to possess these two women into your show?"

Orin removed his wineskin and took a deep drink while anticipating a reply. Two-Bit looked over toward the twins before he gave his response. After choking down several of his crackers, he pulled a water bottle from underneath the bench and drank.

"Well, I found them several months ago," Two-Bit began, "They were near an abandoned hotel two days ride from here. Unfortunately for them, the place burned from a lightning bolt. I was passing down the road by the river when I found them. They were watching the smoldering flame scorch the last of the building to ashes. I offered them both a position in my freak show and ensured they were clothed and fed in return. It's a win-win situation for all, if you ask me, and them. Heh. But you won't get much out by asking."

"What are their names?"

"Well," Two-Bit paused, "on account they are mutes, I haven't been able to find out. I refer to them as Tao and Mao. They seem to respond to those names."

"Tao and Mao," Orin repeated, "so, what do they perform in your freak show of 'Outlandish Creatures'?"

"You like the name of the show, do you?" Two-Bit said, smirking, "fantastic! They perform a marvelous balancing act and contortion. Their famous piece, which gets the crowd hollering, is when Mao stands on one leg while balancing her sister on her head. These ladies earn their keep!"

"I should like to see that sometime."

"Hah! It's a sight to see! We are passing a settlement this evening down the road away. You can watch them perform while helping me collect payment! It is a regular stop for the show. We can usually procure additional trade items before we arrive at Ádyto."

"And out of curiosity, what does the chicken do besides eat little critters?"

"All in due time. Hah! Now, let's start our journey if we want to make it to the hamlet before dusk."

Two-Bit tossed the remaining crackers toward the twins and shut the plank doors on the wagon. He slapped down the alloy latch holding the doors closed. Flashing a toothy grin, he gallivanted toward the front of the carriage.

"Hope you do not mind walking," Two-Bit said, "the mules are tired, and I do not want to add our weight to the caravan if we can help it."

Two-Bit picked up a switch from the small shelf jutting from behind the mules. With a quick swipe, the whip cracked, slapping the rump of the mules.

"Git!"

Orin walked alongside Two-Bit near the burros as the wagon's big rollers gracefully skipped over the clefts in the road. The sun was directly overhead when the men started their journey eastbound. Orin perspired as he walked, and he took a long-drawn drink to cool him.

"How d'you get in the freak show business?"

"Well, it is a lengthy story. But I suppose we have time," Two-Bit chuckled, "I came upon this gig of sorts from a former acquaintance."

"A former acquaintance?"

"He was an older chap who taught me to train hens. He expired from a disease, and I took over the business. After several years of traveling, I put together a stable show of my own. Mao and Tao have helped tremendously in this endeavor as they often bring that *je ne sais quoi*."

"You roam around performing shows, and you can get by on that alone?"

"Indeed, we thrive on this work. These days at least. It wasn't always like that, mind you. A lot of trial and error for the first few years," Two-Bit placed both hands across his potbelly jiggling from his chuckle, "but those days are gone. We have enough material to take the settler's minds off their daily routine for a short while."

"What do you earn from the people watching the shows?"

"I will often go through the crowd during the show with my hat to collect items of value from the settlers. The settlers expect it, and I have my regular stops. The times I step at a new settlement are few and far between. The settlers usually pay without too many issues."

"What do these settlers pay you with?" Orin inquired, "aren't they struggling themselves?"

"The usual. Mostly alcohol. But also seeds and candles. Occasionally a bag of salt or a family heirloom is accepted as payment. Most of the settlers will pay for the chance to escape reality. The monotony of the routine can be a dreadful bore."

"Seems as if you have this running smoothly," Orin marveled, "I look forward to seeing the show tonight. Unfortunately, I have nothing to provide as a payment for the show!"

"Ah, but you will have something to contribute! You are the hired help," a cheesy smile swept across Two-Bit's face, "you will see to it we collect items for payment while also guarding the wagon until we reach Ádyto."

"I could provide muscle for you," Orin nodded with a wink.

"And you will do a phenomenal job, I am sure. With your big and intimidating demeanor, we will collect our payment-in-full, that I know!"

Orin snorted and touched the cherry-wood handle of the revolver he received from Two-Bit. His fingers rubbed the smooth handle, and he traced the engravings. Flies hovering around the mules made attempts of settling on the perspiration around Orin's neck.

"Let's hope you don't have to use that gun," Two-Bit said, raising an eyebrow, "we try to keep things amicable around here. Violence is bad for business."

"What happened with your last guard again?" Orin asked in an attempt to see if the man's story would change.

"He succumbed to the disease after a vicious bite in the mountains," Two-Bit stuck his thumb behind his shoulder toward the mountains, "that was several moons ago."

"Wolves also attacked my camp a week ago."

"Rough business. I am sorry to hear that. Which brings me to my line of questioning. What happened to your camp? Are you the sole member?"

"I belonged to the Squad of Liberty," Orin sighed, "the Righteous Warheads attacked our camp. Many died in the battle, most of my fellow Squad members. I believe my brother may have survived, but I am not sure."

"And you are heading to Ádyto to find this Liam? Magnificent! What a tale!"

Orin nodded while scanning the scenery as they wandered. When they arrived at a t-shaped junction, Two-Bit directed the mules northbound to the left. As they proceeded to the north, concrete ruins continued to become denser.

They observed the world around them silently as the wagon creaked while rolling over gaps in the road. They heard noises of rushing water of a river beyond the ruins toward the west. The sound was beautiful as the withered men were parched from the walk.

"Aye! Halt! Let's refill our canteens. Do you have one other than your pouch?"

"I do not," Orin replied.

"No worries. I have an extra can in the back."

Walking around back, Two-Bit extracted two red squared containers handing one to Orin. The twins sat on the bench, chewing the crackers while holding another with both hands. They stared blankly out at the road behind them.

They did not move much at all, Orin mused.

Two-Bit reached into a box handing the twins a jug of brown-tinted water. Orin cringed as one twin, opened the bottle and chugged the liquid. The other twin rubbed her hands together while kicking her legs and licking her chapped lips.

"It's not dirty," Two-Bit said with a wink, "it has remnants of iodine in it to keep the water purified."

They strolled toward the river leaving the twins in the wagon. Orin stumbled over a secluded rock among the tall grasses near the ruins. Birds cawed as they perched on top of decaying roofs and poles.

"Do they ever leave the wagon?"

"Who, the twins?" Two-Bit rolled his wrist, "when they need too. I don't keep them, prisoner!"

They discovered the rushing river weaving among enormous boulders behind thick cement walls. The men knelt beside the water, splashing their faces and hands with the cooling liquid. Dipping the red containers into the water, they filled the jugs, and Orin lifted his to drink. As a result, Two-Bit slapped the pitcher away from his mouth.

"No! You cannot consume that water yet, Orin. You will become ill from the poisoning!"

Orin stared down at his water. A few specks of soot floating in the water, but other than that, it appeared drinkable. Two-Bit reached into a side pocket and pulled out a bottle filled with tablets.

"These are iodine tablets," Two-Bit proffered a pill to Orin, "put one of these into your jug. It will sterilize any bugs you may get from uncleaned water."

Orin dropped the tablet into the jug and watched as it broke into fine particles. They floated toward the top while the capsule continued sinking toward the bottom. As the pill dissolved, tiny bubbles emanated toward the top.

"Now, shake the container."

"Got it," Orin said, shaking the container until the water turned a light brown.

"You may now drink from the jug."

Lifting the container to his lips, Orin took numerous swallows from the jug. The water felt crisp and refreshing as it flowed down his throat. The men stood there for a moment quenching their thirsts and topped off the pitchers before walking back to the wagon. Two-Bit screwed a cap on both containers, placing them into the cart near the twins. The young women sat on the bench with their fingers folded on their thighs.

After replacing the latch on the doors, the men walked toward the front of the wagon. Two-Bit used his switch to move the mules along the road. They made small talk as they continued marching toward the northeast. They expected the caravan to reach the next settlement by sunset.

CHAPTER 8: COME ONE, COME ALL!

"Ladies and gentlemen!" Two-Bit roared to the crowd, "children of all ages! Come now! Gather round, gather round!"

Children hopped up and down gleefully on rugs in front of the carriage side. People from the hamlet stood behind them, speaking in frantic chatter. The crowd simmered when Two-Bit continued.

"And welcome to Two-Bit's Outlandish Creatures! With your host, me! Two-Bit!"

Orin stood near the side of the wagon, hiding out of view. He monitored the cheers and howls from the crowd. Two-Bit swung doors open on the side facing the group. A mysterious indigo veil rippled in the brisk evening breeze.

"In just one moment," Two-Bit advertised over the continuing chatter, "ladies and gentlemen, we will commence the show!"

Orin looked at Two-Bit, who raced around the rear of the wagon to remove the hen from her cage. Two-Bit nuzzled his face close to the creature, whispering while petting her head, brushing down the silky feathers. The chicken clucked and picked at Two-Bit's tiny chin hairs.

"Shh. Shh, shh," Two-Bit cooed.

Placing the fowl onto the landing behind the purplish curtain, he removed several alloy rings from underneath a bench. Two-Bit attached the rings to a small stand near the chicken. Lantern light sparkled from the metal, and Orin couldn't see how the hen was large enough to fit through the rings. Two-Bit straightened the silvery rings into a line across the opening. He reached into another box, removing three red vessels before placing these cups upside-down on the stage behind the chicken.

The twins sat on the edge of the wagon, stretching their limbs. They both wore their matching golden dresses with frilly white socks displaying flowery designs to their knees. Orin couldn't help but notice how clean they appeared after having traveled for miles. Their matching polished shoes mirrored the flicker of lantern light. The girls synonymously pointed their legs toward the heavens in a fantastic display of their suppleness.

Two-Bit fiddled around with various objects inside the wagon. He muttered something while placing candles of different colors and shapes behind the red vessels. The hen began nonchalantly pecking the platform, creating a hollow thud noise. The crowd just outside the wagon continued their enthusiastic chatter in anticipation of the upcoming events.

Two-Bit removed a brass horn from a crate, rubbing his perspired forehead with his coat sleeve. He placed the old dulled horn to his lips and quickly removed it, staring down at the mouthpiece. Using his sleeve, Two-Bit wiped crud from the corners of his lips before wiping the instrument's mouthpiece. The plump, short man raised the trumpet to his lips, blowing three thundering blasts.

"Ladies and gentlemen," Two-bit roared, "the moment you have all been waiting for! Our opening act of tonight stars Woodstock, our wondrous and outlandish chicken!"

With a slow wave of his hand, Two-Bit pulled the drapes to one side, revealing the hen. The clinking of his jewels was perceptible over the crowd's uproar as he gesticulated toward the opening. Two-Bit provided a proud grin as the group admired the collection of objects surrounding the chicken. Woodstock continued his repetitive raps on the stage.

Two-Bit snapped his fingers twice, and Woodstock punctually jumped through the loop in the core of the floor. The chicken just fit through the ring as it milked its body through the petite round hole. The crowd cheered and whistled, seeing the chicken perform. Woodstock turned to the side, jumping through a nearby hoop before dashing to the platform's other end. He jumped through the final ring and gave a loud *Cluck!* The creature's showmanship delighted Orin.

Laughter exploded from the crowd, and they applauded in excitement. Children sang a silly tune and hopped on their quilts. Seeing the crowd react with fascination, Orin couldn't recollect ever attending a show like Two-Bits. He remembered traveling merchants and the occasional fun show caravan, but nothing with a chicken obeying a man's command.

Two-Bit launched his next act by reaching into a sac on the ground. Removing his hand, he showed to the group he held birdseed in his pinched fingers. Placing the seed under one of the red cups, he moved the metallic rings to the side. His hands moved in rapid motion as he mixed the cups in no precise order to try and confuse the hen.

"Now, watch as Woodstock uses his inherent abilities to find the seed!"

Two-Bit snapped his fingers, and Woodstock wobbled over to the cups, plucking near one on the left side of the stage. Picking up the container, Two-Bit revealed to the crowd the chicken elected the correct choice. Woodstock pecked at the remaining seeds on the platform. Lifting the other two cups to expose nothing underneath, Two-Bit held them high in the air, presenting a toothy grin. Members of the crowd cheered and

whistled while applauding the spectacle.

This is going well, Orin thought as he browsed the animated party.

Orin examined the lively crowd. Faces of numerous skin hues gazed out behind

white, red, and yellowed eyes toward the fowl on stage. Many settlers wore overall attires

covered with dirt along with soiled button-downs. A few also donned caps that flatten out

toward the front of their heads. Some immigrants were smoking rolled cigarettes, while

others sipped from containers. Many of the men in the crowd were older, wrinkled, and

disheveled with unkempt beards.

Removing the stopper from his wineskin, Orin drank a mouthful of the grainy

liquid. Two-Bit closed the curtains while soaking in the applause beside the wagon. The

twins continued stretching behind the carriage. Two-Bit ran around to the back of the cart

and placed Woodstock into his cage. Dumping a large handful of grain into the bird's

cage, Two-Bit chuckled as the bird eagerly nipped its seeds.

"Better slow down, buddy," Two-Bit said.

He reached into the crate petting Woodstock's feathers while the hen shook its

body, allowing a lone feather to float above it.

After having another sip, Orin corked the leather pouch, letting it slap his leg as

he strapped it to his girdle. His grime-covered button-down flannel shirt floated lightly in

the frosty night breeze. Mao and Tao went into position on the stage within the wagon.

Orin winced when he saw the young women deforming their bodies, posing

awkwardly behind the curtain. Their slender pale-white limbs bent in positions Orin

never perceived or imagined possible. Orin couldn't help but stare in bewilderment.

"Orin, my tall and mighty friend," Two-Bit urged, "help me bring this basket around to the settlers while the twins ready themselves for their performance."

Picking up a wicker bin Two-Bit motion toward, Orin stepped to the crowd. Two-Bit resumed placing objects into numerous boxes and discussing something with the young women within the wagon. After a moment, Two-Bit hurried out of the carriage and clapped his hands while standing near the group.

"Now, we are setting up for our next act," Two-Bit shouted, "we would like to take a moment to thank you all for watching our show. Please, place anything you can spare into the container that my fine assistant, Orin, will bring throughout. We accept nearly everything of value, folks! Seeds for Woodstock, candles for the performance, salt, and hooch are all welcomed!"

Chains rattled loosely from Two-Bits clothes as he yelled to the masses. Orin walked among the musky homesteaders. Alcohol splashed onto Orin's boots as he continued to move among the crowd. People placed various items into the basket. A few drunk men tossed in unopened bottles of suds into the bin.

Seemed like a considerable payment to watch a bird, Orin mused.

Once the wicker container weighed heavy, Orin strolled back toward Two-Bit, who was rummaging in his wagon. Two-Bit looked at the first-round of earnings while sifting through the collection of items. Tossing the loot into an adjacent box, he quickly thanked Orin and hastily walked toward the side of his wagon facing the crowd. The jingle of his chains echoed above the anxious voices from members of the congregation. Two-Bit cleared his throat.

"L-a-a-adies and gentlemen! Our closing performance for this evening may have you investigating answers. What is life? How is it feasible? Are they human?! These my kind and weary friends are common questions to ask after seeing what we have in store. And for the fellows out there," Two-Bit suspended and studied the crowd, "you wonder if your ladies can do this in the huts. I'm here to tell you, it takes lots of practice, but it's *possible*!"

The crowd praised while cheering wildly. A few settlers threw their hats high into the night sky.

"So," Two-Bit resumed, "without further ado, let me introduce to you fine folks, Mao on the left, and Tao on the right!"

Two-Bit pulled the curtains to the side as the lantern wavered in the wind. The crowd gasped upon seeing the contorted twins. Uneasy murmurs crept from members of the group. People in the crowd became agitated and disturbed. Orin glanced over toward the twins on the platform.

Mao contorted her knees at an acute angle, pointing toward the ceiling while relaxing her head flat on the platform. She used her arm to brace her body off the box in a painstakingly awkward position. The other twin also contorted herself in a unique position. Tao planted her knees on the platform while bending her body to rest her chin and face them. Tao gave the crowd a broad grin, and Orin noticed a gap in her front teeth.

Several of the faces in the crowd turned a shade of pale and beet red. A few of the women speedily walked several paces away, fanning themselves. Children wailed and cried for their parents holding their arms high into the sky. Shouts of dismay and fear arose from the settlers.

The twins methodically moved out of their original positions and began another pose, propping themselves into a crouching place. Two-Bit squirmed and sputtered as he looked from the young women toward the group frequently. Orin stared at the twins.

This is unlike anything I'd ever seen. I wonder how these women learned to do that?

Mao and Tao moved in harmony with one another in flowing motions. Their slender limbs bent at near any angle. It was clear to Orin the twins practiced these moves many times.

Crouching on the platform, the young women tensed their palms into a fist before leaping from the opening toward the ground. They landed on their feet, narrowly avoiding the kids in the front row. Their clean shoes kicked up billows of dust toward the children. A few of them coughed and cried more emphatically. The crowd became more aroused at the recklessness of the act. Women pulled their babies away from the performers forcibly by their tiny arms.

The twin's golden dresses fluttered in the mountain breeze as they rose up, pointing their hands toward the stars. Lantern light flickered off pale faces as their long charcoal-colored hair hung down to their shoulders. Mao rapidly squatted while Tao lept over her sister. Tao grabbed her sister's shoulders while hoisting herself upside down above Mao.

The young women remained in this position as the crowd shouted at Two-Bit. Several drunk settlers in the group hollered vulgarities at the twins. Orin focused on the faces in the crowd to ensure they didn't try to attack the young women. His gaze lingered on several of the drunk men near the middle who waved bottles over their heads.

A bottle left one hand near the middle, sailing toward the twins. The glass flew between Tao's legs as she balanced herself over her sister's head. Glass shards rained down on the twins as the bottle shattered against the cart. Another projectile soared toward the twins as people shrieked while moving away from the area. The twins fell to the ground, narrowly escaping being hit by the bottle.

Orin rushed over toward the center of the crowd. The remaining settlers backed away, forming a circle enclosing the men. Orin brutally seized the nearest offender by the flesh of his neck while slamming his clenched fist against his nostrils. Blood oozed from the small openings in the middle of the man's face, splattering down his clothing and onto Orin's flannel.

Looking down to examine the stranger's blood covering his flannel sent Orin into a blind frenzy. Without thinking, he forcefully kicked the man's kneecap, sending it shooting backward, resembling an ostrich. The second culprit swung at Orin, connecting with the side of his face. Orin's teeth rattled, and he could taste blood. He staggered back a few steps to catch his balance before leaping toward the man while landing a dominant right-hook to his chest. The man roared while coming in for another punch. Orin caught this blow with a solid block and yanked his arm backward. A loud snap sprang from the settler's forearm, and Orin watched it dangling loosely from his elbow. A piece of small bone particle stabbed through the man's skin.

The men howled and shrieked as Orin placed a hand around the meaty portion of their necks while pushing them toward the wagon's backside. The man with the busted kneecap stumbled several times, but Orin held his grip firm. A few of the remaining settlers protested the treatment of the men. Still, Orin didn't pay them attention as he continued walking. The crowd dispersed back to their main hamlet.

Two-Bit stammered at the dispersing mob as he shook his flipped top-hat toward several settlers. Walking passed the twins, Two-Bit checked to ensure they were uninjured from the events.

"Don't forget folks," Two-Bit said, "We accept payments of all types! Whatever you can give for the twins! Please don't leave without paying for the entertainment this evening!"

Orin pushed the pair toward the dirt once they were behind the wagon. The mules idly grazed on sagebrush nearby. Orin could hear the settlers disbanding and Two-Bit trying to collect what he could from the stragglers.

"Why would you throw bottles at those women?" Orin asked.

"Please, sir. I di-did-didn't mean nothin' by it. I swear"

The one with the hanging arm pleaded as his bone pierced through his skin.

"They were performing their acts," Orin snarled, "adult men should not be throwing bottles."

Orin kicked at both guys as they laid sniveling on the ground. Sobs of snot and dried blood clung to their faces. One man spat his blood on Orin's boot. Enraged, Orin quickly slammed his fist into the man's temple, causing him to go limp with his tongue licking the mud.

He looked over to the man holding his dangling arm. Hovering over the man, Orin glared at him in silence. The man on the ground stuttered and spat onto the ground. Orin leaned closer to the fellow, smelling the tar and alcohol on his breath. Sweat glistened from the moonlight on his pasty forehead as he shook wincing on the ground.

"What is your name?"

"Ja-a-Jake" the man stammered.

"Who is your friend here?"

"Hi-his name is R-R-Ryan."

"Jake," Orin snapped, "don't let me see you nor Ryan ever again. If I do, I will break your other arm."

The man nodded his head eagerly, "N-n-no problem, sir. No problem at all."

Orin patted down the pockets of the unconscious man, removing a flask filled with liquid. A card attached to the side of the container read, "Robert Clement: Pittsburgh Pirates," portraying a bearded man holding a knife in his mouth. Orin tucked both items into his flannel shirt pocket before walking over to Jake, who shook on the ground. Two-Bit shuffled around the corner of the wagon.

"We must continue on soon, Orin," announced Two-Bit hurriedly, "we can't stay in this settlement after tonight's events."

Orin bent over the trembling man, feeling for any items of value in his pockets. He removed a golden flip pocket-watch attached to a tiny chain. Turning the watch over in his palm, he held it up for a closer inspection in the moonlight.

"Pl-pl-p-please that was my father's watch. It-it's all I ha-have."

"It's mine now. For the trouble, you see."

Orin hocked up phlegm and spat on the ground near the man while shaking his head. He hurried over to Two-Bit and helped pack up the remaining items from the show.

The twins sat on the bench with their fingers interlocking into a double fist. They silently watched the men shift the surrounding boxes.

Rearranging the rest of the loot received, Two-Bit blew out the candles and lanterns before placing these items into a box. Orin watched the man in the long coat as he swung the wooden doors shut, putting the rusted latch into place. Orin walked toward the mules and checked to see their straps were snug as Two-Bit removed his switch from a container behind them. Two-Bit smacked the backside of the mules with a quick motion of the switch, causing them to trot forward.

The caravan resumed its journey away from the settlement following the asphalt road to the north. Orin looked back at the men lying on the ground. In this darkness, he could see their silhouettes slowly moving. They laid underneath the glowing jaundiced-looking moon.

They could hear the remaining settlers calling to one another and shouting from the central campfire. Orin listened to a woman cry out into the darkness.

"Jake, Jake, Ja-a-ake!" she howled.

Two-Bit's caravan proceeded to the north, ignoring the various shouts and cries. They walked in silence for a long time before Two-Bit chuckled. Orin looked over at him raising his eyebrow.

"Take anything good from them?" Two-Bit asked.

"A flask and a card of some type."

Orin's temples pounded with each thump of his heart. He removed the flask from his flannel and unscrewed the cap before sniffing the contents. A sour stench wafted from the small round opening, and Orin raised the container to his lips and took a swallow. The liquid was tart and tasted how it smelled. An intense burning sensation flowed down his throat to the core of his stomach. Orin immediately felt relaxed as the alcohol sedated him. He handed the flask to Two-Bit as they continued walking.

"Well, it wasn't an ideal show, but I do believe we can restock in Ádyto," Two-Bit gently pat Orin's shoulder, "you're a good companion, Orin. Thanks for your help this evening."

Orin was not accustomed to being appreciated for his services. He grunted as they kept speed with one another. The wind wafted softly from over the foothills, blowing their coats behind them as they continued down the road.

"We'll camp once we're a couple paces north," Two-Bit said.

They strolled in silence while enjoying each other's company. The moon splashed a yellowish hue across the landscape, which allowed them to see for miles in either direction. The wooden wheels creaked as the caravan rolled down the rough asphalt road. Two-Bit's Outlandish Creatures continued its campaign rolling steadily toward Ádyto.

CHAPTER 9: ÁDYTO

They established camp between massive cement walls containing round pits. Fragments of concrete littered the ground, and Two-Bit used these to create a ring around the fire. Hours passed since Two-Bit's Outlandish Creatures performed for the settlers. Orin believed they were safe from any pursuit from those seeking revenge for Jake and Ryan.

They were scumbags, Orin reflected as he gathered firewood.

He listened keenly to the encircling sounds. The irregular sigh from the mules and hooting from an owl was the only noise above the constant bone-piercing wind. Orin clenched his leather windbreaker around his torso while stacking a pile of wood near the ring of concrete.

When he returned to camp with enough wood to last the evening, he sat on a concrete piece lifting the flask from his shirt. The drink calmed the tremors in his hands. If he didn't keep a steady supply of alcohol, he became dizzy. He also shook with increasing intensity until he quenched his thirst. The worst of it was when his eyes rapidly twitched to the sides. Booze helped calm his nerves enough to subside these tremors.

Staring across the blaze at the twins, he noticed they were unobtrusively eating crackers in a sleeve. Two-Bit flung Orin a package of salted meat with wafers once he started the fire. He thanked Two-Bit, and hastily made himself a sandwich. Orin washed the crackers and meat down with another drink before tossing the remaining contents of the flask toward the plump man.

"You did well this evening," Two-Bit announced as they sat around the fire, "those men got what they deserve. Although, I wish we have resolved it more amicably."

"I'm not sure what amicably means, but you do put on an interesting show."

"I expect we will arrive in Ádyto during the late morning hours," Two-Bit nodded and cracked a toothy grin, "you'll receive your whiskey once we reach the stadium."

Ádyto must be a fascinating place. I wonder who lives there? And where should I look for Liam? Orin removed his wineskin and took sips of the brisk liquor. The wind wailed while sweeping down from the ridges above and around the box wagon. Orin deeply inhaled the crisp scent of roasting pine as he reflected on their destination.

"What is Ádyto like?" Orin asked.

"It's a stadium among the rubble," commented Two-Bit waving his hand in a significant oval gesture, "many people gather there. I wouldn't recommend venturing too far outside Ádyto among the ruin, though. Rift-raft and desperate scavengers cling to their impoverished lives with whatever hope they have remaining. Also, stay away from the bottom level of the place."

"The bottom-level?"

"Yes, the stadium splits into several levels—five in total with the affluent sharing the view from the top while hoarding most of the wealth. The middle levels, three and four, are where you find many shops selling an assortment of items. Great drinking places on those levels, too. When you enter through the central entrance, you are on the second level where stores sell produce and other food wares. In the center field of the stadium, animals are stabled, and crops are grown to sell."

Orin tossed a small log onto the campfire, watching as the embers grew into a low flame catching the additional fuel. The twins finished their meal and silently shuffled toward the wagon. Orin dusted off the cracker crumbs from his jeans while watching the youthful women crawl into the carriage.

"What does Ádyto mean, anyhow?"

"Beats me. Probably something to do with it being a safe-haven among the chaos."

"Like a utopia?" Orin asked.

"Hah! I'm not sure it's that safe to call Ádyto a 'utopia,' but it's safer than being on a settlement, I suppose. The Righteous Warheads, for instance, wouldn't dare attack the stadium. Not with the heavy defenses and guards stationed every few paces."

"How often have you made the trip to Ádyto?"

"Enough times, the stable boy has a reserve spot for my mules!" Two-Bit laughed before continuing, "I come through that entrance, and people say, 'here comes that Two-Bit feller!' Stable his stagecoach pronto!"

"Seems as if you receive the fifth-level service," Orin raised an eyebrow skeptical at Two-Bit.

"And I should, I should think! With how many trades I offer them. The loot my Outlandish Creatures brings in paid for the third-level renovations!" he chuckled while using his chubby fingers to wipe crumbs from his mouth.

"Last time I was there," Two-Bit continued, "Jerry, the bartender at Dee's Tavern, enjoyed my performance with Woodstock so much he let me drink until I passed out," Two-Bit chortled, "when I awoke, he out-drank me until I passed out, again! Hah! They love me at Dee's place, I tell you. And that Jerry is a great fellow. Say, perhaps I can introduce the two of you."

"I would like to meet Jerry."

"Yeah, he's a connected person. I am sure he can help you locate your brother."

People talk loudly and often when drunk. Jerry may help me find Liam. He must know something about the Righteous Warheads.

Orin tossed Two-Bit his wineskin, and the men shared drinks while eating the last of the salted meat. They both chuckled over the ridiculousness of the evening's events. Although the show ended abruptly, Two-Bit felt he made out well with the first round of collections. The men were in good spirits as they drank while Orin listened to Two-Bits tales of his travels. With the alcohol providing a festive buzz, the men retired to padded blankets near the wagon.

* * *

Ádyto's broken arena walls emerged in the distance. The caravan made a slow pace over the fractured pavement as they proceeded toward the stadium. Passing dense pre-war ruins, Orin noticed most looked empty By degrees, the structures grew more condensed as they careened around chunks of blasted walls and hollowed, rusted automobiles.

The wagon squeaked as the mules led the carriage toward the oval-shaped arena. Merchants shouted their wares to the caravan as they passed. Crowds of poor and scroungers huddled amongst the ruins to keep warm. Laborers in tattered apparel pushed modest carts containing various items. Men and women carried produce-filled bushels on their heads. Donkeys and mules pulled wagons loaded with vegetables and grains toward

Ádyto. Carts filled with livestock or whole carcasses of meat; goats and sheep herded in lines, and settlers selling these wares dotted the street. Haggard women were wearing stained bandanas to prevent their stringy hair falling across their faces while pulling buckets of water from a nearby stream.

As the carriage pulled closer to the stadium, Orin noted there appeared to be an entire concourse of people treading through the stadium with various supplies. Approaching Ádyto, the noise and foot traffic steadily increased; when they arrived within a hundred yards of the towering stadium, the sounds rose into a loud whirling roar of movement.

Orin was in shock at the number of people in one place. Raised on small settlements and matured by a loose collection of mercenaries, the number of people surprised Orin. Settlements guarded by the Squad never held over twenty to thirty people within them, occasionally with as few as ten!

Ádyto must have thousands of people!

Orin gawked in wide-eyed wonderment at the sights and sounds surrounding the caravan. He felt a sensation of anonymity among the buzzing crowd. Orin's gaze honed-in on a horse statue standing out of the ground by its neck. The figure jutted from the Earth, exposing various stains and grime down its body. Strange symbols of graffiti scattered across the torso and limbs. Orin stepped cautiously over one of the significant rifts which jutted out from the stallion.

Children gave chase, bobbing, and weaving as they clambered around the horse statue. Orin curiously pondered why people would prop a stud upside-down in the road.

Orin found the sight strange and couldn't help but glue his eyes to the curious statue as they passed.

Gazing up the massive stadium walls, Orin noticed multitudes of birds squawking and circling over concrete spirals running the structure's length. Tiny figures of people shuffled behind the thin veil of curtains on the fifth-level. The lack of curtains on the fourth level allowed Orin to see scores of people performing their work. A section of the wall was blown away, allowing Orin to see blacksmiths pounding on anvils, sending sparks flying with each strike. The singe of metal touching more lukewarm liquids resounded above the noise from the marketplace. Two-Bit muttered something inaudible above the uproar.

A vile-smelling moat coursed the parameter of the stadium. Orin heard water spilling into the ditch. Looking over the bridge, he noticed a rusted pipe spilling lime-colored water into the stagnating river. An assortment of litter drifted in the liquid. Orin gagged as the rotten eggs, and sour mash stench wafted into his nostrils. Orin felt a wave of dizziness sweep through his body and turned away from the water.

The moat could be defensive by the stench of the water. I doubt anyone would try their luck crossing over to the other side of this river, Orin pondered.

"Hot bread! Hot bread!" bellowed a vendor pushing his way in front of their wagon.

"Excuse us, good sir," Two-Bit said.

"Move it," yelled the man as he hurried into the stadium.

Two-Bit's wagon passed through the arched entryway leading to the second-level corridor. The mules appeared accustomed to this routine and continued walking forward toward the center arena. Mud and straw heavily compacted the ground allowing the wheels of the wagon to roll gracefully across the walkway. Small shops and stalls lined both sides of the passage around the stadium. Hordes of people shouted at one another while conducting various transactions.

"Onions, potatoes, tomatoes," a merchant shouted, "come get 'em here, fresh from the garden!"

"Hey! Yeah, you!" another called, "you look like you could use a good meal. Come try my stew!"

"Hot soup! Hot soup!"

One shop keeper from behind a counter waved a wooden spoon toward Orin. The merchant presented a gaping smile beneath his baggy, beady eyes. The man's beard was unkempt, and Orin noticed food particles sprinkled throughout his coarse hairs.

Hardly someone I would buy soup from, Orin thought while examining graffiti painted across the stadium walls.

"Fresh's meats," a bedraggled woman yelled, "get 'yer meats ta here! Sausage, veal, venison, and 'un steaks!"

Shaking a bloodied cleaver into the air, she screeched while staring directly at Orin. A black hole covered one of her eyes, and Orin couldn't help but notice a considerable gnashing scar across half of her face. Orin moved out of the way as the meat vendor continued waving her knife around her body as she cracked a toothless grin. Orin shivered from the woman's sight and kept his pace with Two-Bit as they continued to cross the hall.

"Homemade liverwurst here! I grow the mustard myself! Going fast! Come get it while it lasts!"

As they walked through the center arena archway, Orin couldn't help but notice a lady dressed in silk linens leaning on a low post outside. Her pink dress and floral-laced red stole flowed elegantly in the flurry floating in through the stadium. She brushed a white lacy veil to reveal her sultry smile as the mules walked past. When Orin was within reaching distance, she lightly grazed his arm with her fingers, causing his hair to stand on end.

"Care to have fun?"

The woman gave Orin a sudden wink, and he couldn't turn away. Her sweet rosy perfume lingered in the air, making Orin breathe deeply. He wanted to take it all in. Orin never saw a woman so alluring and captivating. He noticed the bronze pouches under her copper-colored eyes. The way her long eyelashes rolled upward toward the high heavens.

"Not right now, sweetie. We have a business to attend," Two-Bit interjected, "thank you kindly, perhaps I can use your services this evening, mm-hm?"

"Hardly," the woman responded.

"Well, that's no way to drum up repeat sales, I'd say!"

Two-Bit held up his right hand to ignore the prostitute as he tilted his top hat. She crossed her arms with a look of disgust as she glared at Two-Bit. The mules continued leading the wagon down the extended ramp toward the center of the stadium. Two-Bit's jewelry lightly jingled as they walked down the hard-concrete slope.

Orin's eyes stung from the intense sunshine spilling across the arena. He couldn't help thinking about the beautiful woman and the way she emanated. He stole a few glances back toward her, but someone preoccupied her attention.

Orin swore under his breath as his hands trembled. He bungled at his side for his wineskin. Bringing the wineskin up to his mouth, he spilled a substantial amount down the front of his jacket as he tried to drink. The surrounding sensations were overwhelming. He was not used to the roar of a crowd. The grainy whiskey he swallowed helped drown out the commotion and made the experience tolerable. He felt nauseous as he looked at Two-Bit. Feeling exhausted, Orin stopped walking, closing his eyes to stave off, dizzying vertigo. Orin slowly gulped down another drink keeping his eyes closed.

"You okay?" Two-Bit asked.

"I'm fine," Orin gasped, "just needed a drink."

After several deep breaths, Orin took a moment to examine the sea of tents in various sizes and colors leading up the rows of steps around the stadium. People were attending to their chores among the tents. Orin watched as some hung laundry, washed in bins, and others used the open latrines off to the side. Taking a deep sip from the wineskin, Orin admired the organized chaos. It was enough to allow him a moment to appreciate the resiliency of humankind.

The intensity of energy within the stadium amazed him. Cloth banners in faded peach and cerulean hues hung down from towering poles around the stadium. Orin could not read the signs nor understand the strange symbols covering the flags. He noticed the closest ones displayed small horse heads and wondering if that had anything to do with the statue outside.

Perhaps they held horse auctions here. Or maybe horse races, Orin pondered as he corked the wineskin.

"Why do they hang flags from the towers?" Orin asked.

"They represent the lineage of the high-society of Ádyto. Each name derived from the founding members of this city. Though the original high-society has passed to the other side," Two-Bit paused waving his round fingers, "the descendants enjoy the luxuries of the fifth level."

The mules arrived on the grassy field, and Two-Bit clicked his tongue while guiding them toward the stables. Orin inhaled the foul stench of defecation from the animals roaming the nearby boarding pens. Two-Bit raised his open palm toward the wooden structure off to the side.

"These are the stables; we will rent a stall for the wagon here."

Seizing the reins dangling in front of the mules, Two-Bit led them toward the giant structure. As they entered the building, Orin noticed a dense blanket of straw bedding sprinkled across the ground. Wooden stalls divided the corridor of the structure with a few containing various farm animals. Horses neighed, and goats cried out as the caravan creaked through the large stable doors. Orin coughed into his arm to clear the stench of excrement.

A small, thin stable boy with a dark brown furrowed face approached the men as they entered the stable. A broad toothless smile stretched across his pockmark-laden cheekbones. A tall, scraggy man twice the boy's size came into the corridor from behind dragging on a pipe. They both wore patterned flannel shirts and tattered overalls. A haze of smoke hung above the man as he greeted Two-Bit with a friendly wave.

"Nice to see you again, Jessiah."

Two-Bit grinned while rubbing the top of his hat. The stable boy grabbed the reins from Two-Bit, leading the mules and wagon further down the passageway. His clothing was uneven, with many rips running down the shin from the boy's knees.

"And you Two-Bit," the stable master replied casually, puffing his pipe, "the usual, I presume?"

"Yes, Jessiah. Park the wagon, and I need to retrieve a few items. Also, I have a pair of twins in the wagon. If you would be so kind as to unlock the doors to allow them to stretch their legs."

The seasoned man lifted his bony fingers toward the brim of his straw hat, tilting it toward Two-Bit with a nod. The hat resembled a hat worn by the settlers on the front range. Orin noticed the similar curved recess in the middle, unlike the usual flatten cotton caps worn by those near the entrance. Jessiah appeared to work in the sun every hour of his life as his skin darkened and was profoundly creased. His patchy gray hairs dotted the bottom of his chin and neckline. Jessiah dumped the remaining contents of the pipe onto the ground before stuffing it into his faded overall pockets.

"Your boy is looking healthy! What have you been feedin' 'em? Hah!" Two-Bit exclaimed before laughing and whistling while leaning backward on his boot heels. The young boy glanced over his shoulder, forming a gaping grin revealing a small rotten stump of a molar. The boy was charmed with the complement.

"Jonas is growing by the day I tell yah," Jessiah hesitated, "turning into a big pain in the rear! Hah!"

The man chuckled as he cracked his joke. His son's grin quickly transformed into a sour expression at the insult. There was a slight whistle in Jessiah's tone as he talked between significant gaps in his teeth. Spittle sprinkled Orin's face as the stableman was sent from his laughing into a hacking fit.

"I will need the mules to be reshoed and promptly if you'd like. I was hoping to leave this evening for a settlement to the north."

Two-Bit reached his hand into his coat pocket, producing a packet of seeds before tossing it over to Jessiah. The man caught the seeds, looking them over carefully.

"Ah, a bean sprouts, carrots, and corn! This will do fine," Jessiah shook the seed pouch, "not a problem, Two-Bit. We should have 'er done before dusk!"

Jonas unhitched the mules from the wagon once parked in a vacant stall. The stable boy led the creatures to a neighboring booth across from the carriage. Using a pitchfork, Jonas gathered hay into a pile for the mules and shut the stall doors. Two-Bit tossed the keys to the wagon toward Jonas and instructed him to open the back. The boy beamed and scurried around the end of the cart.

"Say Two-Bit," Jessiah continued, "have I ever told you what it means to find a horseshoe?"

"I'm afraid I don't know Jessiah, what does it mean to find a horseshoe?"

"Finding a horseshoe means some poor horse is walking around in his stockings!"

Jessiah let out a hearty laugh, which quickly escalated into a choking cough. The man pulled out a handkerchief and blew his nose, continuing to laugh between gasps of air. Orin could hear a shrill cackle crop up from Jonas near the wagon as he fumbled with the lock.

"Say old feller, did you make that up on your own?" Two-Bit grinned.

Orin smiled at Jessiah's attempt at a witty, stable joke. The man reminded Orin of the joyous nature he was accustomed to with Liam. A tinge of worry swept through him as he remembered his brother and his eyes welled up with tears.

"That I did Two-Bit!" Jessiah responded as he finished hacking up phlegm.

"Take it easy on the smokes, will you?" Two-Bit said, "I need you around! Who else will stable those stubborn mules!"

"Wi-will do!" he choked between hoarse, hard hacking spasms.

The stableman leaned against a wooden post to support his balance and catch his wheezing breath. Two-Bit slapped him on the back, attempting to help the man hack up the mucus. Jessiah held a palm up to Two-Bit, showing he would be fine as he covered his mouth.

The twins walked over to the group with Jonas. They looked the same as they did in the morning when they left the camp. One twin curiously glanced around the room as they approached.

"Now, head to the market up the ramp and search for the largest squash and potatoes," Two-Bit said, handing them a pouch, "I have something in mind for supper tonight."

The twins both grinned as one accepted the pouch and scampered with their long, stemmy legs toward the stable doors. Orin watched both young women turn toward Two-

Bit to bow together near the doors. Jessiah waved a sizeable dark hand in their direction as he regained his composure.

They do everything in unison. It's as if they read each other's minds, Orin admired, *and how they accept being cooped up in those cramped conditions for so long. Unbelievable.*

Two-Bit led the assembly over to the wagon reaching inside one box. He slipped a few items into his pockets and handed a treat to Jonas. Jonas eagerly accepted and clapped his hands excitedly.

"Almost forgot, this is for you, my dear friend, Orin!"

Two-Bit handed Orin the pristine bottle of honey-colored whiskey. The liquid sloshed in the container as Orin admired the label, "Turnerburg's *Distilled Whiskey*."

This whiskey was packaged before the war! How this bottle survived the last fifty years?

Orin's hands shook with his excitement, and he rubbed his tongue across the roof of his dried mouth. He thanked Two-Bit before placing the bottle into his bag with the cans of food hanging from his belt. Orin wanted to taste the whiskey but did not wish to share, and so he instead opened the cork of his wineskin. Two-Bit chuckled as he watched Orin drink.

"No," Two-Bit said, "thank you for getting us here safely!"

"Good sir, we are bound for Dee's tavern," Two-Bit said, turning toward Jessiah, "take care of those mules! And if those twins turn up with my food, kindly set it to the side and direct them to wait for my arrival. I shan't be too long!"

"The mules be all right, now y'er hear?"

A hacking fit erupted from Jessiah's lungs as Orin followed Two-Bit toward the entrance of the stables. The mules whined as they saw Two-Bit walking away. Orin breathed slowly through his mouth to avoid inhaling the rank odor of confined animals and tobacco. His drink burned the back of his throat while giving a warming feeling in the pit of his stomach. Orin was satisfied with the outcome of his journey with Two-Bit. He reached down and felt the bottle in his bag, which clinked against the aluminum cans.

Somehow, booze makes life more tolerable.

Orin waved to Jessiah, who was hacking up phlegm near the wagon as they exited the stables. The pair proceeded up the ramp toward the second-level foyer. Looking at the other half of the field, Orin noticed it contained gardens with vegetables and fruit trees neatly plotted. People plucked the crops, placing them into bins and others carrying them toward the market. Animals lazily cried as the sun beat hot upon the field. The settlers built wooden enclosures to keep animals isolated from one another. To a man accustomed to working the land and helping settlers fend off wolves or the occasional bandit, Ádyto was surreal.

"Seeds for the blind?" a beggar croaked.

The man's face was grotesque, containing open sores with oozing puss dotting his arms and neck. His silvery beard and greasy sun-bleached hair touched the concrete ground from where he sat against a post. He rattled a tin cup toward the men as they stepped up the ramp to the marketplace's entryway.

"No, we do not," Two-Bit replied.

"I swear," Two-Bit said, gesturing toward Orin, "you offer them one seed, and the problem worsens. Kindness attracts the panhandlers and like flies to a honey trap."

Orin felt remorseful for not helping the beggar, but he didn't have much to give. Once they entered the foyer of the second-level, they turned to the east and walked the passageway. Mingling with the crowd was effortless. People seemed to be preoccupied bartering for goods or eating meals to notice them.

Orin pushed his way through assemblages of people converging in the middle of the walkway. Off to the side, beggars and feverous people asked for food and seeds. Other groups sat around beating empty buckets with their fists creating a rhythmic thud. The repetitive beats were heard down the corridor above the chorus of chatter and shouts.

"You trust the twins in this mess?" Orin asked.

"Yes, I do because," Two-Bit said as he pointed toward two guards standing off to the side between merchant stalls. The guards wore dark green uniforms covering their bodies with black gloves and gas masks. Green caps were tightly worn on their scalps, similar to those worn by some Squad members. Each of the guards firmly gripped a powerful rifle pointed toward the ground. Orin only saw these types of weapons occasionally and never out in the open.

"Aren't they a beauty," Two-Bit whistled, "those guards will shoot anyone dead if they messed with those young ladies."

They walked toward a set of stairs near the outer wall of the stadium. The soreness Orin felt from connecting his knee to Denk's spear almost wholly subsided. Orin placed his hands on his thighs as they walked up the stairs for support.

When they reached the third-level landing, Orin took a moment to study the various shops selling clothing and antiques. Several shops presented graffiti advertising card games in the back rooms. Several scruffy adolescences shot dice against the wall, throwing down little pouches with each turn.

They walked along this corridor, which was as full as the one below. People rushed around while attending to their business. A few individuals carried boxes of items or piles of clothing in their arms while hobbling down the hallways. After moving through the sea of people, they came to a large sign advertising alcohol.

Filled with excitement, Orin took a moment to examine the bar sign. Graffiti art covered dull cement blocks above a large wooden door read, *"Dee's Tavern,"* and right below it, *"the only place with the pipe bomb drink!"* An eroded painted image of a bomb with a wick sparking at the top appeared after the last line on the blocks. Orin somehow knew he was destined to find this place.

CHAPTER 10: LOOSE LIPS, SINK SHIPS.

Dim lanterns illuminated across the dozens of round wooden tables. A spacious

bar with a shaded chestnut backdrop lined the far wall of the room. Candlelight flickered

from the glass bottles lining the shelves. Orin's parched mouth salivated at the display of

all the alcohol. He followed Two-Bit toward a row of cushioned stools wrapped in red

fabric.

Within Dee's Tavern, people sat around tables drinking alcohol and playing card

games. Patrons filled the room with merriment, song, and excessive smoke. Orin gazed

around the room, occupied with people from all walks of life. Some wore neat suits and

dresses, while others presented the typical attire of blind assorted fabrics.

"All in, you donkey biscuits!" exclaimed a man crashing his fists on the table.

Two-Bit continued toward the bar, motioning with his hand toward a well-dressed

fellow cleaning the inside of a glass. Orin hacked a cough into his arm and tried not to

notice the ensuing disturbance over at the table. He sat on the barstool next to Two-Bit.

"Jerry! The one, the legendary, my man!"

"Eh, hey there you. It's a' been a while Two-Bit.," Jerry replied, "how've you

been, yah know with the circus thing and all?"

"It's a freak show."

"Say, you gon' get one of those, eh what you call it, uh the lions and bears?"

"Splendid idea, Jerry! One problem, where would I get a lion or a bear?"

"Eh, I saw it on paper. And might know a guy," Jerry shrugged his shoulders

quickly while smacking his teeth, "you know, Two-Bit, we're, uh, still recovering from

the last incident. No outlandishness this time, capisci?"

"Jerry, the outlandishness stays in the stables," Two-Bit presented his open palms, "we are all good. Orin and I would appreciate a couple rounds if you don't mind."

"You got payment this time?" Jerry asked as he glanced Orin over.

"Jerry, a man after my heart and purse, you see, I thought we had an understanding?"

"An understanding, eh?"

"Yes!" Two-Bit exclaimed, flashing a grin while raising his eyebrows, "remember two fortnights ago when I entertained your fine patrons because you ran out of malted bubblies?"

"Doesn't matter, I'm in a lousy way and need payment."

"Is that so?" Two-Bit asked.

"It is so, and that is how it will be! I need payment this time Two-Bit."

"Calm down, Jerry, my friend. I am just jiving with you. I am good for it. And you know I am. Here are a couple seed packets, and there's more in the wagon. You'll be paid," Two-Bit lowered his voice, "now, can my friend and I, please have two of your finest scotch beverages?"

"Who's this guy?"

"Orin and he is a zealous fellow might I add," Two-Bit responded with a chuckle.

Looking Orin over, Jerry agreed and grinned. Reaching behind the back bar, he removed two glasses, which he set in front of the men. Jerry swiftly pulled a bottle with a caramel-colored liquid from the top shelf and poured it into the glasses. Without spilling a drop, the plaid-suited bartender capped the bottle and placed it under the counter. He resumed his chore of cleaning another glass with a stained rag.

"Let me know if you need another, Two-Bit. It's good meeting you, Orin."

They raised their glasses as Jerry walked to the other side of the bar. Two-Bit smiled at Orin and shook his head enthusiastically. After an abrupt pause, Orin noticed tears in Two-Bit's eyes and his lip quiver.

"To our journey, you have been a proper companion. I hope you find your brother," Two-Bit stated.

"It has been an experience."

"Not without the risks. If I could do it again, I would," Two-Bit's red eyes welled with tears.

"To our health, wealth, and prosperity," Orin said.

Orin lifted his glass with shaking hands. The salivation he experienced upon entering Dee's Tavern had withered, and his throat became itchy. Through stinging eyes, he clinked his glass with Two-Bits.

Downing the dark liquid, Orin welcomed the mild lightheadedness he felt. His sight became a familiar haze, and he looked over his shoulder across the room. A man in the corner plucked the strings of an elongated, curved wood instrument. The vibrating sounds emanating from the device were soft, low, and pleasant.

"Jerry!" Two-Bit shouted down the bar, "Jerry, my friend, Jerry! Come down here for a minute!"

"What's it this time?"

"My friend, Orin, and I would like another round!"

"Are you paying for it?"

"I will when I get back to the wagon, we agreed to this."

"We agreed to the first drink," Jerry said, leaning under the bar, "but I like this quiet Orin guy. Maybe you can learn a thing or two from Orin, eh, Two-Bit?"

"You never mentioned how you are in a lousy way," Two-Bit recommenced.

"I didn't volunteer the information."

"Come on! We're all friends here!" Two-Bit exclaimed, taking his glass from the bartender, "drink with us for a moment, will you?"

Jerry poured Orin a glass of the spirits before removing another empty half-pint from behind the back bar. As he poured his own drink, Orin watched the booze splash against the bottom of the glass. Orin enjoyed the way it curled right near the top like a wave crashing down. He was familiar with ocean waves from the picture books he read as a child. Jerry raised his glass in a toast, which snapped Orin out of his daydream.

"Salute!" Jerry announced.

"Salute!" they repeated.

"Listen, Jerry, Orin is in a lousy state too," Two-Bit said while imbibing his drink, "maybe you can chat and help each other out? And if he can't help you, ah what the hell, talking is a form of medicine. Or was that laughter?"

"Ah, Two-Bit if there's one thing you're good for, it's talking," Jerry laughed as he downed his liquor before slamming the glass on the counter, "okay, so listen. I have an earner who didn't want to pay me."

Jerry leaned in close enough for Orin to inhale his stale cologne. His fedora hat tipped forward as he gave a wink. Tapping on the counter twice, Jerry poured them another round before pointing his finger at Orin.

"You know, Orin. I don't like it when I don't get paid. Yah dig? It's not good for business."

"What do you mean you didn't get paid?" Orin asked before draining his drink.

"Sent a bagman to rob the shipment during our weekly drop-off," Jerry's face turned red as he slammed his liquor, "can you believe the nerve of the guy? Now, I'm out a dozen cases of liquor and must deal with a dead man. Cazzo!"

"Pour yourself another drink, Jerry. Penumbra knows you need it," Two-Bit said, "and while you're at it, pour us another."

"What did you say?" Orin shot a penetrating look toward Two-Bit.

"I asked our friendly bartender to pour us another round. Settle down, settle down."

"Penumbra?" Orin asked, raising an eyebrow over his empty drink glass.

"Heh," Two-Bit became fidgety, "it's no-nothing, really. Merely a figure of speech is all."

"And you," Jerry poured another round out of the bottle while pointing at Two-Bit, "you will pay me for these drinks. Or your friend can retrieve my merchandise. Salute!"

Jerry clinked his glass with the others as they raised another round high in the air. Cards shuffled and chips scattered across tables behind them. The musician in the corner continued strumming the strings of his wooden instrument. Cocktail waitresses flirted with patrons hoping to receive extra payment. Glasses clinked around them above the chorus of conversation. The room was lively, and the sensations overwhelmed Orin as he swayed on his barstool.

"Sounds like you and Orin have similar needs and interests," Two-Bit said.

"Is that so?" Orin asked.

"Well, sure! You're both looking for someone," Two-Bit turned toward Jerry, "Orin is looking for his brother and can help you find your ex-earner, shall I say? Tell him, Orin."

"Where is your brother?" Jerry inquired.

"I believe the Righteous Warheads enslaved him," Orin responded solemnly.

"Not so loud," Jerry hissed, "I may know something about the location of Kraken," Jerry waived his glass, "see, I need to find my earner and collect what's rightfully mine. You need to find your brother. Let's say we help one another out?"

"How does he know that you know the whereabouts of the Righteous Warheads?" Two-Bit questioned.

"I'm a bartender," responded Jerry, "I overheard something said a couple nights ago."

"Fine," Orin whispered.

"I'm sorry, what was that?"

"I said fine, dammit!" Orin shouted, slamming his glass on the counter.

"Hello there! Take it easy, will you? I will make the arrangements this evening," Jerry said, "but watch that temper, Orin. Some wise guy, eh?"

Jerry shook a finger in Orin's direction while glaring at him as he walked to the other side of the bar. Orin sat on his barstool and reviled while finishing his drink. Watching Jerry, Orin shifted the weight of his rifle as he saw a man pass the bartender a note.

"Don't sweat him, Orin," Two-Bit rapped the bar counter lightly, "that's the way he does business. He will come through for you, you'll see."

"We have a way to collect," Jerry said, walking back toward Orin, "if you're still interested in finding Kraken, that is?"

"Let's hear it," Orin replied.

"The bagman, Sparks, is meeting with an associate of Big Jim, the big earner, tonight near a settlement just to the west away. You see? Now, I need you to head over there when the moon is directly overhead, that's when the deal will go down. You let the deal go down, you collect the goods from both parties. The place is a slight distance outside the city. So, don't go wandering over there too soon. Capisci?"

"What type of goods?"

"Anything you find of value. I need you to find a jar of pills, mostly antibiotics. The bagman should have it on him. Grab the medicine and any seeds, salt, or liquor bottles you can carry, get those too."

Shaking Jerry's extended hand, Orin accepted the deal. He asserted he would retrieve the antibiotics and any other items of value. Jerry poured them another round as he gave a sizeable gaping smile.

"Great man, you got here Two-Bit. Tell you what," Jerry continued, "Two-Bit you still owe me for the other drinks. But this next round is on me."

"You agreed Orin's errand would cover these drinks."

"Shh, Two-Bit. It's not classy to complain. No, Orin's paying for information for his brother. You still owe for these drinks."

Two-Bit stammered as Jerry held up a palm. Orin's head was swirling from the spirits. He hadn't been this intoxicated in months, and it felt good. He embraced the mild buzz as he held up his glass filled with caramel-colored sour drink.

"Salute," Jerry stated.

"Salute," the others echoed.

Two-Bit slurred thanks to Jerry for the drink as he shifted his attention toward other patrons down the bar. Orin felt content as he observed people engaged in their gambling endeavors. A few carried chips over toward the bar cashing in for bottles of liquor. The solo band in the corner continued plucking the strings creating a reverberating sound across the room.

"I tell yoush, Orin!" Two-Bit slunk onto the bar, "you hear me?! I tell you, you're no you sir, are the fi-i-nest, FINEST, man I have met in a long while."

"Thanks, Two-Biiiirrtt," Orin belched, "I appreciate you showing me around Ádyto."

"Oh, don't mention it," Two-Bit's rosy cheeks were bloodshot, "le-let me tell you somethin' else that happened in here!"

Two-Bit smacked his knee while squinting, gaping mouth as he laughed. His laughter turned into a hacking cough as a bout of hiccups overcame him. Orin slapped him on the back hard until he held up a hand.

"This fellow Jerry," Two-Bit continued while smacking his lips, "Hah! He needs a cut of damn near everything' round here! He does! Well, one night, not too long ago! Hic! I swindled a patron of his out a pound of salt! I did it!"

"So," Orin raised an eyebrow, "what's the problem?"

"Didn't you listen? Jerry takes a cut of everything involving his bar, and I didn't give it to him! If only he knew."

"... reaching the Utopia."

Orin's attention shifted toward the table behind them. The discussion they were having was challenging to discern above the excitement in the barroom. Orin turned his head to the side, diverting his focus away from his companions' drunken story.

Could this be the same Utopia?

"… I don't know 'bout it."

"shall see..."

One man banged his mug down onto the felt-covered table. He scooped his chips into a sack and scooted his chair across the concrete floor. Orin steadied himself with one hand on the bar counter as he turned around on the stool.

"Say!" Two-Bit exclaimed, slapping Orin's leg, "did I ever tell you how I met those twins, Orin?"

"No, you haven't."

Orin remembered Two-Bit sharing his tale how he found the twins under a tree. He decided to entertain his acquaintance and let him tell his version of the story while intoxicated. Atticus used to say to members of the Squad that the truth came out with booze. Orin figured Two-Bit would tell him the truth now.

"Well, I was-h walkin' 'long a rushing river one lonely night," Two-Bit began in a whisper, "not too far in the foothills over yonder. There I was minding my business and alone in my thoughts. I had just finished a show in Nightingale near the mining caves. Suddenly, I heard a blood-curdling scream in the darkness near the road."

"And what happened?"

"Two men raided a caravan. One of them killed the husband. The mother wailed and pleaded for the twins as the butchers bickered over which one of them would have their way with the ladies."

"What did you do?"

"I directed my mercenary to shoot those thugs," Two-Bit laughed, "then, I took the twins and left the mother to her own."

"Why didn't you leave the twins with their mother?"

"Well, I figured that if the mother weren't fit, you see, for taking care and protecting the twins. That I was doing both a service!"

"You kidnapped those twins, you bastard," Orin snarled, "they don't belong to you. What happened to you finding them watching a building burn to the ground? You are a liar!"

Orin's furiously clenched his fists. A patron at an adjacent table stood up and delivered a right hook flying toward Two-Bit's face. The connection dazed the stout man as he dropped from the barstool. The stranger kicked Two-Bit repeatedly in the stomach as other patrons cheered and hollered. People raised glasses around the bar as they supported the fight.

Orin hesitated before intervening, rather enjoying the sight of this dishonest man now disheveled. Once blood dripped from Two-Bit's mouth onto the concrete, Orin pushed the man off the freak show operator. He grabbed Two-Bit by the shoulder as he hoisted him to his feet.

"Hey, hey, you two," Jerry shouted, "stop that now!"

"You get your friend," the man spat at Orin, "take him out of here. Disgusting fat pig."

Two-Bit picked up his hat from the ground, dusted it off and placed it back on his head. The low murmurs of voices gradually emerged into a surge of chatter from tables across the room. The bassist in the corner plucked the strings of his instrument in a slow rhythmic manner.

With his arm around Two-Bit's back, Orin clenched his neck while leading him toward the entrance. Orin opened the door, pushing Two-Bit outside to the ground.

"Don't let me see you again," Orin hissed shaking a clenched fist at Two-Bit, "if I do and you still have the twins performing in your act, I won't go easy on you as they did."

"B-b-but wait!" Two-Bit stammered, "what about?"

"And I'm keeping the gun!" Orin spat while touching the cherrywood handle tucked in his waist.

Turning toward the bar, Orin closed the dense wooden door shut behind him. He left Two-Bit out in the corridor and denounced his name. Orin thought Two-Bit was a scumbag for kidnapping and enslaving the twins into his performance. To top it off, he felt betrayed and lied to by his former companion.

Orin sauntered toward the bar and watched the patrons resume their drinking and gambling activities. He ordered another glass of scotch and drank it down slowly. Sitting at the bar, Orin stared at the crowd and soaked in the room's atmosphere. His thoughts turned to Mao and Tao and what they may do outside Two-Bit's care. He then thought of the cultists he escaped and Two-Bit's mentioning of Penumbra. As he sipped his drink, he cursed the Righteous Warheads for Liam going missing. His thoughts never returned to Two-Bit for the rest of the evening. Not even once.

CHAPTER 11: AND THEN THERE WERE NONE.

The distant howling of wolves pierced the calm night above the chorus of cricket tunes. Hunched low as he trudged through the sagebrush, Orin headed toward a sand dune overlooking a rocky ravine. A campfire bounced light across the desert fields and crumbled structures as he kept himself concealed in trenches of the dunes. Thankful for the cool breeze sweeping in over the foothills, Orin concealed his footsteps and advanced along the sandy ridgeline. Orin looked behind him, examining the shadows of the spiral columns around Ádyto. The pillars towered in the distance as the moonlight outlined its silhouette across the horizon.

Orin peeked his head just over the dune toward the campfire below. Several men in suits warmed themselves by the glow. Orin saw them speaking with one another but couldn't discern what they were saying. A fierce gust from the foothills flung particles of dust at Orin's eyes. Using his jacket, Orin shielded his face while glimpsing through a sliver in his arm toward the people below. He transferred his weight to one side while stumbling over toward a decayed brick wall near the ridge.

Orin had a clear view of the deal from this vantage. He was sure he could remain undetected while preventing wind gusts from blinding him with sand. Cupping a palm over his ear, he strained to listen above the constant screeching of crickets and howling wind.

"You think he's running late?"

"Calm down," another said, "it isn't even time."

"Yeah, well, he's late."

"You know a wise man once told me patience was a virtue that would help me live longer. You should learn it."

The man lecturing the others wore a pinstripe suit with a black bowtie and smoked a thick cigar. The man removed a match from his pocket and struck the bottom of his heel. Large puffs of smoke from the cigar blended with the campfire as it dispersed into the night sky.

"Right, Sparks."

One man carrying a long rifle did not reply while staring into the fire. The well-dressed man puffing the cigar shifted his weight as they went silent. Orin watched as the initial speaker continued to look toward the shadows of the gorge.

"Big Jim is never mistaken with the people he brings on board," Sparks said, "trust me. If he says, this guy is good for it. Then we can expect him to be good for it. He's a reliable judge of character. You hear me?"

"Yes, Sparks. I'm just saying we're standing out here in this pit is all."

"Would you rather be moppin' floors? Huh? How about cleaning Ádyto's latrines, eh?"

"No, Sparks," the anxious man replied, lighting a cigarette, "it's no problem, truly. I didn't mean nothin' by it."

Orin strained his eyes to see what types of weapons the other two may have on them. As one henchman looked around the darkness, Orin noticed the gleam of metal from the man's waistline. Sparks had his back to Orin, and he couldn't identify his weapon but figured he also carried a handgun under his coat. Feeling a coolness in the toe of his boot, Orin noticed a tiny hole forming near the bottom. He swore as sitting close to the campfire the evening before melted a hole in his boot. Orin looked toward the anxious henchman, noticing his clean brown boots.

Past the henchman who continuously looked around were several large wooden crates. Orin figured each container would hold up to twelve bottles of liquor. Licking his tongue across his cracked, dry lips, Orin fantasized about feeling the alcohol's burn. He untied the leather straps of his wineskin and loosened the cap. Bringing the nozzle up to his chapped lips, Orin drank the booze. The returning buzz dulled the wind bursts against the tip of his nose and earlobes. Orin continued scanning the group while sipping from his wineskin as clouds obstructed the moon.

Sparks' attention shifted toward the south side of the gorge as several silhouettes appeared. They resembled the first group in stature and attire. Orin noticed two members of the group holding double-barrel shotguns pointed toward the ground. They strolled with deliberation toward the initial group near the crates.

"You're late," Sparks said, taking a drag of his cigar, "it's not like you to be late."

"What's it to you? Something held us up a way back. But now we're here."

"Ah, phooey," Sparks spat on the ground, "that's not how we conduct business. Anyway, you got the goods?"

"Yeah, we got 'em," one man said, turning toward another and nodded, "how about you?"

A man appeared from behind the group setting a rectangular metal box on the sand between both parties. Silently, he transferred the weight of his shotgun before stepping back behind his group. Sparks nodded and pointed toward the box on the ground. The anxious henchman stooped forward with a knife to pry the lid open.

"Good, very good," Sparks said, looking at the contents, "well, at least you are resourceful. But we will take both this loot and our crates off your hands."

"Now, you listen here, you son of a bi-..."

The gleaming handgun made a tumultuous noise as Sparks squeezed a cartridge from its chamber. The man speaking to Sparks clutched his abdomen as he dropped back to the ground. His comrades attempted to raise their firearms to shoot at Sparks. Orin ducked his head behind the brick wall as gunshots pierced the night. Stray bullets smashed into the side of the ravine wall sending tiny whiffs of dust into the air.

Orin cursed the pandemonium now ensuing around him. He listened to cries of anguish and wails of distress as the guns continued to boom within the narrow ravine. Dense smoke lingered above the gorge, covering the rocky area below. The canopy of smoke made it challenging for Orin to see anything, let alone take a precise shot.

Might as well let them slaughter each other, he mused.

The commotion was over within seconds. When the last shots sporadically split the night, Orin glimpsed from behind the collapsed brick wall. He noticed several bodies strewed about in the ditch with pools of blood seeping out from underneath the frames. Orin waited as Sparks lifted his body from the ground and scrambled toward the alloy box. Orin lifted his rifle into position and guided the bagman in his sights.

Sparks fumbled around with the container on the sand. Once he opened it, he emptied the contents into a rucksack. Gasping, Sparks crawled toward the boarded crates. There was no movement from the other bodies on the ground. Orin heard a groan as Sparks lifted himself to his feet using the containers for support. Aiming for the middle of the man's back, Orin took a deep breath and held it.

Aim for center mass and continue shooting until he's down.

Orin held his breath as he squeezed the trigger. The blast from his weapon sent his target flying forward to land on the crates. Orin shot repeatedly watching Spark's shoulders twitch as the cartridges tore through his skin.

CRACK! Orin's ears rang loudly as a shot soared inches from his ear. He ducked his head behind the wall as another cartridge slammed into the brick. Orin shifted his weight to ensure he covered his entire body. Peeking his head slowly, he noticed one man on the ground aiming a long rifle toward him.

Sparks manically cackled while shouting obscenities between bursts from a weapon. Orin's felt the oscillations from his heart throughout his body as he steadied his rifle toward the henchman on the ground. He tried to calm his shaking hands by slowly breathing and pressing his body closer to the soil.

Orin felt a pinch at his waistline while holding his position on the ridgeline of the ravine. Reaching down, he shifted the cherry-wood revolver before repositioning his rifle, surveying the clearing below. Bullets sporadically flew in Orin's direction, but he held his breath while gripping his gun firmly. Upon inhaling, Orin squeezed the trigger of his rifle, sending two cartridges consecutively sailing toward the man propped on the ground.

Blood sprayed from the man's neck, and Orin watched him collapse on his back before dropping his weapon. In his peripheral, he detected movement and sidestepped as Sparks shot his handgun toward Orin. Hiding behind the brick, Orin checked his ammunition, noticing he was running low. He used the revolver instead to conserve his remaining rifle cartridges.

Pausing for a moment, Orin listened as four bullets landed on the other side of the wall inches from his head. Sparks coughed and continued shouting obscenities at Orin. Above the howling wind and persistent ringing in his ears, it was difficult to discern what the man was yelling. Orin steadied his breathing to qualm his heart rate. Once Orin detected a break, he jumped over the brick wall and climbed down the ridge.

Pointing his revolver toward Sparks, he saw the bagman struggling to brace himself against the crates while indolently pointing his pistol toward Orin. The henchman who shot at Orin earlier laid dead on his back with his eyes showing white. Orin wanted to ensure the man was killed and so he pointed the revolver toward his skull and fired.

Pieces of brain matter and bone fragments splattered from the projectile impact. Orin looked down at the man in contempt before training his revolver on Sparks. As he walked toward the man, he listened to his sobs.

"Why, you… why did you… do you know who I am?"

Sparks sputtered spittle down the front of his pinstripe suit. Blood oozed from his wounds, covering the front of his clothing. After a brief moment, Orin looked at the man and sniggered. Delighted with the outcome, Orin was eager to inform Jerry of the news.

Crack! Sparks fired his pistol, which sent a searing pain shredding across the side of Orin's bicep. His arm went weak, and he dropped his rifle. Looking down at his arm, Orin saw that the shot grazed his skin. Blood slowly trickled from the tear of the wound. Recovering from the initial shock, Orin dove to the ground picking up the revolver.

"Body armor you fuckin' moron," Sparks spat blood to his side as he slunk against the crates, "you are a dead man walkin'. You hear me?"

Orin pressed his face to the ground as two bullets sailed over him into the blackness. Orin steadied his aim on the man in the pinstripe suit.

Orin squeezed the trigger sending the cartridge, leaving his rifle at twelve hundred feet per second spinning toward Spark's face. A distinguishing crunch sounded as the shot ripped through the man's tissue, muscle, and skull bones. The bagman's head slunk forward, and he dropped his pistol with his arm drooping limply to his side. He made faint gurgling sounds before becoming still.

Shifting the weight of his rifle on his shoulder, Orin lifted himself off the ground, walking toward Sparks. Checking to see if his chest moved, Orin leaned in closer toward the bagman. A mixture of saliva and his blood dripped onto his pants. Orin ran a hand across his pockets, retrieving a flask half-full of liquor. Unscrewing the cap, Orin lifted the flask in the air and nodded at the dead man.

"Don't mind if I do," Orin spoke.

Orin took several long swallows of the cold liquid. The alcohol dulled his injury, and he continued draining the flask. Once it was empty, Orin picked up a nearby knapsack, tossing the container into the bag. Stepping over the bagman slunk on the ground, he rummaged through the crates. Removing twelve bottles of liquor from the top container, Orin stuffed these into the knapsack. Nudging the bottom boxes with his foot, he felt they were empty. Tossing the top wooden crate to the side, he noticed someone loaded the bottom ones with hay.

So much for a fair deal, Orin contemplated tightening the straps of the knapsack.

Orin checked the pockets of the other associates wasted on the ground. He found a gold wristwatch on one but nothing else of value. Slipping the watch into the knapsack,

Orin ambled toward the henchman with the coffee-colored boots. He removed the man's boots before sitting on the ground and replacing his own.

The new boots fit Orin perfectly as he took a few trial steps around the henchman's corpse. There were no holes in the soles, and he could no longer feel the wind numbing his toes. Orin found a box of ammunition matching his rifle's caliber and a full clip from a pistol. He dropped these items into his plastic bag before adjusting his gun across his shoulders.

Wincing from the tenderness in his arm, he thanked the dead man and climbed the hill out of the ravine. Orin heard shouts echoing in the distance from behind him, and he hurried his pace toward the shadow of the stadium. Keeping low among the sagebrush, Orin made his way steadily back to Dee's Tavern.

* * *

"You're back! And not dead!" Jerry blurted.

Orin felt delirious as he rambled toward the bar plopping the rucksack on the counter. With a heavy sigh, he pulled a barstool closer and sat down. Shifting the weight of his rifle, he brought a hand to his forehead and waved at Jerry.

"Here's the goods."

"Not bad," Jerry said, looking through the bag's contents, "and you got my booze back! Here, let me pour you a drink."

Placing a glass on the bar counter, Jerry filled the cup with liquor. As Orin lifted his drink, he revealed the tear in his coat where the bullet grazed him earlier. Jerry raised his eyebrows as he eyed Orin's injury.

"Looks like you got nicked good! Lucky it wasn't any closer," Jerry smirked, "am I right?!"

With a grimace, Orin swallowed the booze. He breathed a sigh of relief as he welcomed the familiar burning sensation. He savored having come out on the winning side of that conflict.

"Your bagman's dead along with his men. And the others."

"Eh, don't fret over it. Those bastards had what was comin', I say."

"About the location of Kraken," Orin responded.

"Gee, right to the point, aren't you," Jerry laughed again, pouring another drink, "I like you, Orin. You got a real pair on you, you know?"

"Anyway," Jerry continued, "I overheard a couple guys talking about joining up with Kraken near Lake Abyss. About a day trek up through the main pass and another half a day south."

"How will I know when I'm near?"

"Beats me. I'm not a tour guide. But perhaps you'll get lucky again, eh?"

"Thanks, Jerry."

"But wait, Orin. You can't seriously expect you'll wander there and rescue your brother, do you? I've heard crazy stories, but that my friend is insane!"

"What would you propose?"

"There's a group out in those woodlands," Jerry replied, "they call themselves outcasts, outlaws, or something of that nature. Well, I hear they don't enjoy Kraken close to their territory. Let's say you link up with them, you may discover they could be worthy allies."

"I need to find my brother," Orin said as he drank his spirits, "sooner rather than later. I don't have time to run any more favors."

"WOAH, Woah, Woah, listen, Orin, I am not asking for a favor here. You already did one for me. And for that, I am indebted," Jerry placed a hand across his chest, making a sweeping gesture, "hence the free booze. I wanted to give you some advice. You wouldn't last two ticks taking on the Righteous Warheads alone. No offense, but you're gonna need support. And they could be the ones able to offer," Jerry refilled their drinks, "when you get the courage, they're over near Khione's Glacier. That's all I'll say about it," Jerry paused, "thanks again, Orin. And let me know if you fancy another drink."

"As a matter of fact, Jerry, this wineskin is full of grain–I don't know what–would you fill it with a proper beverage for my journey?"

"Sure, let me have it."

Jerry took the wineskin and flushed the contents. Pulling a bottle from a shelf, Jerry poured until the leather pouch was plump. Screwing on the cap, he handed it back to Orin with a toothy grin.

"Thanks, Jerry."

"No problem, Orin. See you around, maybe. Don't get yourself killed out there!"

"Don't count on it."

* * *

Leaving Dee's Tavern, Orin traveled to the fourth level to see what type of weapons they have for sale. He figured if he were to take on the Righteous Warheads, he would require an enhanced gun and body armor. Earsplitting slams of hammers on anvils echoed from the floor above as daylight broke the horizon. Once he approached the landing, he noticed heavily equipped guards barring the entrance to the stairs leading to the fifth level.

"Off-limits."

"What?" Orin asked.

"Keep moving," the guard crisply replied while idly tapping his baton against his palm.

On the fourth level, people proceeded about their business. No beggars were asking for seeds, booze, or food on this level. He peered out across the landscape from the expansive windows. Sunlight splashed across the arid desert region. Orin noticed concrete ruins with rebar pried out for miles around.

Orin's eyes moistened as a tinge of stinging vapor wafted throughout the level from the smoldering coals behind the blacksmiths. He understood why they didn't have curtains on this level.

This stench could kill a man!

Orin walked close to the windows to breathe the fresh air. Stopping to admire the view, he looked to the west. Obscurations of the looming mountains appeared a short walking distance from his vantage within the stadium. People began their day outside the stadium below, going to and from tents and transporting an assortment of items.

At least I am alive. But for how long?

Orin looked along the corridor at numerous shops selling weapons, armor, and miscellaneous survival accessories. Shops and blacksmiths were tucked into the cinderblock walls along the corridor. Painted graffiti advertised the shop's wares or various special rates.

"Guns, ammunition, armor," yells from blacksmiths commenced.

"Armament, large-caliber!" Another merchant shouted, "for those pesky critters or men! Hah!"

Merchants shouting their wares grew into a chorus of conversations as bodies filed into the passageways. Noticing a shop with armor vests and rifles on the walls, Orin walked toward the counter.

"What'll it be, kid?"

"I'd like to look at your armor on the wall," Orin answered.

"Sure, what you got to trade?"

"And let me see the rifle," Orin said.

The merchant raised his eyebrows suspiciously at Orin but did not move. Orin reached into his coat, tossing the golden watch onto the counter. Upon seeing the trinket, the man's bushy eyebrows reached his receding hairline as he studied the golden wristwatch.

"Sure thing," the man said, clapping excitedly, "it would be my pleasure."

"You have any knee and elbow pads?"

"Yes, oh, yes!"

The merchant removed the rifle and armor, placing these items in front of Orin to inspect. Reaching below the counter, the man produced a box full of knee and elbow pads. He handed Orin a pair that appeared to fit.

Orin's attention turned toward the rifle on the counter before him. Orin examined the curvature of the stock and double iron sights.

"She's a beauty, isn't she" the merchant grinned, "I'll even throw in a mounted sight."

The bolt-action rifle would jam less often than Orin's current level-action gun. Picking up the arm to inspect it, he noticed a stripper clip which would provide the ability to reload rapidly. It would be difficult to part with his rifle, gifted to him by Atticus. But Orin also couldn't risk being at a disadvantage when the time came to rescue Liam.

Placing the rifle back on the table, Orin strapped the body armor around his chest. He pulled his flannel button-down over the corset to conceal it. His chest bulged out uncomfortably from underneath his coat, but Orin knew he needed the added protection. Strapping on the knee and elbow pads, he felt untouchable.

"I'll take it."

"All of it?"

"Yes, all of it."

"Well, that'll cost you more. Say, how about your cherry-wood handgun?"

"Not for trade."

"Oh, everything is for trade here in Ádyto!"

"This is not."

"Fine, fine," the merchant rubbed his palms together, "sentimental, are we? How about the antique rifle across your back? I could fix it up and resale it. Fair is fair."

Orin hesitated while considering the usefulness of carrying both rifles. As much as he didn't want to depart with Atticus's gift, he knew he needed a more powerful gun when venturing into the mountains' forests. If he were to have any chance of finding

Liam, he needed to face any threat. His rifle was exceptional at hunting animals, but it usually took him a few shots to down someone shooting back.

"Fair is fair," Orin replied, "would you also pitch in ammunition? I'll trade what ammunition I have for this rifle."

"Deal!"

Spitting into the palm of his hand, the merchant extended it toward Orin. Reluctantly, Orin shook his hand, and the merchant gave a generous grin. The man reached underneath the counter, producing a box of ammunition for the new rifle.

"One box of .308 cartridges and a pack for the pretty gun tucked in your jeans. I'll throw the revolver ammo because you're a good sport, and you look like shite," the merchant hacked a chortling cough, "oh, and one last thing. I made a new batch of self-igniting party starters this morning! I'll throw those in for free if you tell others about my shop! Stall 448, quality wares for trade!"

"You bet."

The merchant's smile stretched wider across his face, and his eyes sparkled as he rubbed his hands together. Placing a red tin box on the counter, he opened it to reveal clear bottles filled with liquid and stuffed with a soiled rag. Orin seen members of the Squad use similar bottles of ignition when fending off packs of wolves.

"And you said these are self-igniting," Orin asked, "how so?"

"The secret is in my recipe," licking his lips, the merchant continued, "you throw it against a hard surface with enough force to break the bottle, and it will explode. Poof!"

"It will not explode while I am carrying it?"

"Oh nonsense," the merchant casually waved his arm, "you must throw it with force for the chemicals inside to mix properly for ignition. It's harmless to carry, trust me!"

Orin stuffed the items into his bag along with his remaining rations of food. The munitions boxes ripped a section of the plastic bag. Cursing under his breath, Orin tied the bag in several places to contain the items.

"I'll take one. And where can I pick up a bag?"

"Fantastic! Oh, tell me how it works for you," the merchant said, removing a bottle and handing it to Orin, "be careful you don't bang it around in the stadium! Hah! There may be somewhere to buy bags down a level."

"Thanks, you've been generous."

"Ah, don't mention it. I'll see you around."

Orin turned and headed down the nearest flight of stairs to the third level. Pushing through loitering crowds, he walked along the corridor in the opposite direction of Dee's Tavern. The compact masses made it challenging to see the shop's wares. Orin adjusted his rifle along his spine to prevent it from hitting people he passed. Keeping his hand on the handle of his handgun, he walked methodically through the swarm of people.

Characters with dense dreadlocks reached toward Orin from along the wall. They smelled horrid, and flies circled around them. When Orin made eye contact, they flashed a toothless grin and became excitable.

"Pleesh, sir. Have a drink for us?"

Orin ignored the beggars as he continued looking toward the stalls advertising various items for trade. A few shops promoted drinking and gambling within. After passing shops selling everything except backpacks, he discovered a booth with many

bags hanging on the walls. Small wicker baskets on the counter displayed various

survival items.

Flint fire starter will come in handy out in the woodlands.

"Ca-an I he-elp you," a croaking voice rose from the back of the store, "wha-t is

it, hm, yo-u ne-ed?"

An elderly woman approached the counter from behind a low wall. A large bump

protruded from the middle of her back, causing her to arch over as she walked. Orin

noticed a giant mole on the tip of her nose. Leaning her weight on the counter, she gave a

toothless smile.

"I'd like to see that bag," Orin said.

"Oh son, th-at bag," the woman heavily breathed while sauntering over toward the

bag, "just le-t me fi-nd that l-le-ver."

Removing a long slender metal pole with a hook on one end, she attempted to

grab the bag off the wall. Her stringy white hair swathed her shoulders, and a few strains

floated in the air. Orin didn't want her to struggle with it and offered to help.

"Oh, oh, son. I don't need help," she swatted an emaciated arm in his direction,

"if I can't do this, I may turn it in."

Turn it in. What an odd statement.

Orin cringed as he watched her struggle to raise the backpack and plop it

deliberately on the counter. Orin hoisted the bag to inspect the number of pockets within.

The quality of stitching on the bag impressed Orin.

"Did you make these yourself?"

"Oh, no son. Someone made those in the old days. Before your time, I reckon," the old woman giggled, "now will you need anything else?"

"Yes, I need fire-starter flint."

The woman casually pointed to a basket near Orin. Looking among the contents, he spotted a C-shaped steel band and a sack of flint rock loosely tied to it. Orin also removed a small ball of string, placing these next to the flint rock.

"I think I need a new flannel."

"Yes, I'd say a new flannel would be an improvement, my dear," the woman cackled, "I thought you'd never ask, help yourself!"

She placed a pile of shirts on the counter next to Orin's items. Sifting through the mildewed collection of clothing, Orin found a dark blue checkered flannel. Removing his leather jacket and flannel, he buttoned up the new shirt. The fit was snug, and Orin felt cleaner than on his travels. He figured the flannel would provide the protection he needed from the biting wind. Orin stuffed his worn button-down flannel into the backpack before donning his leather jacket. Slinging the rifle over his shoulder, he placed Spark's flask onto the counter.

"Ve-ry nice," the merchant licked her cracked lips, "is that for me? I could use a dr-ink. I am parched."

"It may have a little liquor left."

"Wonderful. Thanks, son. Oh, your food bag looks meager. Here."

"It's okay, really. I don't have enough to trade." Orin said.

"Nonsense, son. I insist," the woman said, removing a sack full of food items in labeled cans, "you need food for your journey young man. Place these in your backpack. I'll accept it as fair trade if you let me sip on your wineskin."

The woman continued smooching her dry lips. Orin unscrewed the cap from his leather pouch, offering the merchant a drink. Her hands shook, and she spilled booze down the front of her blouse.

"Oh, oh, dear. I've made a mess."

"Do you need my," Orin said before she held up her palm.

"No, dear. Thank you."

Orin looked through the can food items the woman provided. Yams, corn, green peas, green beans, black beans! Each one with a picture of the food item enlarged on the label. Orin's mouth watered at the sight of these food items. He hurriedly placed the cans into his backpack before zippering it up.

"Thank you again. It means a lot you would give me these food items."

"The pleasure is mo-st mi-ne, handsome! You remind me of my son," a tear formed in the corner of her eye as her smile vanished, "I wish he wo-uld come to see his mother more of-ten! Any-ways yo-you takes care, dear. Blessings of the High Heavens to you."

Orin shook her frail extended hand and turned toward the nearest flight of stairs. He wanted to reach over the counter and pull her closer. She looked and sounded helpless at that moment. But he thought better. Besides, he needed to be on his way to find Liam. The crowds were bustling during the late morning hour. A roar of conversation swept through the corridors on all levels of Ádyto.

Once he arrived at the central entrance, he stood for a moment to survey the landscape. Several dozen caravans headed down the winding road toward the stadium. He rose to the side, inhaling the stench of the moat. Shifting the items on his shoulders, he adjusted his backpack straps to ensure they were snug.

Standing on the ramp leading into Ádyto, Orin felt that his luck was changing for the better. Orin planted his heels firmly in his brown leather boots while adjusting the plump wineskin hanging on his belt. His backpack full of food items weighed on him. As he lightly tapped the cherry-wood handle of his revolver, it filled Orin with a surge of excitement and anticipation for his journey. More confident and determined than he ever was, Orin took a long breath and pushed through the remaining mobs toward the foothills to the west.

CHAPTER 12: REFLECTIONS

The blistering sun roasted the begrimed asphalt causing Orin's boots to stick with each stride. Corroded husks of vehicles endured along the sides of the road. Passing these automobiles, Orin made a habit of inspecting inside. He was not fortunate enough to discover anything other than rubbish. Still, it provided him something to keep his mind occupied on his expedition. Beyond the path, sagebrush, juniper, and pine trees extend from the desert between compact rubble heaps. Rebar and random litter floated in the flurries bearing down from the looming foothills.

Orin walked for miles listening to the squeaking sound his shoes made as he peeled them from the sticky asphalt. Removing his jacket, Orin noticed his flannel was wet from sweating. With a pulsing in his temples, he removed the cork on his wineskin to drink alcohol. He realized he would eventually have to find a stream or other water source to avoid dehydration.

As Orin walked, he reflected on stories Atticus told the Squad about weather patterns decades ago. Back then, the weather constantly shifted where it could snow, rain, flood, and dry out before the sun went down. Gazing up toward the fiery ball in the sky, Orin longed for precipitation from the looming greyed clouds in the distance. The wind blew at his face sending a shiver coursing down his spine.

These days, the sunlight beats down hot while at night, the icy wind pierces the bones, Orin reflected.

Orin's hair rippled in the flurry behind his shoulders. He reached up a hand to feel clusters of hair dreading in several areas. His facial beard was also thickening and itched. Scratching along his prominent jawline, Orin took another gulp from the wineskin. He figured if he maintained this pace, he could reach the foothills before the sun slipped behind the peaks.

Orin hadn't seen this region of the countryside as he never ventured this far northwest. Trees occasionally protruded from among the concrete rubbles. Large birds perched atop lengthy poles jutting along the side of the pavement. They would cry to one another as Orin continued making his way toward the west. Scanning both sides of the highway, Orin remained alert for potential predators or bandits.

Occasionally, Orin noticed a lonely caravan or traveler heading toward Ádyto. They each had a distracted look about them as most ignored Orin. With every mile, settlers he passed became fewer. Orin's concerns turned to the events of the fateful battle with the Righteous Warheads. He cursed himself for not being there to help his brother or fellow members fight off those savages. Remembering Marlow standing in the field, Orin tried reflecting on the last time he saw his brother. Attempting to recall this hazy memory made his temples pulsate.

Hiking along the serpentine highway, Orin heard droning to the north. Hovering above a small patch of tall grasses sticking among deteriorated structures, six enormous black and yellow-striped wasps faced the street. Orin knew what these creatures could do to a person. A single injection from the needle at the rear of their torso was enough to drive someone into a painful delirious death. Squad members told horror stories around the encampment of swarms of these insects across the plains.

Orin stared at the massive yellow jackets with their stingers hovering above the grasses. He was unsure how to proceed in this situation. If he decided to run, he'd risk them chasing him down. There was a limited opportunity of refuge around. Shooting at them would anger them into a frenzy. Orin wasn't confident in his ability to kill all six creatures with his rifle or revolver.

Bobbing in the air, they slapped their wings swiftly, appearing stagnant to the eye. Orin slowly slunk his shoulder down to remove the rifle, leveling it toward the wasps. Drawing a heavy breath, Orin stood on the road with one leg extended forward to hold his balance. He continued holding his breath as he trained his sights on the nearest yellow jacket. Pulling the trigger, Orin released his breath as the rifle recoiled, and the cartridge sailed toward the target.

The blast rang loud, causing Orin to hear a tone in his ear. He spun toward the insect as the shot ripped through its wing, sending small fragments of chitin floating into the air. The buzzing developed into a symphony as the wasps flew toward Orin. He pulled the trigger rapidly, hitting a creature once, which only thumped it back before continuing pursuit.

What should I do? Orin's mind scrambled, and his hands shook, holding the weapon, *not today. Today is not the day I turn it in.*

Orin's mind clouded as he reacted by reaching near his backpack at his feet and snatched the merchant's 'party starter' container from a side pocket. Without hesitating, Orin flung the jar toward the edge of the grasses.

The glass exploded with a thunderous boom that vibrated the asphalt. A fiery mushroom cloud jolted toward heaven. Orin's eyes enlarged as he saw several wasps immolated from the blast. Their sizzling charred corpses fell from the air as their wings evaporated. Grasses around the explosion blew slightly outward from the concussion before immolating ablaze, quickly spreading across the fields.

Flying through the thick smoke, the remaining wasps continued their pursuit toward Orin. Orin turned toward a broken vehicle with one door swinging loosely near the ground. Picking up his pack and slinging the rifle over his shoulder, he bounded toward the car with gigantic strides. Tossing the door open, he plunged inside before holding the door shut behind him as the wasps slammed into the windowpane. The door could not be completely closed and was loosely held onto the frame via corroded hinges. Orin held the handle to prevent the door from flying open. The wasps repeatedly rapped against the window glass with their stingers.

The humming from the wasps persisted as they struck their enormous bodies against the vehicle. Loud knocks from the fiberglass frame reverberated with each contact. Orin noticed sections of the car become dented from the wasp's entry attempts. The buzz was deafening and sounded as if they were in the vehicle with Orin. Orin looked up toward the front windshield as a wasp slammed its stinger through the glass, splintering it like a spider web.

Afraid the windshield would shatter, Orin pushed his boot heel onto the hole to prevent it from caving in. The wasps continued striking against various parts of the vehicle to reach their mark. The wildfire created by Orin's self-starter blast died down, turning into a smog across the field.

Seconds turned into minutes as Orin held the door shut with his hand while pressing a leg against the windshield. The wasps steadily grew tired, and taps from their stingers became less persistent. Watching the creatures intently, they hovered back toward the burnt grass field.

Orin sighed a massive breath of relief as a broad smile crept over his face. Cackling uncontrollably, he couldn't believe his fortune of making it to the vehicle unscathed. Realizing he was safe for the time-being, Orin watched the wasps move further away from the car. Briefly pondering who owned this automobile, Orin whispered thanks while knotting a shoestring from his boot around the door handle. Tying the shoestring to a metal strip underneath the windshield, he dug in his bag for food. Taking out a can of peas, he used the steel ring device he received from the merchant to pop holes into the container.

As Orin ate his meal, raindrops splattered steadily onto the roof of the vehicle. The thumps of rains turned into a symphonic roar as heavy clouds blanketed the sky. Thunder boomed from the impenetrable gloom as lightning struck red rocks. Orin watched the wasps hover away from the area in proportion to the volume of rain roaring onto the roof.

And here's the rain, right on cue, Orin thought while peering out the window toward the burnt grass.

The storm was convenient, and Orin gratefully finished his can of peas before sipping his drink. The liquor helped lower his heart rate, allowing him a moment of reprieve. Leaning back onto the strains of fabric comprised of a seat long ago, Orin gazed out toward the yellow jackets. The merchant's concoction worked well enough for the situation. He made a note to inform him about it should he ever see the merchant again.

Stall 448.

Laying his head back against the seat's frame, he sat awhile, listening to the patter of rain against the rusted hollowed temporary shelter. Taking several swigs from the wineskin, he recorked it before tying it against his belt. The raindrops' sounds were calming, and Orin relaxed, knowing the door was secured to the dashboard. A wave of exhaustion traversed over him as he realized he hadn't slept since his evening with Two-Bit. Closing his eyes, Orin allowed the cadenced thumps of the rainfall and thunder drift him into a deep slumber.

* * *

When Orin regained awareness, he found himself in the evening's shadow. The moon replaced the sun splashing its light across the nearby fields. He smacked his parched lips and drank a small sip of booze before untying his shoestring and opening the vehicle door. It creaked noisily, and Orin silently gazed around for signs of danger. Readying himself, he devoured a can of corn before shifting his attention toward the gap in the foothills.

Following the uneven pavement for miles, Orin listened to the echoes of crickets and owls in neighboring pine trees. The fields of grasses and ruins blended into a variety of tall earthy pines and dense juniper trees. Ascending the pathway into the foothills, Orin gazed in bewilderment at the enormous buttress cliffs on either side of the road. He noticed various shapes lined the horizon of each crag.

Orin pulled his leather jacket closer toward his torso as the wind whistled through the gorge. Seeing his breath forming puffs in front of him as he wandered, he swiftly rubbed his palms. The biting wind was a constant factor as Orin walked among the rocky cliffs and towering trees. Frequently, while looking overhead, Orin thought he saw the shadow of a wolf. Other than the hooting of owls and wailing wind, the night was eerily quiet.

Taking a sip from his wineskin, Orin felt the alcohol warm his bones throughout his body. He watched as the moon steadily dipped behind the western crest. Orin cursed himself for not trading gloves or water from one of the merchants in Ádyto as his hands shook and head pounded. Orin's thigh muscles ached as he sauntered along the mountain pass.

When his legs burned and ached to the point where he considered resting, Orin noticed a tarnished sign with a white arrow pointing northbound along a precarious dirt trail. The sign read, "Kh-on Gla-i—r." Filling in the blanks, Orin knew this sign provided direction toward the Outlaw camp. Reflecting on his conversation with Jerry, Orin knew he would find the Righteous Warheads to the south of this place. Continuing north on the trail, he would meet with the Outlaws. The choice wasn't difficult, and Orin turned toward the dirt path winding up the cliff and into the timbers beyond.

Walking along the snaking path, Orin inhaled the fresh scent of the pine trees. Daylight began piercing through the woods from the east as he continued his ascent. He speculated about what the outlaws might be like from his conversation with Jerry. Figuring they may be woodland savages, Orin kept his revolver accessible. For all he knew, they may seek to rob him of his items and leave him dead in these woods.

When the sun loomed overhead, Orin came to a clearing in the woods where the trail seemed to arrive at a dead-end. A fragrant of sizzling meats floated among the pines. Looking around, Orin noticed a billowing smoke rising over the enormous trees through the clearing. Walking off the beaten path, Orin saw clapboard structures high into the trees. These appeared well-built and organized in a fashion where roped ladders planked to the other structures.

A city in the trees.

The enormity of make-shift structures amazed Orin with how they appeared blended into the surroundings. The houses begot small openings for an entryway and rectangular windows around the structures. A few held potted plants or beaded drapery in the various window panes. Accustomed to seeing settlers residing in hastily made shacks, Orin's eyes and mouth widen as he stared around him into the trees. Nailed wooden boards ran up the trunks of the trees leading up to the structures.

"Hello?" Orin shouted, cupping both hands over his mouth.

The sudden noise sent birds scattering from nearby pines. A crow cawed a solitary cry from a branch overhead. Orin glanced at the bird before cupping his hands around his mouth.

"HELLO!" Orin called again.

The trees around him stretched toward the cyan-colored sky. The density of the towering trees provided limited visibility in all directions. Orin walked across the expanse to try attracting attention. He didn't want to catch these Outlaws off-guard.

As Orin walked across the clearing, he noticed peculiar symbols etched into the trunks of the trees. There were animals and strange lettering which appeared chiseled into the base of the tree, spiraling around them. Figuring the images told stories about the Outlaws, Orin stopped to examine a tree. He noticed several creatures appeared near a stick-figure of a person with a bow.

Perhaps a description of a hunt? Orin wondered as he proceeded deeper among the trees.

As Orin continued wandering, he heard a low noise vibrating through his boots. The sounds became a steady percussion as Orin overheard growling cries between the rhythmic beats.

"Ey-ey-yea-ya! Ey-ey-yea-ya!"

A dark, withered man appeared from among the dense pines wearing red and black-colored feathers on a distinguished headband. Both men paused for a moment staring at one another. The strange man displayed painted markings across his face and down his arms. His thin black hair hung past his waist. Orin saw bone jewelry around his wrists and ankles, which jiggled softly with every step. He wore deerskin pants and a leather vest with an empty bandolier covering his hairless chest.

"Well, what brings a shit-licker into our humble abode," the stranger broke the silence with a full grin, "not looking for any items of value, are you? The last man who stole," his eyes widened, "we ate him."

"Excuse me?"

Orin placed a hand on his gun while inspecting the man suspiciously. The guy methodically strolled toward Orin with his palms outward. When he was close enough, Orin inhaled the stench of decaying flesh on his breath, and the savage's eyes gleamed.

"I said," the stranger's yellowed teeth shot spittle into Orin's face, "what brings a pus-sack like yourself into our humble abode? You've got the city-stench all about you!"

"You'll have to do better with the insults," Orin glowered at the man, "I've seen too much in the last week to care what you call me. I am not looking for trouble. I wish to speak with the Outlaws."

"Of the Forest?"

"Yes, of the forest or woods, whatever."

"It's 'of the forest.' Although 'of the woods' has a subtle flair to it, doesn't it?"

"I like either name."

"Hah! A diplomat. What did you say your name was?"

"Orin, yours?"

"White Feather."

"White Feather, huh," Orin echoed, "how d'you earn the name?"

After noticing a gnashing scar across the man's face, Orin's attention turned toward his own wound on his arm, which itched. Trying not to pick at the scab, Orin ignored the urge to scratch to avoid infection. He'd seen people die from minor cuts becoming infected. Orin extended his hand toward White Feather, and the two shook hands. White Feather slapped Orin on the shoulder and pointed in the direction he came.

"That's a story I may share after we drink jungle juice. Hah! Come, Orin, you've found our group, the Outlaws of the Forest. We are celebrating Mea'n Fo' mhair and giving back to the forest. Partake with us, and we will chat by the fireside after the feast."

Orin smirked and acquiesced as he followed White Feather through the thick pines. The steady rhythmic thuds became thunderous as he stumbled over protruding roots. White Feather gracefully made his way around the pines toward a massive flame. The vibrations dulled the pounding in his temples as Orin crossed through shrubs arriving into an expanse. Avid people of all shapes and sizes dressed in leather garbs participated in various activities. Orin couldn't help but chuckle at the situation. He found the Outlaws of the Forest.

CHAPTER 13: OUTLAWS OF THE FOREST

Stepping into the expanse with White Feather, Orin noticed flames licking the tops of great pines. The morning sunshine radiated from between the pine twigs. Several massive wooden tables held containers filled with produce of all types at the center of the clearing. Orin never witnessed such a variety of foods spilling out of bowls onto a table. Squashes, pumpkins, corn, radishes, lettuces, and cucumbers piled out of vessels. Near the fire, a fleshy boar with an apple stuck between its teeth slowly rotated. A sweet scent of charred boar emitted from the carcass, making Orin's mouth fill with saliva.

The Outlaws of the Forest appeared an eccentric band of savages. An assortment of colored garbs hung from their bare bodies as they danced in a flurry. Vibrant feathers along with bones draped from their wrists, necks, and ankles. Each person was crusted in mud, ash, and paints across various skin and hair dyes. Some members were clean-shaved while others stuck bones and feathers into their dreaded hair.

Not adapted to such diversification, Orin questioned if he could convince them to help rescue his sibling. Eyeing the bones which whirled across their bodies, Orin knew these savages could hunt. Assortments of vegetables on the table signified the Outlaws knew how to sustain themselves. Orin gazed at snapping yellowed teeth as they flailed their arms to a steady beating rhythm. Across the clearing, a row of percussionists slammed massive clubs on top of hollowed containers creating a prominent blast. Animal skins hung from the sides of the instruments, which emitted a thundering racket with each strike.

"Fazel! You act like a mangy dog," White Feather shouted at one man on the table, "drink from the water! You've had much jungle juice half-sack!"

"Ah o'yee," the man gnashed his teeth, screaming, "tir helaeth!"

"Y'Goedwig!" the Outlaws chanted above the rhythmic thuds, "forest of great abundance!"

The Outlaws of the Forest performed dances as White Feather, and Orin stood and watched. Food flew in the air as the members thrashed their bodies wildly around the fire. Orin saw an Outlaw pour a red liquid into another's opened mouth. The Outlaw, originally shouting on the table, ran toward an enormous silvery container. Twisting a spigot, he lowered his head, allowing a clear liquid to pour from the box.

"Can't let 'em get much drunk-on juice, never know where they end up! Hah," White Feather beamed, "d'you enjoy celebrations?"

"I've never encountered one," Orin answered.

"Well, join. Take a load off. We will talk later."

"What were they chanting?"

"It's a motto of life. We praise the land for producing a wealth of resources," he took a cup from a nearby outlaw before continuing, "we proudly proclaim our status as the Outlaws of the Forest."

"What are you all celebrating?"

"We call it, Mea'n Fo' mhair. Celebration of the forest during this season of giving. The forest provides for us. And we provide for it. A balance to the chaos."

"Here, Orin," White Feather resumed handing him the cup, "drink our jungle juice and join in the celebrations."

"I think I may stick with my wineskin," Orin casually replied while watching the others dance, "but I appreciate your offer."

"Oh bullshit," White Feather spat, "you will drink the juice. I never trust a foreigner who doesn't partake in jungle action. Now, drink."

Peering down into the mug, Orin swirled the drink, watching tiny bubbles appear along the rim. Lifting the cup to his lips, Orin took a deep gulp. The liquor was smooth and tasted tart as it moved down his throat. A fruity aftertaste followed, and Orin noticed he couldn't feel the burn of alcohol.

Not long after taking the drink, Orin was dizzy and felt a surge of energy. Orin's blood boiled to the tips of his fingers, and he clenched a fist. He felt as though he could single-handedly take on the Righteous Warheads. Orin tilted around as he tried strolling alongside White Feather. From the liquor, his strong buzz made his thoughts dulled. The jungle juice made it increasingly difficult for Orin to put together a string of coherent thoughts.

"Lightweight, I see," White Feather chuckled, "figured as much. I've got matters to attend. Go join the others in the festivities. We can discuss relevant matters after the feast."

Observing the crowd flailing their limbs, Orin sauntered toward the drummers to the clearing side. Everyone in the clearing seemed to have a cup overflowing with jungle juice. Orin gawked with swollen eyes as a few of the savages danced in place with arms stretching overhead. They stared off into the distance with a glazed expression. It was as if the jungle juice placed people into a delirious trance.

Orin wondered how the Outlaws of the Forest would fare against the skilled Righteous Warheads. Watching these savages dance around in a trance, he thought there was something strange in how they performed their dances. Perhaps the unexpectedness that seemed to appear from these forest savages would provide the upper-hand to defeat the Righteous Warheads. Orin believed it was worth trying to convince White Feather of the need to join his cause and rescue his brother. Shivering at the thought of what was happening to Liam, Orin realized he didn't have many options. If both groups were barbarians, Orin figured he may as well try to have them battling each other.

"O'yee! O'yee!"

The tribesmen chorused while dancing to the beats and slapping their thighs with their palms. The rattle of bone ornaments enjoined with the vibrations as the dancers stomped the soil with bare feet. Orin noticed a few clasping from tree branches, shaking their bodies in all directions over the long plank table. Orin grinned while looking at the surrounding festivities. He couldn't help but bend his knees somewhat to the uniform hammering of the buckets.

Standing by the percussionists, Orin sipped from his cup. The red drink swirled, bubbling as Orin stared at it. Picking out a pine needle, he looked toward the water container to see a few people pouring the clear liquid into their gaping mouths.

A few savages hung around the table, chewing forcefully on foods as they continued dancing to the rhythm. With grungy, dirt-crusted fingers, the savages picked various vegetables from the table and shoved them into their mouths. Yellowed-fangled teeth smiled at Orin as he watched the ruffians eat from the banquet. After a swift bite, they would resume their flailing with the others. Pine needles flew as they stomped and thrashed around the clearing. They appeared enchanted while moving around the bonfire.

As Orin drank the red liquid, his vision blurred, and he leaned against the nearest trunk. Tilting his cup back to finish the jungle juice, he looked up and saw her. Locking eyes with an olive-toned woman with heavy dreads, he grinned. Yellowed teeth with deep black gaps smiled back at him. Orin noticed her slender grimy figure. She steadily walked toward Orin swaying her hips seductively.

Bones and green gemstones hung on braids around her neck and arms. She tucked a long dagger into a leather sash at her side, which covered her deerskin knee-length fringed skirt. Orin immediately noticed her brown eyes, which mesmerized him. Daylight reflected from a round alloy piercing protruding from her smooth nose. Oversized hoops dangled from each earlobe brushing against her shoulders, creating a sagging round hole.

"I'm Emerald," the woman said, handing Orin another cup, "drink."

"Orin."

"I don't care. Now drink the juice," Emerald giggled, pushing the drink toward his lips, "it'll take that wide-eyed expression off your face."

"What's in this drink, anyway?" Orin asked, staring at the familiar bubbling red liquid.

"Don't bother about it," the woman replied, tilting the cup toward his open mouth, "just drink."

Orin's muscles began relaxing after taking several large gulps of the drink. Finishing the container, Emerald pushed the cup upward, emptying the remaining contents down Orin's throat. Placing an arm around the back of his neck, Emerald propelled his head within inches of her face. As she caressed his leg with hers, Emerald nipped at the bottom of his earlobe. A shiver and excitable passion coursed down his spine. Orin hadn't been with a woman in years.

Feeling a mild buzz, Orin felt the blood flow toward his groin. Her dusky copper-colored eyes had a flicker to them as she tilted her head casually. Her breasts heaved and thrust against his chest. Orin had not felt this turned on in ages. His surroundings whirled into a mixture of background noises and movements. Looking back into her eyes, he longed to kiss this woman.

Pushing her lengthy, dense dreads behind her shoulders, Orin brushed his fingers down her cheekbone. Bringing his lips close to hers, they kissed intensely with tongues tangled. Orin leaned against her soft, round succulent breasts. They kissed slow and sensual, and Emerald readily returned the passion. Her saliva tasted sweet from the jungle juice. They stood for a moment as the vibrations from the percussionists faded from awareness.

"Let's go, love, mm?"

Whispering softly into his ear, Emerald made Orin's scruff hairs rise on end. He felt a spouting sensation near the tip of his genitals. Swallowing the rest of his refreshment, Orin released the cup to the ground. Emerald caressed her fingers through his hair. Taking his hand, Emerald led Orin toward the structures in the trees. The cheers and chants from the celebration faded as they rambled among the dense woodland.

When they arrived at a set of plank steps leading up toward a pine tree structure, she signaled for him to go up first. Instead, Orin held up a hand to support her in proceeding first. Emerald pushed his gesture away with a movement of her hand before running swiftly toward the landing. She leaned over a railing while motioning for him to follow.

Orin climbed the boards leading toward the landing, walking inside the construction. The room was sparsely decorated, aside from a few pieces of wooden furniture. Small green plants grew atop the windowsill along the far wall. In one corner, someone attached storage cabinets to the ceiling forming a space to keep cans of foods. Orin noticed a heavy scent of pine and wet dirt in the room. A bundle of clothing and padded blankets sat crumpled in an adjacent corner of the small structure. Next to the garments, a mattress lay on the ground with Emerald gazing at Orin. She rubbed her privates seductively. With a snap of her fingers, Emerald unbuttoned her leather skirt, revealing plump toned breasts.

Winking at Orin, Emerald smiled a gaping, fangled grin while gesturing with a finger for him to join her on the bed. Orin hesitated, unsure how to react to this unfamiliar situation.

"What are you waiting for," she inquired, "make yourself at home and stay awhile. The others are busy with their celebrations. Let's have one of our own, mm?"

Orin sensed she was right, and the others would plainly be too drunk to notice their absence. Smirking, Orin placed his rifle and backpack on the floor before unbuttoning his flannel. He pulled off his jeans with haste and sat next to the woman, rubbing her soft breasts. Emerald helped him unstrap his armor before placing it on the ground near his coat and flannel. Emerald brushed her palms across Orin's chest. Small goosebumps formed from her light touch. Orin leaned to kiss her neck, inhaling her aromatic scent.

Laying naked in bed, Orin caressed his fingers down her torso. She arched her back as he mopped an index finger along her inner thigh. They cuddled and kissed one another excitedly. Stringy strands of saliva formed a bridge attaching their mouths between kisses. With sweat and eagerness dripping on his fingers, Orin slipped inside Emerald until he couldn't push further. They stroked along to their own cadence until Orin felt a wet, pulsing sensation grip him tight. As the two intertwined and felt each other's pleasure, they heard a man yelling outside.

"EMERALD!"

"Emerald," the voice shouted again, "are you up there?"

They heard wet thuds as someone ascended the planks toward the landing. Orin's heart hammered with every step. Rising slowly off Emerald, he twisted his naked body facing the entryway.

His body tensed as an enormous man with calloused ebony skin stood in the entrance facing Orin. Painted markings were laden across his exposed chest and muscular arms. Orin held his breath while gawking at the man before him. A scowl swept across his face, which quickly vanished into an angry snarl. Orin felt powerless without his rifle. His body involuntarily quivered as he sat on the mattress wearing a confounded expression.

"Just what do you think you are doing," the man tensed his fists, "Emerald is my woman!"

"Ta-Tu! No! It's not what you think!"

Emerald's appeals fell on deaf ears as the man charged Orin with fists approaching his face. Ta-Tu connected a massive punch to Orin's jaw. Orin heard a reverberating collision as he prevented another strike toward his abdomen. His teeth rattled together, and Orin bit his tongue as another fist connected with his cheekbone.

Flying backward against the clothing, Orin brought his arms in front of his face to block the onslaught of punches.

Shaking his head to regain clarity on the situation, Orin looked toward the towering guy as his heel connected with his ribs. Orin had the wind knocked out of him, and he heaved dry coughs. Gasping for air and clasping a hand on his chest, Orin reached up another palm toward the man pleadingly. Ta-Tu brought his foot beating down on Orin's ribcage, sending searing pain through his gut. Sharp teeth from bone jewelry hanging around Ta-Tu's ankles pierced Orin with each thrusting kick.

Knowing he needed to react immediately, Orin seized the man's legs, which sent Ta-Tu stumbling backward. Scrambling to his knees, Orin pushed his weight toward Ta-Tu, causing him to crash against the wall. Ta-Tu punched him repeatedly, but Orin couldn't feel the impact with his adrenaline pumping. Pushing Ta-Tu through the entryway, Orin flung him against the wooden railing. The man fought as Orin sent a crushing knee toward the man's stomach. Ta-Tu lost his balance as the rail collapsed, sending the man tumbling to the ground. Emerald screeched as she ran toward the ledge.

Orin watched the man's head bounce, and the impact reverberated throughout the man's body. Orin heard bellows coming from the pines and glanced over to see several Outlaws running into the area.

Hearing a loud groan, he looked to Ta-Tu to see him struggling to raise his body. Ta-Tu looked at Orin and snapped with a furious leer. Figuring the Outlaw may try to kill him, Orin leaped on top of Ta-Tu and pummeled his face. Ta-Tu received the punches without striving to fend them off while sneering a bloodied grin. Orin felt someone grasp his arm and pulled him forcibly off Ta-Tu.

White Feather's face was expressionless as he stared at Orin. Orin was aware of the throbbing in his hand while White Feather gripped his arm securely. White Feather looked between the men, before frowning at Orin.

"Just what do you think you are doing," White Feather's eyebrows furrowed, "I welcome you into the forest and our celebration of Mea'n Fo' mhair. And this is how you repay me?"

"Apologies, jungle juice...," Orin panted, "didn't mean..."

White Feather held out his hand for Ta-Tu while holding open a palm to silence Orin. Orin heard murmuring among the mob of Outlaws. Ta-Tu stood to his feet and tilted while drooling blood.

"And you, Ta-Tu," White Feather shook a skeletal finger, "our supposed bravest of scouts. To get bested by a nude, unarmed outsider?"

"Orin," White Feather roared, glaring at Orin, "get dressed and meet us in my home near the water purifier. Now!"

"Sure."

Orin sauntered up the plank steps and felt the sea of eyes watching his climb. The Outlaws whispered and laughed as Orin carefully made his way toward the landing. He could hear them joking about his naked body. Orin did not pay attention to their comments. He walked past Emerald into the clapboard structure to collect his belongings.

* * *

Orin methodically climbed the planks toward White Feather's treehouse. Upon entering the home, he saw a flame in a large metal bowl in the heart of the room. Smoke traversed via a begrimed pipe toward a narrow opening in the roof. A thick cloud of sage hung in the air.

Seated on a quilted blanket, White Feather wore his crimson and black feathered headdress with turquoise-embedded deerskin tunics. Orin noticed White Feather appeared stoic as he sat cross-legged on his sheets. His hands never left their position as they hung loosely over his kneecaps.

Next to his leader, Ta-Tu sat cross-legged on a quilted blanket. Ta-Tu's skin glistened with sweat. Orin watched as he silently flexed his fingers while staring into the amber-colored charcoals. Ta-Tu did not rise to meet Orin's gaze. Orin could see Ta-Tu's swollen face in the firelight, and a puffy purple bag was forming under his eye.

"Sit, Orin. Let us chat awhile."

Extending a palm toward the seat opposite Ta-Tu, Orin stepped toward the vacant padded blanket. Orin quickly examined the symmetrical designs on the sheet. He leaned his rifle and backpack against the wall near his seat. The fire crackled and shone angled shadows across the walls. White Feather reached behind him to reveal three cups, which he placed in front of his blanket. Orin heard the faint beats from the percussionists near the bonfire below. The festivities of Mea'n Fo' mhair continued outside, and Orin listened to the chants and sporadic howling from the Outlaws.

"Let us not delay here in rambling chatter while we honor the forest. The energy within this place between the two of you is unstable. We must create unity for the celebration. So, I demand answers to questions. What is the nature of the conflict between you?"

"This son-a-bitch," Ta-Tu snarled, baring his stained teeth, "violated my home, caught inside Emerald!"

"Ta-Tu," White Feather held up his palm, "who hasn't been with Emerald? Damn near half the camp!"

Ta-Tu gasped, heaving a puff from deep in his chest at the insult. He shook his leg and fidgeted with his hands but remained silent while frowning. Ta-Tu bit his lip as Orin looked between them.

"The truth upsets you," White Feather continued, "for often the truth is unpleasant. But to become stronger, you must learn to acknowledge it."

"Look, Ta-Tu. I apologize," Orin began, "I didn't kn-."

"Orin," White Feather looked to him, "do not apologize. You did not know who Emerald was nor where she came from. And who would blame you for not probing during the celebration of the forest? Everyone's easy!"

"Besides," White Feather continued with a snicker, "it makes you appear weak. You're a dirtbag with no common sense, but you aren't weak. The weak don't venture into the mountains, they leave them!"

Handing a cup to each of the men, White Feather motioned for them to drink. Orin looked inside the container, noticing the dark red bubbling liquid. A sweet smell wafted from the cup, providing a relaxing sensation.

"Let us drink to the forest and its ability to heal all wounds."

As he drank the jungle juice, Orin's legs prickled, and his muscles relaxed. The feeling he received when drinking was unlike anything he'd experienced while drinking his booze. Jungle juice made him feel elated and carefree simultaneously.

"So, Orin," White Feather recommenced, setting the cups back in front of his blanket, "why have you come to visit with us? Did you claim you sought the Outlaws? Or have you discovered what you're after, hmm?"

"I wish to ask for help rescuing my brother."

"Your brother? And where is your brother? Is he here among the Outlaws of the Forest?"

"No," Orin said with a trembling voice, "the-they have taken him. By the Righteous Warheads."

"Ah, yes, hmm," White Feather flicked his wrist, rattling his jewelry, "Kraken. He has been creating trouble with our supply convoys. We plan to move against the Righteous Warheads during Deireadh Fómhai in a fortnight."

The echo of someone clambering up the planks leading toward the landing interrupted their discussion. Breathing heavily, an Outlaw appeared in the doorway, holding two cylinder-shaped containers. Firelight reflected from the steel tubes grasped in each of the man's hands.

"Wh-white Feather," he sputtered between breaths, "the ca-carbon f-filters, they're com-completely loaded."

"Slow down, Kanuna," White Feather gestured toward the containers, "Can we regenerate the carbon?"

"Yes," Kanuna said, unscrewing the top of a container removing a soot-covered cylinder, "but it will only give clean water until dawn's meal. We need another container of the crushed shell to remove the sediment."

"The two of you," White Feather said, pointing at Orin and Ta-Tu, "you travel northeast about a half day as the bird flies. You'll find a stone warehouse, chiefly intact, stocked with water filtration devices. We require an activated carbon filter, which you should find there. Four containers will keep us stocked until we achieve a more durable solution."

"Yes, I can do that," Ta-Tu said with his chest puffed.

"Anything else we need?" Orin asked.

"We could use mesh filters if you can find them," Kanuna said.

"We will see you on the return. Ta-Tu, you recall the place. It's near the roundabout road in the core of the old village. Make sure you obtain the correct container. The coconut carbon, not the wood or coal! Orin, we'll talk further when you return. I expect to see you both at dawn. Now, leave!"

Gathering his bag and rifle, Orin followed Ta-Tu around the Outlaw in the entryway and down the plank steps. The celebration continued as the sun settled over the peaks to the west. Once on the ground level, Ta-Tu paused, raising his eyebrows at Orin.

"Hold it. I need my bow."

Ta-Tu ran toward the clearing with the tree structures and returned a short time later. Orin was not entirely sure Ta-Tu wouldn't try to kill him during this expedition. But he also believed he didn't have a choice if he were to receive their help fighting the Righteous Warheads. Ta-Tu wore a polished wooden bow across his chest with a leather quiver against his back. Orin noticed several of the arrows had colored tips.

"Try to keep up," Ta-Tu said.

Following a modest dirt trail northeast, Ta-Tu led them speedily through the pines. It wasn't long before the trees thinned and gave way to broad expanses of land. They came to a clearing, and Orin looked ahead, staring at a looming massive ice sheet accompanying a jagged ridgeline.

CHAPTER 14: WHY DO THE BIRDS GO ON SINGING?

A piercing wintry flurry wafted from over the glacial pass. Orin and Ta-Tu walked in silence as they started their trek near Khione's Glacier's snow line. Ta-Tu recommended it faster to pass over the glacier than head down the winding river cutting through the bluffs. Ta-Tu speculated that there was less possibility of running into predators at higher elevations than along the water runoffs.

Orin observed a layer of ice covering the mountain pass. The glacial head stopped near a vast crystal lake where they plodded along near the edge of the compact snow. Their aim was to reach the top of the pass and decide the best route. At this elevation, the snowbank appeared permanent, making Orin grateful for the boots he wore. With snow high to their knees, they trekked along at a painstaking pace.

Reaching the crest, they realized only a few hours of sunshine remained. Orin soaked in the view as he uncorked his wineskin. For miles around, as far as the eagle flies, vast peaks and valleys sprawled before them. Orin looked down at the lake toward the pathway they traversed. To the northeast, scantier hills between thickets of trees dotted the scenery. Splashes of lavender and dusk-tinted hues painted the sky.

"That is where we need to be," Ta-Tu pointed to the tree-line toward the northeast, "the best passage looks to be a crooked path descending from here and across that valley toward those hilltops."

Orin bobbed his head in agreement as he sipped from his wineskin. He tossed the wineskin to Ta-Tu, who also took a few sips. Ta-Tu slowly wiped his lip, where Orin's fists connected earlier.

"How you feelin'?" Orin asked.

"Been better, but I'll manage."

Ta-Tu spat toward the rocks at his feet. Looking to the north, Ta-Tu began his decline from the frozen peak. Loose stones made for a gradual pace down the side of Khione's Glacier. Orin used his hands for support to avoid sliding too far down the surface during their descent.

Going down a mountain is trickier than getting up, he mused.

As they crossed the valley in front of the tree-line, the wind-blasted continuously from the peaks above. Strong gale-force winds whistled as they mopped the grasslands. A pleasant aroma wafted from purple lilac flowers among the whispering meadows. Thankful there weren't giant wasps hovering nearby, Orin followed Ta-Tu across the lowland.

With the sun setting behind the crowns, the sky turned from pink streaks of clouds to the night's deep indigos. Crickets played their lonesome songs as the air began frosting within the valley. Trudging on without incident, they reached the end of the fields, progressing through the tree-line and into the dense forest.

Enormously thick pine trees overlooked the stars overhead. Dense branches pointed out in every direction, lush with sharp growing thimbles. Withered pine needles and ponderosa cones littered the woodland floor. Along with the cries of a nearby owl, Orin attended the soft crunches as they stepped on pine cones.

With the twilight enveloping them in the woods, maintaining a sense of direction became burdensome. Orin saw each of the trees as indistinguishable and soon relied on

Ta-Tu to point the path. As the night sky grew darker, they appeared in a small clearing and paused for a rest.

Several rabbits ate nearby beneath a rotten tree. Lining up a shot, Ta-Tu let an arrow loose. Piercing his prey through the back of the neck, Ta-Tu pulled the hide off by its legs with a quick and deliberate motion. He hoisted the skin over his shoulder, carrying the rabbit toward Orin by its hind limbs. Impressed with Ta-Tu's shot, Orin gave a smile and offered to prepare the fire.

Orin created fire using the mineral ring and flint in his backpack. He blew the ember within his kindling into a larger flame, taking care not to suffocate as he piled sticks. They cooked the rabbit and then ate together in silence, listening to the crackle of the wood.

As they packed up and stomped out the fire, a howling noise rose from the forest's darkness. Several others joined the original howls, and Orin's pulse raced at the recognizable sound.

Stamping out the remaining charcoals, he equipped his rifle. Ta-Tu slung his bow from across his shoulder, drawing a projectile from the quiver concurrently. Orin glanced at the green bolt tip before facing the direction of the laments.

Moonlight cast shadows through the forests, making it challenging to detect the threat. An obscuration appeared between the dense pines in the distance. Orin cocked his revolver and steadied his aim at the threat's position. He saw the wolves separate, jogging in several directions while weaving among the trees. They growled and snapped as they closed the distance between the men.

Aiming toward one traveling in his direction, Orin pulled the trigger. The bullet missed by inches as it clipped a small branch that snapped off, hitting the wolf. The wolves ran, darting behind the solid pine trunks to avoid getting hit. Licking its chops, Orin watched foaming salvia dripping from the wolf's mouth.

Drawing the string back on his bow, Ta-Tu shot at a wolf closing in on him. The arrow zipped toward its target, connecting with the wolf's left eye. The creature slunk over while providing a loud wail and jerking a hind limb.

Taking aim on a wolf growling at him as it rushed forward, Orin let off another shot. The rifle boomed as the cartridge spiraled to reach its target. Yelping loudly, the wolf fell before picking itself off the ground and stumbling toward Orin. Orin repeatedly shot, finishing the wolf as a bullet connected with its forehead.

Turning toward Ta-Tu, Orin's eyes widen when he noticed a wolf chomping toward his partner's neck. The gnashing teeth of the creature connecting with his flesh, sending Ta-Tu to the ground. The wolf lunged forward, biting furiously toward his head as Ta-Tu struggled to hold it at bay by its nostrils.

Lining his sights on the wolf's abdomen, Orin breathed deeply, releasing as he pulled the trigger. The shot connected with the wolf's torso knocking it away from Ta-Tu. With snapping jaws, the creature dripped saliva from its muzzle as it looked toward Orin. Orin pressed his trigger again, connecting with the wolf's leg. Stiffening its limbs, the animal keeled over falling with a lolled tongue.

"Thanks," Ta-Tu said breathlessly, "Orin, I owe you one."

"Don't mention it," Orin gasped while examining the parameter for additional wolves, "that was a close one."

"Yeah, you saved my life. I'd propose we're about even, you and I."

Dusting himself off, Orin adjusted the rifle across his shoulder. He loosened the cap from his wineskin as Ta-Tu cut the paw off a wolf. Orin watched him stuff the creature's foot into his leather sash.

"We better continue toward the warehouse," Ta-Tu said, "White Feather expects us with the filters by dawn, so there isn't time to delay."

Orin stomped on the ashes and kicked the hare away. The charred rabbit sizzled as it flew into the neighboring brush. A gentle snow flurry fell through the pines as they continued northbound. An icy, brisk wind blew at their backs and wailed through the evening.

* * *

The moon cast soft light across the expanse as Orin and Ta-Tu crawled toward the edge of the hillside. From their vantage on this cloudless night, they looked at the cement blocks of the warehouse. Most of the structure appeared intact, which was not the norm for the other remaining structures surrounding the warehouse. Additional concrete deteriorated in ruins nearby, strewing chunks across the tall grasses. A narrow clay path snaked its way from their hill toward the warehouse through the meadows.

They hiked for hours during the evening to reach the vantage point. Distracting themselves by listening to the symphony of crickets and occasional hoots from an owl, they eventually arrived at a hillside overlooking the warehouse. In the distance, a howl from a wolf deep within the forest pierced through the pines.

Ta-Tu stated he'd been to this warehouse for activated carbon filters before a few seasons ago. As they crouched overlooking the warehouse, he confided the place could contain bandits or critters who may have moved in for refuge. Shifting the rifle across his backpack, Orin leaned close to the ground, attempting to conceal himself in the grasses.

Satisfied there were no predators between themselves and the warehouse, they made their way steadily along the dirt trail. Orin used his hands to steady his balance from the weight of his weapons and backpack as they deliberately took each stride. Once they arrived at the warehouse, both men pressed their bodies near a side door.

"Stay low," Ta-Tu whispered while gesturing toward the fractured door, "it's open."

Ta-Tu lightly nudged the entrance open and examined inside the darkness. Orin could see fragments of light shining into the structure from little broken windows near the roofline. As Ta-Tu opened the entrance wider, the creaking sound resounded with the door scraping the floor. Orin noticed the handle appeared withered and broke as he slipped inside.

Orin followed Ta-Tu while pressing his back against the rusted cabinets and shelves along the wall. The slivers of light spilled into the warehouse on their side of the building, while the other half remained enshrouded in darkness. Mounting shelves lined the floor space, filling nearly every conceivable square inch with assortments of items. Sketched graffiti decorated the surfaces of the building, but Orin could not read its strange symbols.

Holding his knife outward, Ta-Tu crouched low while inching along the edge of the wall toward the heart of the warehouse. Orin found it cumbersome to see further than to the shelves' end, even with the moonlight's small fragments. His mind played tricks as he occasionally saw a shadow in his peripheral. Orin kept pace with Ta-Tu as they methodically made their way to minimize noise. Soft echoing footsteps resounded as they strolled toward the end-cap. Orin's heart pounded in his breast as a clang of hardware in another aisle shattered the silence. A loud screech followed the crash as Orin pulled his revolver from his waistline and cocked the hammer.

Another crash repeated from across the room, followed by scurrying of feet and a rummaging noise. Orin held his weapon pointed outward as he glanced around in each direction. His head pulsated, and his palms perspired. Orin paused to take a deep breath to calm his nerves.

Edging along the passage, they continued heading toward the end-cap. Orin eyed buckets and crates lining the racks while taking broad steps over spilled containers. Spotting a small package containing squared-shape mesh screens, Orin gestured toward them.

"Are those the screens we need?"

"No, those are for ventilation," Ta-Tu hissed waiving his palm earthward, "we require water filtration mesh. They should be near the middle of this place. Let's locate the origin of that noise, first."

Orin moved a few items on an adjacent shelf near eye level to see through to the other aisles. Many of the objects remained on the shelves, which surprised Orin. Orin assumed the interior of this place would be bare from scavenger raids. Most of the structures he'd seen along the foothills were barren, and you were lucky to find a pile of frozen clothing in a derelict room.

Continuing along the path, they came to an end, and Ta-Tu briefly peeped his head around the corner. A third crash originated a few shelves away. A faint tapping sound followed another collapse and shriek from a rodent.

Orin could feel his heart hammering against the interior of his body armor he wore underneath his flannel. A loud shrill cry pierced the sudden silence. The noises came from all around them. Orin had the impression of being watched as they stood near the edge of their aisle.

Orin leaned past Ta-Tu to check the central hall of the warehouse. The main walkway led to adjoining aisles, which lined both sides of the structure. Silhouettes of boxes appeared lifelike in the enshrouding darkness. Following Ta-Tu, Orin walked into the corridor, straining his eyes to look down the aisles.

A scurrying sound continued as they pressed on speechlessly down the hall. They heard items being rearranged in a box down the lane closest to them. Pointing his revolver toward the sudden noise, Orin drew a deep breath and held it while squinting his eyes.

Ta-Tu continued to point toward the middle of the warehouse. When they came near the center, a loud clambering racket repeated from a neighboring aisle. Ta-Tu advanced toward the edge of the aisle, pressing his body along the shelf as a creature with a long roping tail jumped from a top ledge. Both men flinched simultaneously in astonishment as another creature screeched from behind.

Giant Rats!

Orin saw their short fangs hanging from behind their pointed noses. Long whiskers stretched from either side of their snouts. Thick phlegm dripped from their teeth as they studied the men curiously. Orin stood staring at the pest in the aisle until it screeched shrilly. The shrieks from the critter preceded additional scurrying of feet toward their position.

Orin fired rounds toward the nearest fangled creature until the trigger clicked, indicating an empty chamber. The monstrous rat slunk over and died with an awful screech. Ta-Tu drove his knife into the skull of another rodent in the corridor. With a reverberating squelch, the creature keeled over while twitching its legs. Ta-Tu removed the dripping blade as several rats scampered toward the commotion.

Stepping behind Ta-Tu, Orin fumbled his hands, struggling to reload his revolver chamber. As his fingers shook, he forcefully inserted several cartridges into the cells. The vermin shrieked but kept their distance as Ta-Tu waived his knife before him. Orin figured they could be diseased and that a bite from them may prove lethal.

While moving among the obscurations, two rats lunged forward at Ta-Tu. He held his blade high and brought it down forcefully while stumbling backward into an opening. Orin's hands shook while popping his revolver chamber shut.

A colossal rat wriggled on top of Ta-Tu's breast and scratched at him as he stuck his knife repeatedly into its gut. Ta-Tu kicked at the creature sending it flying backward toward Orin. Slapping the chamber into place, Orin pointed the revolver toward the second rat and fired a shot. The bullet connected with the rat's head, and he glimpsed at his partner, who climbed to his feet. Orin shot toward a shadow in the darkness as it moved across the passageway.

Ta-Tu panted while grabbing his chest. Orin saw his eyes expanded as he saw the palms of Ta-Tu's hands. His abdomen was a darkened shade, and Orin knew the rat injured him. They heard numerous clatters of objects from an adjacent aisle as Orin examined Ta-Tu's wounds.

"You okay?"

"I'll be fine," Ta-Tu gulped, "just a scratch, you?"

"I'm good," Orin responded while pointing his revolver into the darkness, "let's get these filters and get the hell out of here."

Ta-Tu searched through items on the shelves, holding them up toward the moonlight's fragments spilling from the upper windows. He tossed pieces onto the ground as he hastily pulled each from the shelves and read the labels. After several attempts, he threw Orin a small container. Unzipping his backpack, Orin, tossed the box into his bag.

Ta-Tu pointed toward a crate near a lifeless rat loaded with mesh screens. Orin grabbed a handful, shoving these into his backpack as Ta-Tu ransacked through additional shelves. Pleased with their loot, they made their way toward the rear of the warehouse. Orin stepped over twisted shelves and scattered cases cluttering the walkway. With Ta-Tu guiding the way toward the entrance, Orin listened to the rats' distant shrieks and squeals.

Once outside, they placed their hands on their knees, inhaling the fresh twilight air—the dank, mildew odor of the warehouse, dissipated outside. Although the shrieks faded behind them, Orin kept his revolver clutched tightly. Looking toward the glowing half-moon, Orin noticed the stars blinking light-years away. Orin realized that he hadn't taken the chance to look up toward the stars in moons, or had it been years?

"Well," Orin gasped, "we've made it."

"Not yet, we have to make it back to camp."

"We could camp tonight somewhere and rest up for the morning."

"No," Ta-Tu shook his head, "the others are counting on us for these carbon filters. People could become ill and die drinking unfiltered water."

Altering the weight of his backpack, Orin took a long drink from his wineskin while listening for the rodents inside. The warming sensation brought forth by the liquor provided enough stamina to continue onward with Ta-Tu.

What I would do to have one day walking the parameter with the Squad, Orin considered as he peered into the blackness of the night sky.

Following the small dirt path, Ta-Tu led them toward the top of the hillside. Lush grasses waved in the breeze, which sent clouds of dirt swirling over the fields. A regular hissing arose as grasses swayed while Orin studied the parameter.

The warehouse stood dark in the distance, and Orin's heart rate returned to normal. As they looked toward the tree-line, Ta-Tu smirked. Orin inquired what could amuse, but Ta-Tu kept quiet as he walked toward the pines. Shaking his head, Orin followed while listening to the distant howls of wolves and hooting of owls.

The moon slowly waned behind the mountain peaks. The howling of wolves grew louder and became more persistent as they drudged on through the dark woodlands. Orin's coat flapped in the flurry while he adjusted the straps of his rifle. Taking another drink as he walked, Orin realized his wineskin was half empty. He paced his drinking as he heard a low reverberating growl behind them. Orin swung his rifle down from his shoulder as he dropped his corked drink.

Ta-Tu readied his bow using a green-stained arrow. The snarls became rowdier, and Orin saw a shadow emerge from behind an adjoining pine. The noises came in each direction as Orin spun his head around. He lifted his rifle toward the nearest creature and discharged his weapon. The bullet missed, and the wolves snapped their jaws while swiftly enclosing the distance between the men. Ta-Tu relieved the arrow, which soared until striking a wolf in its ribcage.

Orin pointed his rifle, firing another round toward a howling cur. A loud growl emanated behind him. Orin turned as he felt the clamp of teeth around his forearm. The stinging pain caused Orin to cry out as the creature's razor-sharp teeth pierced through his skin. Ta-Tu swiftly reacted by swiftly thrusting his knife into the wolf's skull. The wolf unclenched Orin's arm as blood-spattered from its nostrils. Orin watched the creature slump on the earth.

Another wolf kept its distance, seeing the demise of its comrades. Growling, the wolf revealed its teeth to Orin. Ta-Tu removed another green-tipped arrow, letting it loose toward the creature. The arrow pierced through the predator's leg bone, but it continued limping toward them. After several yards, the beast slunk to the dirt while whimpering. As its limbs twitched, the vocals of the wolf softened and ceased. Orin kept his rifle trained on the wolf as he watched its chest heaving.

"Poison," Ta-Tu whispered, holding up a hand, "it won't last long, save your ammunition for when we need it."

Orin shouldered his gun as he heard a reverberating roar from the top of a hillside. His hands fumbled for his wineskin on the ground as he eagerly scanned the tree-line. The roaring noise did not sound as if it came from a wolf.

Another roar soon followed the original. Orin saw an enormous creature prompt on four legs surmounting a rocky edge of the hillside. It was challenging to discern precisely what type of creature it was in the fading moonlight. But Orin knew that whatever it was, it was larger than them and most likely hungry.

"Let's move!" Ta-Tu hissed, guiding them through the woodlands.

"Wh-what the hell," Orin gasped running after Ta-Tu, "was that th-thing?"

Passing through the dense pines, they kept aligned with the moon piercing its rays through pine needles' canopy. They darted over roots and fallen trunks as they scampered from the looming silhouette. Stopping to catch their breaths, Orin withdrew his wineskin and took a long sip.

A rumbling growl rose in their direction, followed by another ear-splitting roar. Orin's fingers quivered as he capped his wineskin and bungled with his rifle strap. He wheezed as he tried catching his breath. Minute tufts of vapor dispersed in front of his face as he squatted down, pointing his rifle outward.

Orin strained his ears to listen for additional signs of the creature. The rumbling noises ceased, and they could hear nothing but their own breathing. A sudden crack of a twig caused Orin to slowly turn his head toward a mass of overgrown thicket. Noticing a hairy snout peering at him with beady black eyes from above the brush, Orin gasped as the beast ducked its head and bellowed.

Orin coolly lifted his rifle, propping the stock firmly against his shoulder. He closed one eye and took aim down the scope as the massive bear charged toward him. Orin fired two shots in rapid succession as the grizzly swiped a huge claw across Orin's breast. His flesh burned as the bear's ebony-colored razor nails bore into his chest. The force of the impact elevated Orin, sending him flying backward through the air. Orin slammed his skull into a tree, causing a distinct cracking vibration in his neck.

Looking toward Ta-Tu, Orin saw him dashing up the high bark of a nearby tree. The bear clamped its mighty jaws across Orin's arm and wrenched its head. Orin heard a snap as the beast dragged him across the rough ground by his arm. Dirt and tree branches snapped underneath the bear's weight as it rambled toward Orin chewing his arm repeatedly. Orin's bag slid from his shoulder as his body sailed into a dense pine tree. His revolver slipped from his waistline, becoming caked in grime and buried among the pine needles.

The massive coffee-colored beast emanated decomposing flesh, and its mouth dripped thick saliva onto Orin's coat. Twisting his body, Orin tried moving out of range from the bear's staggering blows. As the bear clamped its jaws around his arm a third time, Orin's forearm went slack, and the rifle dropped to the ground. He tried punching the side of the bear's head repeatedly as it dominated over him, swiping at his chest. Orin's body armor was the only thing shielding his flesh from being mauled. The beast thrust its head, sinking its fangs into the meaty portion of Orin's thigh muscle. Blood squirted between the bear's teeth gripping Orin's torn jeans.

Orin twisted his face in sheer agony as the searing pain pulsated from his leg toward his back. The bear landed a crushing paw against Orin's face, sending a stinging ache shooting down his cheekbone. Quickly using its jaw muscles, the grizzly bit through Orin's body armor and nipped at his flesh. Orin felt excruciating pain and saw a brief flash of light as he lifted his hands to protect his face. Using his remaining strength, Orin pounded the creature's eyes until it released its grip. With a low roar, the bear turned to face Ta-Tu, who was high in a pine tree overhead.

Turning to lay on his stomach, Orin reached out, digging into the dirt to try to wriggle away. Noticing his movement, the bear hurled a paw against his ribcage while biting the back of his thigh muscle. Orin cried as the injury sent another fiery sensation accompanied by a flash of light. His leg went numb as the bear continued biting Orin's leather jacket. With a thrust of its strong muscles, the grizzly ripped Orin's coat from his back. Glancing up toward his partner, Orin saw Ta-Tu looking down on him with wide eyes and gaping mouth. He looked horrified at the carnage occurring below.

Biting the lower section of Orin's backside, the grizzly hauled him across the ground, planting him several feet away. A shrill scream escaped Orin as the massive teeth pierced his muscle while sending him airborne. A mighty paw crashed down on his back, ripping his flesh along his spine. Orin figured the bear would kill him, and he tried squirming away with all his remaining strength. Orin cried through clenched teeth as he tore at the ground before him in despair.

Digging his fingers into the giving soil, he slipped away from directly underneath the looming creature. The gigantic bear tore at Orin's arm again with its claws before providing a thundering snarl. Foaming saliva dripped into Orin's wounds as he struggled with a numbed leg and limp arm. Biting into Orin's buttocks, the bear ripped through his skin, sending another bout of searing pain along his posterior. Orin felt faint, and the ground tilted as he looked ahead. Lifting Orin into the air with its clamped teeth, the bear shook him forcibly before dumping him to the earth.

Exhausted and nearly succumbed, Orin spread his limbs outward in each direction. His heavy breaths decreased as he inhaled the musky earth scent. Trying to fiend death, Orin did not move as the bear inspected him. Hot air rushed from the bear's snout as it smelled Orin's head. Orin could feel the warm saliva dripping onto the back of his neck and matted his hair. Laying a paw on the back of Orin's neck, the grizzly clenched its nails sinking into his scalp. As the claws pierced the skin on his forehead, Orin tried breathing through his clenched jaws. Unable to handle the sharp sting, Orin provided a choking gasp and tried moving out from underneath the massive paw.

With a low grunt and several clicks of its tongue, the bear continued breathing hot air toward Orin's head. Orin gagged as he inhaled the foul mineral stench of rotting flesh. The breath of the beast was enough to make Orin want to keel over. The grizzly continued sniffing at Orin's head as it squeezed its paw harder into his scalp. Orin swallowed lumps of dirt as his mouth pushed deeper into the earth.

The bear backed away from Orin soon after becoming disinterested. Placing its paws on Orin's backside, the bear sniffed at his legs following a low rumble. After shifting to look in each direction, the bear sauntered over to the thicket from which it charged.

If I make it out of this, I need to kill that bear. Ta-Tu is not much help. I must kill that bear.

Prompting himself with his right arm, Orin twisted his torso to face the bear. He tossed his limp arm toward his nearby rifle and pulled it toward his body. Positioning the gun to point the muzzle toward the immense predator, Orin steadied his arm. Orin took a deep breath and held it as the bear looked his way.

Making eye-contact, Orin fired two rounds toward the bear's head. He couldn't tell if he hit the bear as it roared and charged him. Standing over Orin, the grizzly crashed its paws into his chest. With its weight, the bear pressed Orin deeper into the earth, knocking the wind out of his lungs. Its nails scratched at his torso while shredding the remnants of his flannel from his body. The bear flung Orin's rifle to one side, sending it clattering against a pine. Orin cried out as the bear bit into his chest while sending him airborne again toward a patch of trees.

With the bear over him, Orin slammed his fists on top of the bear's head. Repositioning himself beneath the creature, Orin raised his hand as the bear clamped down on his arm. Screaming as the sheering pain traveled to his neck, Orin felt his arm uncontrollably shake in the creature's mighty grip.

Swiping at Orin's ribcage, the bear positioned Orin to remain flat on his stomach. A burning spasm passed through him as the bear bit through the rest of his armor. Twisting his head, attempting to dodge the beast, Orin looked up to see Ta-Tu holding his blade outward. Hoping he would pounce on the bear to stab it, Orin reached his arm upward at his partner. With its claws stuck through Orin's body armor, the grizzly flung Orin through the air to land in a neighboring brush. With a low growl, the bear snorted as it slowly backed away from his prey.

Orin continued reaching out toward Ta-Tu longing for help. Ta-Tu kept his knife firmly gripped with the blade outward before gently tossing it to land near Orin's feet. Orin winced as he positioned his arm within the grasp of the weapon.

Grasping the handle of his blade, Orin twisted himself to face the bear. The colossal grizzly roared while speedily charging Orin. As the bear approached, Orin repeatedly thrust his knife into the skull of the bear. Blood spewed from the bear's wounds as it moaned from Orin's strikes. Placing a paw on Orin's breast, the bear struggled to stand himself up to ward off the stabs. The bear leaned its head near Orin's face with gnashing jaws. With the creature within range, Orin forcefully brought the blade down into its eye socket. A soft crunch emanated from the blow, and the creature backed away from Orin. Juices from the bear's eyes ran down its muzzle as it violently twisted its head while crying a soft groan.

Orin watched with eyes wide as the grizzly sauntered toward a nearby tree with the blade stuck in its eye. Heaving and groaning, the bear stumbled while trying to scratch at the weapon implanted into its skull. With a few helpless swats, it tumbled into the pine tree and whimpered between low growls. Birds chirped as the bear's cries of agony grew quieter, eventually ceasing to produce any sound.

Ta-Tu climbed down from the tree and ran swiftly toward Orin. Orin coughed up stomach bile as he tried catching his breath. Spitting on the ground, Ta-Tu placed a palm on his chest, groaning as he felt his wounds. Ta-Tu patted Orin's shoulder lightly as his world spun around him. Orin gawked at the sky as it turned a bright crescent of pink with the morning rays splitting the eastern horizon. As he closed his eyes, Orin tried lying back and catching his breath. Ta-Tu crouched over him, inspecting his wounds.

"It will be okay, Orin. You killed it. I can't believe it," Ta-Tu announced as he secured a tourniquet around Orin's thigh, "you're going to be okay. It'll be fine."

Chills coursed throughout Orin's body as he laid peering toward the sky between the pine needles. He tried counting the number of pine needles on the closest branch above his head. As he laid there in the wet soil, Orin felt light-headed, and his body became weightless. He tried shaking his head in disbelief of the events which transpired. Orin was in shock; he killed the grizzly.

His sweats made him cold, and his body shivered. Ta-Tu draped the vestiges of his coat and flannel over his torso as he looked around. Walking over to the bear, Ta-Tu removed his blade and struck the creature in the head to ensure it was dead. Orin watched as Ta-Tu cleaned the knife before plucking his backpack from the ground.

"Listen, Orin," Ta-Tu said, patting Orin tenderly, "you aren't in any shape to travel, and I need to get back with the supplies. I will come back with help. You have my word. Lay here and try to be still."

Ta-Tu poured a jug of water onto Orin's face and propped his head for a sip. Orin choked down water and began sputtering while gasping for air. Ta-Tu placed Orin's wineskin near his hand.

"You'll make it," Ta-Tu said with a grin, "drink if you can. I'll be back with help."

The lofty pines pointing to the sky above whirled around, blending together. Gasping and recoiling from numerous injuries, Orin tried transferring his weight to drink from the wineskin. Ta-Tu ran through the trees and was soon out of sight. Orin's agony was excruciating, and he hacked up phlegm and stomach bile.

Orin felt his discomfort subside in gradual bursts, seeming to melt away like butter. A euphoric sense washed over him as he stared at the magenta sky. His head pounded as Orin realized how inconsequential he was in the grand scheme. *If I perished today, who would commemorate?* The pine needles and branches overhead surged into a conglomerate of molds. Orin's world pulverized a heavenly orchestra as his consciousness sank to obscurity.

CHAPTER 15: MARCHING ORDERS

Orin awoke heaving for oxygen as his fists clenched tightly around the soft, moist soil. He wasn't sure how long he laid on the ground, but from the sun's position, he could see it was near high noon. While straining to turn his body on the sheet of pine needles, he heard sporadic shouts spring above rustling wind.

Smelling the mineral stench of blood, Orin glanced over toward the bear to see it hunched over. Deep gashes covered the creature's neck and head. Dozens of scars scattered across its pelt, a sign it fought fearlessly. Groaning from the pulsing twinge, Orin elevated his head. Overcome with a wave of vertigo, he fell back toward the pine needles in exhaustion.

"Here, he is!"

"Over here!"

The Outlaw's yelling became more resonant as they appeared. Orin's head pounded, and he closed his eyes to prevent the tree branches above from whirling with the sky. Settling into the earth, he listened to the snapping of branches around him.

"Easy now, rest, young one," White Feather stooped over Orin while placing a hand on his forehead, "you have done a remarkable feat, and the Outlaws observe your sacrifice."

"Can you lift him?"

"Two on his shoulders," White Feather yelled, "come on. Let's go!"

"We've got his revolver here. It's caked in mud."

"Grab it. You two, shave that bear. We could use the meat and hide."

They sent the whole camp after me, Orin thought as they hoisted him.

Orin's body spasmed as he welcomed the Outlaws grasping his limbs. He promptly yielded as his blood swiftly surged toward his skull. His temples continued a steady pulsating as the assembly carried him over the terrain.

With an Outlaw carrying him by each shoulder, Orin tripped in an attempt to balance himself. The sun crept toward the western peaks; the Outlaws stopped momentarily to allow Orin to catch his breath. The trek was an exhausting and arduous process traversing the forest and frozen ridges toward the camp. Keeping his eyes on his boots, Orin tried focusing on not losing his balance as they directed him across the region. He continued to fall in and out of conscious awareness, moving toward the Outlaw's camp.

Once at the encampment, the Outlaws chanted as they carried Orin through the clearing. Orin noticed the wooden tables were now barren. As they headed toward the tree structures, he heard them cheering his name.

"You are a champion of these woodlands, Orin," White Feather said, "they cheer because you slew the beast."

Ta-Tu assisted carrying Orin toward a cloth contraption that hoisted him toward the structure in the trees. Keeping his eyes closed, Orin tried staving his dizzying spell, which quickly overcame him. As they raised him, Orin looked around, noticing he was near Emerald's dwelling. The Outlaws placed Orin on the landing, and he could feel someone grabbing him by the torso and lifting him inside. They gently placed Orin onto a padded blanket, and a wet rag applied across his forehead.

Orin blinked and brought a hand across his eyelids. He knew he was in Emerald's home from the fragrance of honeyed musk. Glancing around the room, he looked at the cabinets in the corner. Outlaws were conversing near the entryway in a whisper as Orin groaned from a piercing ache in his ribs.

"Rest," Emerald spoke, hovering over him, "you will survive. Most of your wounds appear superficial. The armor saved you."

Emerald's brown eyes gleamed as she smiled at Orin and swabbed his face with a cooling fabric. Baring her yellowed teeth, Orin didn't feel the same attraction to her as he had the day prior.

Perhaps it was the jungle juice, Orin recollected.

"I told you we'd be back," Ta-Tu's voice bellowed from a corner, "get back to health. We need someone with your courage on our side. No hard feelings. You acted with a spirit such is the way of the Outlaws. You've earned my respect, Orin."

"Rest easy," Emerald raised a cup to Orin's lips, "you will sleep now."

Orin drank the milky liquid in several gulps. It tasted sweet like nectar after abundant rain. Not long after finishing the cup, his muscles relaxed and melted into the padded blanket. He propped his head and stared at the roof above his head. The bare walls around the room were soothing. He listened to the murmurs of the others as he closed his eyes.

* * *

After a fortnight passed of being mended, Orin felt well enough to help with the duties around camp. He didn't want to seem useless to the Outlaws if he were to ask for their help in finding Liam. Orin became close with Ta-Tu over this period and learned how to live from the abundance within the mountainous terrain.

Emerald patched and washed his original flannel, which Orin carried with him in his backpack. She tried to sew his leather jacket, although, with the tightness of the thread, Orin's jacket fits snugly. Outlaws polished his rifle, and he found it almost pristine, aside from a few scratches. He couldn't seem to find his revolver and figured he lost it in the forest's brush. Orin hadn't gotten around to inquiring about it, thinking he'd be better off with his rifle.

Walking back to camp, Orin carried a bucket of water for the distillation chamber. White Feather approached wearing his familiar red and black feathered headdress. He held a palm toward Orin, implying he wanted to converse.

"How are you feeling today, Orin?"

"I'm fine," Orin placed the canister on the ground, unscrewing the cap from his wineskin, "a little sore, but I'll manage."

"She's all cleaned up for you," White Feather beamed a grin handing Orin his cherry-wood revolver, "the gun's a beauty. A lot more than I can say about you. Where did you get it?"

"I ran security for a freak show caravan along the foothills awhile back."

"Let me guess, Two-Bit's magical or wonderful creatures," White Feather chuckled, "something of that nature, right?"

"How d'you know?"

"Oh, he's known. Every few months, he stops by for a swig of jungle juice," White Feather folded his hands across his abdomen, "a bit of a lightweight. Like you, Orin. Two-Bit gets drunk from a single sip and does his show for free! Hah!"

"Two-Bit is a shit," Orin spat, "what he did to that family. Enslaved those twins. If I see him again..."

"Save that energy, Orin," White Feather looked at Orin's clenched fists, "we've work to do. Kraken and his men reinforced an area around a lake south of our location. The end of our harvest is near, and we have supplies we need to trade if the Outlaws are to survive the solstice. We cannot risk any of our supplies being stolen by those barbarians. We will help you find your brother," White Feather continued holding a palm across his breast, "you will help us drive Kraken away from these forests. The time to strike has come. The Outlaws of the Forest move against the Righteous Warheads tomorrow at dawn. Are you with us?"

Orin shook hands with the leader. White Feather enclosed the space between them, wrapping his arm around Orin's shoulders. Orin inhaled the mineral stench of musk and blood. He wasn't sure if the smell came wholly from the Outlaw leader or himself. Orin's heart raced at the thought of finding his brother.

"Tonight, during Deireadh Fómhai, we feast! You will have a place beside me at the table," White Feather paused and held up a finger as he strolled away, "oh, and Orin, if you drink the juice tonight, stay away from Emerald."

* * *

The constant pounding on emptied buckets echoed into the night behind the high wooden table. Outlaws filled each seat along the split-log bench. Laughter filled the air as they told stories or insulted one another. On the table, assortments of fruits and vegetables piled over bowls. The jungle juice poured from ceramic jugs and spilled out of the Outlaw's mugs.

Flames licked the pine needles hanging on branches above the feast. The Outlaws who were sitting closest to the fire fed it continuously dense branches. From Orin's position near the middle, he observed the Outlaws down the line. Ta-Tu and Emerald both sat on the opposite side of White Feather. Each person's spirits were joyful and full of anticipation for battle. The Outlaws of the Forest appeared hopeful of their pending fight with the Righteous Warheads as they gloated about how to direct the most efficient attack.

"I say we go in over the north saddle," an Outlaw yelled, "and down the ridge."

"Nay! We make our point of attack from the southwest of the Lake Abyss," another Outlaw exclaimed with slivers of meat falling from his teeth, "we can surprise them and sneak around the rear."

"Aye! I agree with Himlick," a silvery man snarled while biting into his root plant, "we go 'round the lake. That way, we can take 'em by surprise!"

"Nonsense," hollered another, "the saddle will give us the vantage point. We can see everything in the camp!"

"Righteous Warheads have terrorized settlements and communions along the foothills for a long, long," White Feather's booming voice echoed while emphasizing his point, "a very long time. Kraken pillages and abuses settler's livelihoods. Some of your livelihoods! And for what? For his own greed and narcissistic virtues! And they call themselves 'Righteous'?

"Kraken leads his people as if he were herding sheep to the slaughter. He cares not for his people, but for his ill-gotten gains. The forest consumes the greedy," White Feather's gazed lingered on each person around the table, "today, brothers and sisters celebrate Deireadh Fómhai! May we reap our harvests for another rotation. But for us to do so, we must drive back against this unwanted scum. We cannot allow them to rob and pillage our forest!

"We will attack the Righteous Warheads," White Feather continued pounding his fists, "and we will strike from all sides! If we attack in unison and take them by surprise, we can overwhelm them even with their numbers. I believe many of them may run from their fragile cause during the attack. Victory is assured!"

Cheering loudly in the dark forest, the Outlaws sent birds flying into the sky. They resumed their pounding on empty buckets with greater force. Thundering booms echoed through the dense woods above their roars and cheers.

"Feast tonight, brothers and sisters," White Feather grinned at the dread-headed Outlaws, "for we dine in observance of our harvest! We have a trek south over peaks and valleys as straight as the crow flies. Prepare yourselves for the journey. We leave at first light."

Cheers from the Outlaws flowed readily into a boisterous conversation as the jungle juice and food were devoured. Orin joined in the laughter and ate his share of delicious meats and vegetables. Glancing over toward White Feather, he noticed him sitting back sipping on his beverage.

"Thank you, White Feather," Orin stated, "I appreciate your help."

White Feather appeared worried by his inscrutable gaze. Orin knew first-hand the brutal capabilities of the Righteous Warheads. Their armory was powerful, and they were cunningly ruthless. Kraken wasn't bashful about taking prisoners to farm crops and establish camps. Orin figured this could be his best chance of exacting vengeance for what Kraken did to his Squad members and save his brother.

Looking around the table, Orin examined each of the faces. These savages had been kind to Orin, mending him in his time of need. As he examined their faces, he saw a group wanting to flourish in these forests. Making eye contact with Ta-Tu, he smirked while bending his head. Ta-Tu complimented the exchange, and the two held up a cup of jungle juice. Drinking from his cup, Orin settled back on the bench enjoying the liquor's warmness running its course. His temples throbbed to the strike of the percussionists as he tried masking his anxiety with the alcohol. Orin was the closest he had ever been to finding Liam, and nothing else mattered.

* * *

Dawn light broke across the eastern peaks, penetrating through the dense throngs of pine needles. Carrying food, water, and his weapons inside his backpack, Orin proceeded southbound with the others. They adhered to the narrow dirt path toward the paved road. Their destination was past the highway and through a valley until they reached another mountain range.

It was a beautiful morning with a gentle cooling breeze drifting through the trees. The wind caused the pine branches to sway as the group passed underneath. Birds chirped overhead while flying from the limbs. Orin could see the turquoise-painted sky peeping through the thick tree limbs.

Pleasant day for a battle, Orin considered.

While strolling through the forest, Orin counted nearly three dozen heads. The Outlaws impressed Orin with the number of weaponry they carried with them. Most of the Outlaws carried rifles, pistols, and bows with green-tipped arrows in quivers. A few even slung automatic rifles across their backs. Orin briskly walked past the Outlaws toward the front of the pack alongside White Feather.

"Ta-Tu ventured out earlier to scout the way. We'll meet up with him along the paved road," White Feather spoke.

"Ever heard of a place known as Utopia?"

"Utopia?" White Feather asked.

"I've heard rumors of a place in the mountains where crops grow lush, and the rains don't blister. People along the foothills refer to this place as 'Utopia.'"

"No," White Feather whispered while shaking his head, "I have not seen such a place myself. However, there have been reports from supply runners of a strange place deep in the mountains' heart. The Outlaws do not venture toward the west more than a day's hike. I do not believe there is anything over that way which we cannot provide ourselves in these woods."

"Once we find my brother, we plan to go to this Utopia. Liam's convinced Utopia is safe within the mountains and can provide all we need to survive."

"You're fond of your brother. That's a good thing to see. It's not very often these days people take their family, to be a family. Us Outlaws, we are a family, but not by blood. There is something special there…"

Singing songs and the pounding of the drums, the Outlaws continued down the dirt path toward the blacktop road. They did not have to walk very far before they came to the opening. When they reached the middle of the paved road, White Feather held up a hand, and the Outlaws stopped.

"Outlaws," White Feather shouted as Ta-Tu approached from the clearing, "let us pause while we gather our resources."

"There is a passage that snakes southward before reaching the peaks," Ta-Tu said, "we would have a vantage point overlooking their encampment on the saddle. A small path follows along the precipice, which leads to a ridge along the southern border. The main entrance is toward the south, and they have wagons and horses coming through a widened dirt path."

"How do their defenses look?" White Feather asked.

"They haven't established the posts around the parameter of the lake. I also located a smaller reservoir southwest of the camp. The Warheads have not secured the far side of this lake either. On the western side, they have gaps between the fencing which we could squeeze through. But White Feather…"

"Yes, Ta-Tu?"

"The Warheads are well-armed," Ta-Tu expression was grim, "heavy ammunition and what appears to be a mortar crew."

"We will have the element of surprise," White Feather's eyes expanded, and creases formed around his lips, "one group on the saddle and a smaller force toward the south ridge. A diversion may be sufficient to overcome and drive those bastards from our forest."

White Feather shut his eyes and took deep breaths. His red and black feathered headband swayed in the refreshing mountain breeze. Orin could see his age in the morning sunlight shining across his wrinkled face. White Feather's expression did not change as he chanted in a soft whisper. He slammed his stick onto the road and turned to face the Outlaws. Opening his eyes, White Feather studied each of the faces before him.

"Himlick grab fifteen Outlaws. Split from the main group and follow the ridgeline toward their southern post. We will attack all sides."

"Aye! You damn right, I will, White Feather," an Outlaw with thick dreads caked in mud shouted, "let's kill those bastards!"

"When you hear the drums from the north, that's your cue to attack. Create as much of a shit-storm as you can!"

"Yeah, got it!" Himlick answered.

"We leave once we redistributed supplies and have filled our stomachs with food and drink. Outlaws, prepare for battle."

The Outlaws roared and whistled while holding various weapons high above their heads. Jungle juice flowed from jugs directly into the open mouths of the Outlaws. From across the road, Orin listened to the hooting and cheering as the group's energy rose. He glanced toward the sun, rising over the eastern peaks, and beating down on the asphalt.

Sitting against a thick tree along the road, Orin searched through his backpack for food before removing a can of peas and drinking from his wineskin. His heartbeat quickened in anticipation of the upcoming events.

So close to finding Liam. These drunken savages are the best option I have for finding him. It's now or never. And if I get a shot at Kraken, I can't wait to take it, Orin reflected.

"AYE," exclaimed an Outlaw while cackling, "it's that clanky bastard, Two-Bit, and his caravan!"

"Yeah," another yelled, "have 'em put on a show for us before we make for battle!"

Orin looked toward the east along the curving pass to see the small silhouette of a man wearing a top hat leading a pair of mules. The carriage creaked as it approached rolling over fractures jutting from the highway. Orin squinted his eyes in disbelief. His blood warmly coursed through his veins as Orin recalled their last conversation.

"Two-Bit, a show! Perform something for us!"

"Good morning, my fellow Outlaws," Two-Bit made a twirling gesture as he sat atop his bench behind the mules, "and what brings the group out to the pass on this remarkable day?"

"Hunting!"

"Eating and drinking," shouted another, "don't you know it's Deireadh Fómhai?"

"Ah! Yes, that's right! Seems so, hmm," Two-Bit paused while examining the crowd, "and would you like a brief act? Perhaps see Woodstock do his tricks? Hmm?"

"Yes," Himlick laughed while shaking his bone bracelets above his head, "take out the chicken!"

"Ah-hah! Very good, very go-," Two-Bit's expression became vacant and his face flushed as he locked eyes with Orin, "on second thought, I am late for my trip to the settlement. Yes, indeed!"

"Hold it, Two-Bit," Orin reproached as Two-Bit cracked his whip at the mules.

Cracking his whip again with greater urgency, Two-Bit pretended not to hear Orin. With his mules pushing through the congregated Outlaws, the carriage creaked forward. Orin reached into his waistline, removing his cherry-wood revolver. He pointed it directly at Two-Bit's head and moved toward the front of the wagon.

"I said hold Two-Bit!" Orin thundered.

"Or-Orin," Two-Bit stammered, raising his hands into the air, "I-I-I didn't see you there!"

"Get down from the wagon."

"Wh-what for? I nee-," Two-Bit stuttered.

"Get down," Orin grit his teeth as his face turned deep red, "or I will put a bullet in you!"

Approaching behind Orin, White Feather applied a modest pressure on his arm to defuse the situation. Orin shook his gesture away and kept his revolver on Two-Bit. The chubby man in the long coat and top hat clambered down from the bench. Once on the ground, Two-Bit backed up against his wagon, holding his shaking hands in the air.

"Open the wagon," Orin demanded with a wave of the revolver toward the rear.

"Wh-what?"

"I said, open the door!"

"Orin," Two-Bit's eyebrows furrowed as his fingers fidgeted with his collar, "with my gun?"

"It's my gun, I earned it," Orin tone remained stern, "now open the damn wagon, Two-Bit. I won't repeat it."

Two-Bit's chains rattled as he sauntered toward the back door of the wagon. With his hands shaking, Two-Bit fumbled on his chain for a key. The Outlaws stood around, watching the scene in silence. With a resounding clink, the hatch unlocked, and Two-Bit swung the wagon doors open.

Woodstock jumped in his cage, tucked between large boxes. Sitting on the bench, Mao and Tao blankly gawked forward. Orin snapped his fingers in front of their faces, but they didn't react. Not even a blink. The twin's black eyes stared toward the crates lining the inside across from them. Gripping his revolver firmly, Orin looked toward Two-Bit while spitting on the road. Two-Bit's chains clinked as a gentle breeze wafted down through the mountain pass. Trembling in fear, Two-Bit held his hands in front of his face as he crouched lower to the ground.

"Pl-plea-please Or-Orin. I was pla-planning to get rid of them. I was!"

With a swift thrust of his arm, Orin brought the handle of the revolver crashing across the side of the cowering man's face. He heard bones cracking as Two-Bit's hat flew from his head. Two-Bit dropped to the asphalt with a muffled thump. Blood gushed from the side of his mouth as he spat teeth onto the ground. Tucking the revolver back into his waistband, Orin pummeled with both fists until Two-Bit's face swelled purple.

Holding Two-Bit with one fist around his collar, Orin punched him until his knuckles split and bled. Orin dropped the sunburned man toward the hot blacktop and surveyed his hands. Looking toward Two-Bit, Orin saw his skin turning a vibrant purplish-blue color across his face and neck. Stepping aside, Orin looked toward the Outlaws who stared back, surprised.

Extending a hand toward the twins, Orin waited for the twins to react. Silently, they remained sitting staring at the cases across from their bench. Orin motioned his hand and nodded his head encouragingly until Mao extended her arm to receive help down from the wagon. Her sister followed afterward, and the two women stood beside Two-Bit's unconscious body. They still wore the same yellow chiffon dresses, which were worn upon meeting Orin. Mao and Tao both bore the same expressions of pursed lips as they squinted curiously at Orin.

"You two, go," Orin pleaded, waving his hands toward the eastern pass, "go elsewhere, far away from here. Back to Ádyto or find your mother. Get out of here and away from Two-Bit. He is exploiting you for his gain. Don't you see?"

"Go!" Orin shouted again, pointing toward Two-Bit, "you can't come with us, but you shouldn't stay with him!"

"You two can settle up at our camp," White Feather interjected, "Outlaws are remaining up the trail, you are welcome there."

Motionless, Mao, and Tao did not change their expressions as they continued staring at Orin. They clasped their hands tightly together over the front of their flowing dresses. Sunlight reflected from the tops of the twin's polished buckle shoes.

Sighing and shaking his head, Orin pat Two-Bit's pockets and removed jewelry from his coat. Orin found a cracked pocket watch and rattled the device near his ear. The pocket watch hummed a soft buzz as the more extended hand vibrated in place. Orin tossed the clock to the ground, hearing a soft clink as it hit the asphalt. He handed White Feather his loot from the unconscious freak show merchant. Patting White Feather on the shoulder, Orin sauntered into the crowd, gradually moving away to allow him to pass.

"Let's move out," White Feather ordered.

The Outlaws, with their faces painted in mud and tree sap, howled as they pounded the buckets and continued down the ridge toward the southern forests. Orin could see through the woods toward the rough terrain ahead. He briskly walked toward the front of the group alongside White Feather and Ta-Tu.

As they progressed deeper into the forest, Orin glanced behind them toward the ridgeline at the carriage. The twins stood beside Two-Bit and had not moved. Their tight lips and squinting eyes peered back toward Orin. The wind blew their long ebony hair from their shoulders and bulged their chiffon dresses.

Orin felt the tinge of guilt, gripping his chest as they proceeded far into the woodlands. He wondered if he allowed his impulses to yet again cloud his judgment. A single teardrop formed in the corner of his eye, and Orin blinked profusely to prohibit it from falling. He couldn't afford to demonstrate weakness at a time like this when they were heading for battle.

Were the twins better off without Two-Bit? Two-Bit seemed to keep them fed and clean. I wonder if I made a hasty decision.

Orin's concerns continued to roam as he tried regaining focus. Orin looked from the rocky slope back toward the mountain pass ridgeline, facing the trees' break to the south. When he glanced back at the wagon, he saw the twins continue to stand in the same spot, staring back at him. Orin felt their beady eyes, observing him as he continued traveling with the Outlaws toward the Righteous Warheads location.

CHAPTER 16: KRAKEN

Marching along with the thundering drums, the Outlaws proceeded through tall grasslands toward a steep precipice. Making the incline along the bluff, they single-filed along the rocky ridge toward the saddle overlooking the Righteous Warhead's camp. When the Outlaws neared the position, the steady pounding on the buckets ceased. White Feather directed several to quiet down as stated he believed scouts may roam the area. Orin stole a glance around the destitute rocky vantage point. Below, the valley was covered in lush green forage. In contrast, upon these cliffs, the occasional flower sprouted from between huge jagged boulders.

Life could not sustain itself above a certain altitude, and it was clear where this line was based on where the trees stopped growing. Orin observed the tree-line resembled a straight line around the mid-section of the surrounding peaks. Magnificent predator birds flew over their heads as they stood on the side of the looming foothill. Above him, Orin saw rocks of various sizes leading up the saddle between two gigantic peaks covered in snow.

Reflecting on his recent encounter with Two-Bit, Orin thought about the impulsive rage which consumed him at the moment, clouding any form of rationality. He wasn't entirely convinced freeing Mao and Tao from Two-Bit was necessarily the best idea. For all he knew, Orin believed he may have done more harm to those young women than good. They were stranded far from Ádyto in the mountains. Their best course of action may be to follow the road back toward the stadium or along the dirt path to the Outlaw's encampment.

The rear end of the group passed through the trees below, where they gathered on the mountainside. Small rodents with dark stripes along their backs darted from behind various rocks in a ceaseless tag game. Cushiony clouds blew quickly across the amazonite sky between the towering peaks.

The air was becoming thinner as the Outlaws proceeded along the slope. Using his hands to guide himself alongside massive boulders, Orin shuffled his feet and faced the rocks in front of him. He didn't want to experience the sickening feeling of vertigo while on the side of this mountain. When the path became too steep for the large group to continue, they convened and waited for White Feather's direction. Orin watched as some Outlaws heaved their chests as they tried catching their breath in this altitude.

Searching around for a small clearing, White Feather pointed toward a flatter portion of the mountainside where the group began to unload while waiting for the remaining Outlaws. White Feather instructed the assembly to take a short break and drink water rather than the jungle juice. Ta-Tu shuffled over toward Orin, tossing him a water jug. The two sat on a protruding rock while quenching their thirst. Emerald seated herself on another boulder overlooking the pass as she watched the Outlaws walk up the narrow pathway. The flurry gently lifted her dreads from across her shoulders. Looking around for miles, Orin admired the landscape. From his vantage, he could see Khoine's Glacier and pointed the landmark to Ta-Tu. Pulling his wineskin up toward his lips, Orin took a swig of whiskey to wash down the water.

With the Outlaws resting, White Feather reminded the group of the plan. Himlick's group would follow the ridgeline toward the southwest slope. The remaining Outlaws were to attack from the top of the saddle. Attacking from opposite ends of the camp would ensure the Righteous Warheads were overwhelmed. With the groups in position, White Feather would indicate the start of the attack by the pounding on the buckets.

Shouting acknowledgment of the plans over the relentless wind, the Outlaws resumed their journey up the narrow pathway. As Orin looked toward the top, it seemed like the slope led them straight into the sky. Climbing higher in elevation, they began to see heavy clouds leveling off in the distance. Gusts blew fierce down from the peaks on either side, sending Orin stumbling more than once. Pulling his flannel shirt and jacket tighter around his torso, Orin grit his teeth while pressing onward.

Once they arrived at the top ridge overlooking the Righteous Warhead camp, the Outlaws paused out of sight. They said their words of encouragement to one another. Himlick's group gathered together and began creating a plan for their position. Orin watched as fifteen Outlaws crouched low following Himlick across the saddle toward the southern precipice. A small grin formed in the corners of Orin's lips as he noticed the Outlaw's wild flailing of their arms as they walked. Their eagerness for battle was inspiring.

Orin counted twenty-one remaining heads as they slowly crept toward the ridge overlooking the Righteous Warhead campsite. White Feather wore a stoic expression as he squinted his eyes while scanning the camp below. Looking toward the center of the valley, Orin saw two shimmering lakes with sunlight piercing directly at his eyes. Shielding a hand over his eyebrows, Orin noticed dozens of people below scurrying about like insects. Wooden fence posts loosely dotted the parameter of the camp with many of the voids filled with plankboards. Several significant gaps were noted on the parameter toward the west. Orin heard an Outlaw confirm the weaknesses in their fencing above the slapping wind.

Periodic shouts over the gusts sprang up. Orin heard several short bursts from trumpets above the commotion along the ridgeline. His heart began beating through his flannel as he realized the Outlaws didn't carry trumpets. Peeking his head over the ridgeline to view the activity below, he noticed people running around the camp and moving objects along toward the parameter. Orin knew they were establishing their defensive positions and stole a quick glance at White Feather. His stoic expression did not change as he continued scanning the camp. However, Orin saw beads of sweat forming along his forehead under his feathered headband. Emerald's hand clasped Ta-Tu's fist tightly, causing her knuckles to turn a pale white as the two stared down into the camp.

Pulling his rifle from around his shoulder, Orin pointed the sights down toward the camp. Peering through the scope, he began taking a closer examination of their defenses. Mercenaries scurried around below, but it was challenging to discern specific objects from this ridge. He shifted his focus toward the various objects being moved from within the camp.

Large tents enclosed a massive fire that was surrounded by half-cut logs. A few wagons were placed around the parameter of the camp. The Righteous Warheads covered the back of these wagons with scrubs and juniper branches, shielding its contents from Orin's view.

"Wagons with something in them," Orin said and glanced at White Feather, "they have wagons covered along the camp walls. Toward the front and rear near the lake."

Plumes of snow swirled from the peaks being carried across the saddle before dispersing into the sky. Orin noticed there wasn't much snow on the rocks where they were crouched, except in the shadowed portion between larger ones. Shifting his rifle toward another section of the camp, he peered through to examine the mercenaries below.

Several people barked orders at others around the camp. Orin noticed their body language seemed erratic as they waved their arms vigorously in the air. Some held rifles in their hands at the ready while scanning the ridgelines of their campsite. Several mercenaries wearing cowboy hats with the crease in the middle circled the camp's parameter holding long rifles. Shifting his weight, Orin moved his gun to check the entrance of the encampment.

A man wearing a long trench coat rode around the camp on a large black stallion. Orin watched as the man's thick beard fluttered in the breeze while shouting at the Warheads. Orin's eyes began watering as a wind gust flew in fierce, causing his vision to become blurred. Repositioning his scope on his shoulder, Orin peered back down to see the man on horseback remove a revolver and pointed it at a man cowering with his hands raised. A second later, a shot rang out from the camp, and the cowering man dropped toward the rocky terrain.

A vision invaded Orin's thoughts as he remembered the fields and seeing Liam for the last time. Intuitively, Orin knew who the man was on horseback. Shaking his head to clear the vision, he saw traces of a man on horseback coming through the fields' dense smoke. Orin squinted his eyes and regained awareness as he looked toward the one towering above the others on his stallion.

Kraken.

Above the howling wind, Orin could hear the Outlaws begin to whisper amongst themselves. Orin's eyebrow glistened with sweat, and a clinging drop hung just above his eyelid. He used a sleeve to wipe the tear away as he adjusted his jacket. Using one hand, he reached for his wineskin and felt the leather. It was comforting to know he had his drink nearby as his heart raced with anticipation.

"Himlick has reached his position," an Outlaw shouted over the wind gusts, "shall we signal?"

"Not yet," White Feather firmly stated while holding a palm in the air, "we wait."

With his stringy hair piercing his corneas, Orin jerked his head to the side and shifted his rifle. He focused the scope on several structures propped along the opposite side of the camp. Breathing slowly to control his racing heart, Orin watched people scurry around the campsite wearing leather skins while engaging in various tasks to build their defenses. Moving the gauge around the scope, Orin zoomed in and tried examining the Righteous Warheads' faces. His heart leaped into his throat briefly as he spotted his brother.

This man had the same body structure as his brother but now displayed an abundant thick beard to his chest. His hair was pulled back behind his head into a bun. Orin watched this man as he appeared to also give orders to those around him. He found it odd that his quiet and timid brother would be ordering someone else around. Orin muttered a curse under his breath that his scope couldn't provide greater focus on the target.

"I think I found my brother," Orin shouted over the whistling wind.

"I need ten of you to make your way down this slope when I give the signal," White Feather spoke, furrowing his eyebrows in the direction Orin pointed.

Several of the Outlaws acknowledged with agreements over the relentless gusts. White Feather pointed to the drummers and held up a dark wrinkled hand. An Outlaw handed White Feather a long-ranged rifle with red and black feathers tied together at the end of the gun.

"Outlaws! The time has come. Let's drive these vermin from our forest lands! They may scavenge and pillage along the foothills. Still, we will not allow them to fortify themselves near our sacred forests," White Feather jerked his rifle over his head as he spoke. The feathers from the gun and headband flapped in the bone-piercing wind, "do we have Outlaws ready to charge the camp post?"

"Aye!" Shouted members of the group along the ridgeline while thumping their chests and raising their weapons.

"My brothers and sisters. Today, we arise! Through the forest's strength, the light of the sun, radiance of the moon, and splendor of fire! Attack with the speed of lightning and swiftness of the mountain breeze! TO ARMS!"

The Outlaws cheered and pounded the buckets with low thuds resonating into thundering booms. Orin watched as several members from the Outlaws crawled down the slope holding their weapons before them. Through his scope, he could see Righteous Warheads behind the camp walls sprint toward defensive positions.

Outlaws with Himlick's group were visibly sliding down the slope toward the southwest. The Righteous Warheads blew their shrieking horns while removing shrubs and branches concealing the tops of wagons exposing large machine guns. The Outlaws remaining on the ridge, which included White Feather and Ta-Tu, fired their weapons toward the camp. Orin blasted a couple shots at the men attempting to climb onto the wagons to mount the heavy weaponry.

Orin grinned as a bullet connected with the arm of a Righteous Warhead mercenary, causing him to fall from the wagon. Another man quickly took his place, shielding himself behind the large gun while swinging it toward their position. Clamorous thuds hammered the rocks along the slope toward the descending Outlaws. Orin's ears rang as he heard the crackle and zips of seemingly endless bullets ripping into the mountainside. He ducked his head in time to avoid a few stray cartridges raining up toward him.

Hearing cries from the Outlaws just below him descending the ridgeline, Orin peeked back over and continued firing down into the campsite. Looking through his scope, he caught sight of Kraken, who roamed the camp's parameter with his handgun drawn. Kraken was firing steadily in the direction of the Outlaws, who were advancing. Orin removed his eye from the scope and rubbed his socket while staring down toward his comrades. As he did so, he saw an Outlaw's leg ripped from his body as large-caliber bullets from the machine gun tore through the men like a paper target. Entrails of muscle and tissue flew from the exposed limb. The man screamed in agony as he immediately fell toward the boulders in his path. Laying on the ground, the man reached for his missing leg with a bloodied hand to no avail.

"HELP!" Orin heard the Outlaw cry.

The remaining Outlaws were descending toward the camp scattered behind large rocks as the commotion caused a ringing in Orin's ear. Those on the ridge continued to fire down at the Righteous Warheads, and Orin could see a few of their men fall to the ground clutching their limbs and torso. Horns continued to blast between exchanges of gunfire on the rocky slope.

Lining his rifle toward the man on the machine gun raining up toward their position, Orin slowly inhaled while steadying his hand. Once his sights were focused toward the Righteous Warhead's head, Orin exhaled his breath. His target jerked around from the recoil on his machine gun, causing Orin to have to refocus on his upper chest. Taking another deep breath, Orin held it while counting slowly. On three, he released his breath while simultaneously squeezing the trigger. The man's head flew back, and a line of blood sprayed in a spiral arc as he stumbled from the back of the mounted weapon.

Outlaws continued descending toward the campsite while firing at the Righteous Warheads. To keep cover, Orin watched them hurl their bodies behind huge rocks. Kraken and his Righteous Warheads returned fire as another member of their group began mounting the machine gun. Kraken shouted orders while taking a direct shot toward the closest Outlaw. Quickly taking aim at another Outlaw who exposed his body from behind a boulder, Orin watched in terror as Kraken promptly disposed of the man. The Outlaw dropped to the ground with his rifle clattering down the slope.

Positioning his rifle toward Kraken, Orin breathed in deeply. On his exhale, he fired simultaneously, but the bullet ricocheted behind the man, scaring his steed instead. Kraken's horse began to buck, causing Kraken to swiftly rub its neck to calm it down. Turning around, Kraken rode back toward the center of the camp through an opening in the parameter posts. Several Righteous Warheads poured out through the opening, firing both automatic and semi-automatic rifles up toward Orin's position along the ridge.

Several Outlaws from the original twenty on their side cried out in agony over the constant gunshots splitting through the gusts of howling wind.

"I'm on it!" Emerald shouted above the commotion as she dipped over the ridge holding a wrapped linen cloth fluttering in the wind.

Orin watched as she stumbled and slid a few yards down the ridge before catching herself on a giant rock. Crouching low, she made her way toward the nearest Outlaw as bullets continued raining overhead.

The remaining Outlaws returned cover fire down toward the Righteous Warheads from the ledge. Peering through his scope, Orin scanned the area in which he last saw his brother. There was more than one Righteous Warhead, which matched his description of long dark hair and thick beard. Using his sleeve, Orin wiped the end of the scope as he tried discerning the various figures below. He didn't want to accidentally shoot his brother in the commotion. As he pointed his rifle toward the far parameter of the campsite, Orin noticed a man who ran with the same awkwardness he knew of his brother. Watching intently, Orin saw this man firing at the Outlaws relentlessly toward the southwestern ridge.

Adjusting his scope, Orin peered toward the section of camp nearest the Outlaws from the ridge. A movement in the corner of the sight caught his attention. Positioning his rifle on his right side, he saw several Righteous Warheads setting up a mortar cannon.

BOOM!

The blast sent massive chunks of rocks and debris flying out from the side of the slope. Orin shielded his face with his arm as tiny rocks rained down onto the ridge.

Emerald flew and slammed hard against a bulky boulder before sliding approximately forty feet toward the wooden posts. Shrapnel tore through the muscle and bone of the Outlaws in the vicinity from the blast. Orin's ears rang sharply, and he brought a hand to the side of his face to feel a warm liquid seeping from a wound.

Ta-Tu shouted with impulsive rage while jumping over the ridge and stumbling down the slope toward Emerald's body near the bottom. White Feather tried to call after the deranged man, but Ta-Tu scrambled toward Emerald as quickly as possible. Orin felt a twinge of pain and frustration as it appeared the Outlaws were fighting a losing battle. He knew he couldn't allow this opportunity to find his brother go to waste.

Turning the scope toward Liam's last known position, Orin vehemently scanned as bullets whizzed and crackled overhead. A cartridge landed just below his arm. He noticed a plume of dust spiral to the sky momentarily blocking his vision. Once the dust blew away, Orin repositioned the scope and quickly identified Liam firing a handgun toward an Outlaw who was pinned behind a boulder along the southwestern slope.

Scanning the camp's parameter closest to his position, Orin spotted an opening between the wooden posts. The opportunity appeared large enough to squeeze through and navigate behind tents toward Liam's last-known location. Deciding to head toward his brother, Orin scrambled over the ridgeline and down the slope making his way toward the defensive posts.

He glanced across the slope to his right, identifying Ta-Tu, who was also scrambling behind boulders as he made his way toward Emerald. Clouds of dust billowed around the man's feet as he proceeded while narrowly avoiding the gunfire. Orin watched his comrade for a moment as he also continued to stumble his way down the steep rocky mass.

As Orin slammed into a large rock to avoid falling down the slope, he watched a mercenary on horseback pointing his rifle toward Ta-Tu. Orin's mouth gaped open in horror as the mercenary lowered his gun and fired.

"No, Ta-Tu," Orin gasped, "look out!"

Time seemed to stop as Ta-Tu stood and faced the man on horseback with his bald head shining in the sunlight before he dropped his rifle to his side. Orin was stunned as Ta-Tu fell to his knees, staring wide-eyed at his attacker. Placing his scope dead-centered on the mercenary, Orin fired his weapon. The bullet disappeared into the man's torso, and he fell off the horse, which reared onto its hind legs before bolting across the camp.

BOOM!

Another explosion along the slope thundered into the night, sending debris and shrapnel flying into the distance. The ground shook as if an earthquake split the land. Orin fell to the Earth as rocks began raining down on him once again. Collecting his bag which was ripped from his shoulder, Orin began to stumble down toward the fence.

"Cernunnos guide you," Orin could hear White Feather shout, "give them hell."

Orin lined another Righteous Warhead mercenary in his sights as he edged along a giant boulder. Once he squeezed the trigger, he heard a clicking noise, and nothing seemed to happen. He popped out his magazine quickly and reloaded another full of cartridges. Taking aim, Orin pulled the trigger and immediately saw the mercenary grab his shoulder and wince from the sudden pain. Orin shot again, which sent the man stumbling backward toward the ground. Satisfied with the outcome, Orin quickly shouldered his rifle along the torn strap while shifting the weight of his bag before proceeding down the slope.

Glancing over his shoulder, Orin noticed Ta-Tu clutching his abdomen as he crawled toward Emerald. Emerald looked a shade of purple, and her limbs were sprawled along the slope in an awkward pose. Bodies of Outlaws scattered along the mountainside. Dodging the crackle of bullets, he closed the distance between his position and the defensive parameter.

As he reached the fencing gap, Orin looked up toward the top of the ridge and noticed White Feather only discernable from the red feather poking above the rim. He squeezed his body through the opening while crouching in the brush beside a large tarped tent. Wooden structures haphazardly built within the camp were dotted with thick juniper bushes. Orin concealed himself while pausing to ensure he wasn't noticed during his infiltration. When he was confident his entry went unobserved, he slowly moved his head around the tent's corner from which he saw Liam.

Liam knelt behind a wagon while firing his handgun toward the Outlaws to the southwest. Looking toward the ridge, Orin noted the Outlaws who hid behind massive boulders while firing down into the camp. He listened to the loud blasts and the crackle of gunfire from all directions.

"Liam!"

Orin hissed through gritted teeth. Liam did not notice his brother as he continued returning fire at the Outlaws. Orin felt the ground shake as another blast blew rock and debris from the mountainside.

"Liam!"

Orin hissed again with spittle flying between his teeth. He leaned around the tent flap to expose his head and chest. Incoming bullets ricocheted from the wagon near his brother and tore through the tent canvas. His ears rung again in a loud symphony, and for a moment, the sounds around him deafened. Shaking his head, Orin began to hear the pings as bullets slammed into metallic objects and tore through the clapboard structures.

Picking up a small pebble from the ground, Orin tossed it toward his brother's back. Liam turned toward his direction, and Orin gazed at the scruffy man with a great beard clinging down to his chest. Orin had never known Liam to have a beard, and so he was slightly bewildered by his appearance. Liam knelt closer to the ground as another shot rang overhead and crashed into the nearby wagon. As the two locked eyes, Orin recognized the soft, emerald-colored spheres above his pointed nose and round protruding chin.

"Liam, come here!"

Liam appeared to stare off in the distance, seemingly not recognizing Orin. Orin watched as Liam resumed firing at the Outlaws along the mountainside. Orin twisted his body around the corner while diving for cover near his brother's position. As he slid, he felt the stinging pain of rocks scraping his skin from his arms and legs. The sounds of gunfire became more sporadic as the battle raged on. A cooling sensation crept from underneath his flannel as his arms scraped the hard surface.

Crouching behind the wagon next to his brother, Orin studied his face for what seemed an eternity. Liam appeared rough, weathered, and barely recognizable. His skin was wrinkled as if he aged years since the last time Orin saw him. His dark brown hair, which once hung to his shoulders, now clung down to the bottom of his chest. Liam's face displayed hints of exhaustion as Orin noticed the wrinkles around his eyes and lips.

Smoke thickly hung over the camp, making it difficult to see more than a dozen yards in either direction. Cries and shouts could be heard beyond the opaque cloud hovering above the brothers. They stood silent while studying each other. As Orin tried walking several steps toward his brother, Liam gripped his handgun and pointed it toward him. Orin placed his rifle on the ground as a sign that he meant no harm to Liam.

"Liam," Orin's voice shook, and his hands trembled, "brother. It's me, Orin."

Orin's raspy voice quivered as he spoke these words, unsure if his brother would recognize him. Liam kept his gun trained on Orin while staring blankly through him. His gaze appeared to pierce through Orin as the two remained silent, crouching within feet of one another.

"Liam," Orin repeated softly and displaying the palms of his hands.

Gunfire around them began to fade into the background in a hollow echo. The ringing in his ears began subsiding as seconds seemed to pass like hours. Orin placed a hand to the side of his ear and felt a wet sensation. Looking down at his fingertips, he could see they were covered in a sticky dark-red substance and knew it was his blood leaking from a wound.

"Kraken!" Liam suddenly shouted above the surrounding commotion, "I've got one for you!"

"Kraken!" Liam yelled, "Kraken! I have one here for you!"

Orin could not understand why Liam was calling for Kraken. *Doesn't he know who I am? I am his brother! I am here to rescue him!* Orin was confused and shook his head to try and defeat the ringing in his ears momentarily as he sought to think through the problem.

"Kraken!" Liam shouted between clenched teeth.

Listening to shouts closing in on his location, Orin could do nothing but stare back at his brother in despair. For a moment, Orin believed this ordeal to be nothing more than a bad dream from which he would awaken. Orin pondered his pending fate while standing encapsulated by the echo and sharp bells hammering the space between his ears.

Feeling a heavy hand grab the back of his shoulder, Orin spun around away from his brother. He peered up toward a man on a dark steed. He immediately recognized the trench coat caked in grime and dirt. One eye was as dark as the abyss while the other looked back at him with the color of fresh snow. A deep gnashing scar ran diagonally across his pocked face.

Orin felt a chilling shiver course throughout his bones as he stared frozen back at the man towering above him. His heartbeat thundered from his chest as his palms were covered in a clammy sweat. Inching his quivering hand closer to his weapon, Orin was met with a blunt concussion to his temple's side. Falling toward the ground from his position next to the wagon, he realized Liam's betrayal.

Why Liam? Orin thought as his head hit the Earth, and darkness engulfed his world.

CHAPTER 17: NOBLE CAUSE

Orin awoke with a constant throbbing and pinching laceration above his ears. His hands were bound behind him in what felt like a flimsy plastic tie wrapped around his wrists. There was a thick frayed rope around his chest, holding him back to his seat. He coughed as he sat there, looking at his knees while trying to focus his pupils in the darkness. A mixture of blood and saliva hung in a slow drip from the corner of his lips.

He tried to look up, but a sharp pain in his neck caused him to jerk downward. Orin's eyes could not open more than a squint. Panicking, Orin started to furiously rub his wrists together to decrease the resistance of his bindings. The darkroom allowed a sliver of piercing light through the outline below the door. He couldn't move more than an inch or so while twisting and straining at the bindings.

Orin heard someone wince and gasp to his right side. Straining his neck and fighting through the piercing pain, he saw the silhouette of a man next to him. The man sat on a chair with his hands bound. Orin noticed the outline of feathers on top of his head in the darkness.

White Feather!

A searing pain shot down his body as he strained his head further to see the Outlaw leader clearer. He could hear the murmur of voices beyond the door as the Righteous Warheads discussed plans nearby. Orin sat still on his chair while trying to grasp the past events and listening to the Warheads.

I was with Liam taking cover behind the wagon. But, but, why was Liam shouting for Kraken? Where is Liam? Where am I?

White Feather winced again as a groan rippled in the darkness. As Orin strained his neck, he bit down on his lip to keep focused. The hairless head's shape provided evidence that Ta-Tu sat in the chair closest to the far wall.

The door opens after several moments of groaning arising from Ta-Tu. Orin shook his head to silence an itch above his eyebrow to no avail. The tingling intensified, and Orin violently shook his body in the chair. He noticed a dull throbbing ache in his side, indicating he cracked a few ribs during the battle.

"Em-Emerald," Ta-Tu called out in the darkness, "Emerald!" The man spat blood down to the dirt floor.

"She didn't make it, Ta-Tu. We need to stay strong and focus," White Feather said calmly in between short breaths.

A tall man thrust the door open, shedding sunlight into the room. Orin looked around at the barren place. The cabin appeared to be used for meetings of some sort. A polished wooden table stood leaning against the wall closest to Orin. Aside from the chairs in which the men were bounded, there were no additional items in this tiny dusty room.

The mercenary stood in the doorway for a moment and slapped a metal bat against the palm of one hand. The stranger chuckled a moment before stepping aside and allowing Kraken to enter the room. Kraken stood in his black trench coat, and vision of him by the wagon stole into Orin's mind.

Kraken stroked his scroungy shadowy beard, and a curious reflection emanated across his pale eye. After a moment, Kraken spoke, "what have we here?" A smug grin reflected across his chubby cheeks.

"New soldiers? Hmm? Misfortunate savages? Threats to our noble cause?" Kraken began pacing in front of the men as he continued, "Why did you attack my people? Hmm? We did nothing to you. We let you play your petty games among the trees. Hmm?" Kraken waved his hand frivolous.y in the air.

The room was silent, aside from a slight groan emanating from the corner of the room. Orin could hear others moving about the camp outside the structure. There were no crackles or snaps of gunfire. *The battle was over, and we are the captives. We may be the only ones left*; the chilling thought swept over Orin as he stared back at the looming figure pacing before him.

"ANSWER ME!" Kraken roared, "what gives you savages the right to attack my people and disrupt our noble cause?"

"Your cause isn't noble," White Feather replied calmly, "you rape and pillage all that you see."

Kraken nodded to the other mercenary in the room, holding the bat, and the burly man plunged the end of the club toward White Feathers' ribs. The Outlaws' leader winced from the blow, and Ta-Tu began whimpering upon seeing his leader helpless.

"We do no such thing!" Kraken demanded while pounding a fist into his hand before continuing, "we allow anyone who surrenders with honor to join us in our cause. We share the resources we plunder from those less deserving amongst ourselves. Our survival is my primary concern. I care for those who serve under the Righteous Warheads. Nothing else matters." Kraken paused and studied Ta-Tu in the corner.

"Your man here appears to cower before the sight of me. Has he no courage?" Kraken pointed a hand gently toward Ta-Tu.

"Screw you, swine," Ta-Tu muttered, gasping between heaves of breaths.

"Screw me?" Kraken said, pointing an exposed pale hand toward his chest. "No, savage. Screw you!" Kraken lifted a gun from his holster with his right hand and pointed the barrel toward Ta-Tu's head.

"Let this be a lesson in civil behavior. May your next life bring you more fortunes than this," Kraken finished as he pulled the trigger. The shot echoed in the hollow structure. Kraken straightened and looked at Ta-Tu, who hovered toward the front of his chair. Squinting, Orin could see Ta-Tu's head drip blood onto the dirt-covered ground below his chair. Ta-Tu didn't move as he leaned his head toward his legs. The steady drip continued onto the floor like the filtered water tap he saw back at the Outlaw camp.

"Oh, goodness, what a mess. Hah!" Kraken abruptly cackled as he holstered his weapon. White Feather and Orin said nothing in the small room as Ta-Tu bled on the ground.

"Well, it appears you two aren't in a talkative mood. And I am late for the evening meal. I shall return, but in the meantime," Kraken paused, and a broad grin crept over his heavy beard, "do let us know if you require any comforts." The large man laughed as he turned and walked out of the tent.

The mercenary with the bat looked at Ta-Tu and grunted. He left Ta-Tu, dripping his blood toward the ground as he turned and followed Kraken. The mercenary closed the door, and darkness engulfed the room once again. White Feather and Orin silently contemplated their fate in that dusty room as their companion crouched over dead in his chair.

The murmurs occasionally turned into cheers as the Righteous Warheads celebrated their victory from the battle outside the structure. Orin had absolutely no idea how we would get himself out of this situation. Although Liam had initially betrayed him, he still had the urge to find him and talk some sense to his brother. Orin and White Feather sat bounded in the room, trying to subside their pain with occasional grimaces and deliberate breathing exercises as the Righteous Warhead festivities raged outside. As he sat bounded helplessly in his chair, Orin could not eliminate the itch on his eyebrow. He began to fantasize about what he would do for an iced drink of whiskey.

* * *

The festivities simmered outside while the men were bounded with plastic ties and rope in the darkness. Orin was unsure how late it was as he sat facing the ground watching the shadows move across the sliver of light under the door. He began to shift his weight toward the front and back of his chair to loosen the ties that bound his wrist. The chair rose a few inches into the air on either side as Orin began to rock steadily. He could feel the straps becoming loose around his wrists as he shifted his weight. They did not cut very deep into his skin.

Orin heard a loud thud against the door, and it swung open, revealing a broad outline of a man with a bat. In his routine, he took a step toward the room's side to allow Kraken to appear with a gnarled toothy smile. The man with the bat began to lightly slap it against his palm as he stood facing the men bound to the chairs. Kraken stepped into the room, puffing on a large cigar and drinking from a flask.

Orin's mouth began to water at the thought of tasting booze. He looked down and could not feel his wineskin on the side of his waist or the metal flask against his chest.

His heartbeat quickened as he thought he lost his belongings in the conflict. He began to feel a tinge of anger, and his blood coursed through his veins as Kraken blew a puff of smoke at the men.

White Feather began a hacking cough upon breathing in the foul cigar smoke and shook in his chair against his restraints. Orin tried to steady his pulse with a few deep breaths through his nose to prevent the stinging in his throat from the cigar. Kraken lifted his foot and set it down forcefully on White Feather's thighs. White Feather winced from the pressure as he thrust his chest in a massive hacking fit.

"For the leader of a savage group, you aren't so tough," Kraken mused as he continued to puff cigar smoke toward the feathered man, "look at you," Kraken smirked as he took a swig of whiskey, "pathetic. Your 'Outlaws' are dead. I have your guns, your women as servants, oh, and your makeshift instruments. Hah! It is only you two who remain, and I am trying to define ways of dealing with you both. Your cause, forest-dwellers, is done." Kraken turned toward Orin while drinking a few more sips from the metal flask.

White Feather lifted his head to spit blood toward his battered feet. Kraken turned away from Orin and tilted his face inches from White Feather. White Feather attempted to lift his head back to avoid Kraken's hot breath.

Kraken puffed on the cigar for a moment before continuing, "see, I've heard of you as you have of me. You led your troops galivanting in the woods in search of resources. I led my people to a safe and secure location, surrounded by the region's highest peaks. And you! You come into my land and kill my people! And for what? Was it worth it?" Kraken said as he spat on White Feather and walked toward Orin.

"Who are you?" Kraken turned toward Orin. Orin continued to stare at the ground between the shadow of his knees. He was peripherally aware of the obscurities in the reflections of Righteous Warheads strolling around the fire outside. The throbbing pulse in the corner of his eye made it difficult to hold his head up, let alone maintain eye contact with the looming figure before him.

"Orin," he replied curtly as the cigar smoke swirled around his head, stinging his lungs.

"Orin, I believe this flask is yours. Now, I didn't need one see, but I always say one can never have enough hooch!" Kraken smiled his signature toothy grin as he took another swig from the flask and spat it toward the ground in front of Orin. "Didn't like that, did you? Tell me why you would storm into my camp, hmm?"

Orin tilted his head toward the side to try and avoid the toxic fumes on Kraken's breath. "I only wanted to see my brother," Orin plainly stated as he heaved for a deeper breath. White Feather began to thrust against his restraints, and Kraken waved his hand in the air toward the mercenary with the bat. The man promptly hit White Feather again in the same spot as before, which sent White Feather cringing forward as if he were practicing yoga.

"Your brother?" Kraken inquired with a sharp tone as he stood up in front of Orin, "and who is your brother? Liam?"

Orin nodded his response to the question.

"Speak up!" Kraken demanded as he sent a pale hand crashing across Orin's face.

"Let him b-," White Feather started.

"I don't remember asking you a damn thing," Kraken shouted quickly at White Feather before turning his attention back to Orin. Kraken stared at the man as he slowly puffed on his cigar, waving it frivolously around. Orin was forced to watch as Kraken slowly drank from his flask inches from his face. Orin's lips went dry and cracked as he imagined tasting the sweet, cooling liquid, which sent a familiar pleasant burning sensation down his throat.

Kraken sneered before continuing, "Liam, is it?"

Orin nodded again and said in a crackling voice, "Yes, Liam is my brother."

Kraken backed away from Orin and yelled, "LIAM!" He then began to pace between the two men bounded in their positions as he drank from the flask.

Liam, in his ragged clothing and scruffy beard, stood in the doorway facing the men. He had a spaced look across his face, and Orin wondered if he were on drugs or sedation medication. His brother, while shy, was usually a happy person with some spunk. The Liam he knew brought a smile to those around him with his energy. Liam appeared to be a shell of his former self as he gazed his eyes blankly into the dark space before them. Liam didn't say a word as he stared straight ahead toward the men bounded in the chairs.

"Liam!" Orin gasped as he struggled with his bindings holding his hands behind the chair, "Liam! It's me!"

"He's a loyal mercenary, your brother," Kraken said with a musing smirk. "In fact, if I recall, it only took a week of isolation, and he was fully committed to our cause. I believe he joined up, as it were," Kraken paused and puffed the cigar twice while wiping his squared chin with his arm, "ah, yes! It was during our raid on one of the settlements to the east of here."

Memories of their time with the Squad began to flood Orin's mind as he struggled with the bindings. Kraken tilted his head back and laughed maniacally while taking a long drag on the cigar. He turned toward White Feather and blew the smoke into his face, which sent the man into another hacking fit.

"All you have to do is pledge your loyalty to the cause. That's it," Kraken turned and pointed toward Liam, "once you become a Righteous Warhead, you become family. We look out for our own. And with as bravely as you both fought even with being outnumbered, I would gladly accept you into our ranks." Kraken took another swig of the flask before holding it toward Orin's mouth.

Before Orin could taste the liquid, Kraken pulled the canister away and waved it in the air. "What's it going to be, gentlemen?" Kraken declared as he looked back toward White Feather. Liam continued to loom in the doorway, causing the light from the campfire to cast angelic rays around his body.

"Pledge yourself to our cause, and you will live. Don't, and you will die. Whichever you choose is alright with me," Kraken finished and stood, staring at each of the men before him. Orin could smell the cigar's stench heavy in the air and the musk of the men weary from battle. Rhythmic taps from the mercenary slapping the bat against his palm split the silence within the room.

White Feather heaved deep breaths while staring down toward the ground. The noise attracted Orin, who looked over and watched as light rays reflected from a teardrop as it fell toward White Feather's thighs.

"Outlaws of the Forest have lost this battle. I will fearlessly walk with my people down the path deep among the pines. I have lived a good life all things considered. What I won't do is bow down to your whims. Your cause is nowhere near natural!" White Feather stated in between heaving sighs. White Feather then looked at Orin and slightly nodded before he said, "goodbye, Orin. Good luck on your journey. It has been a pleasure knowing you."

"Says the savage!" Kraken shouted as he took one last puff on the cigar before putting it out on White Feather's face. The man in the red and black feathers tried to wince out of reach and screamed loudly when the burning ember contacted his cheek. A searing sound was briefly heard before the glowing ember was extinguished while White Feather continued to cry.

Kraken threw the cigar remains on the ground beside the bounded Outlaw before pulling Orin's cherrywood revolver from his belt. "Look what I found, Orin. I believe this was yours. Now watch as I kill your leader." Kraken sneered as he pointed the revolver toward White Feather's head.

The old man began to protest Kraken's next actions with a few stammers as Kraken squeezed the trigger. White Feather's head bounced backward momentarily before he slumped forward in the chair. Blood began to ooze down the side of his leather skin vest. Orin could hear the constant pattering drips of the blood onto the leader's deerskin pants as the echo of the blast wore off, and ringing subsided in his ears.

"Orin, what will it be?" Kraken turned his head toward Orin as he waived the revolver handle to reflect the light rays from the doorway, "don't forget the path your brother chose. Think about it, reunited at last. That is, what you wanted all along, is it not?" Kraken grinned as he looked down at White Feather, "as you see, your friend chose the wrong path. Let's hope he finally breaks away from those forests in the next life, hmm?"

Orin stayed silent for a moment, contemplating the choices that led him to this moment. *The best way out of this situation is to play along.* He reasoned as he sat there and watched the blood slowly coagulate in a puddle near White Feather's feet. Liam stood silent in the doorway, watching the situation unfold.

"Tick, tock Orin!" Kraken exclaimed and pointed the revolver toward Orin's face, "I need an answer. I've got things to do!"

"I'll-I'll join," Orin stammered as he felt the revolver nozzle's warm metal against his forehead.

"What was that?"

"I said I'll join the Righteous Warheads." Orin hesitantly replied as he looked at his brother wearing a solemn expression in the doorway.

"Good. Very good. You will be kept in here for some time until we are convinced you will be loyal. Until then, you will be fed and provided security detail to ensure your safety," Kraken looked over at his two victims helplessly leaning forward while bounded, "I'll let you say goodbye to your friends. Oh, and Orin, welcome to the Righteous Warheads." Kraken said with his toothy smirk as he looked toward Liam in the doorway.

"Liam, come with me, I've got work for you before we call it a night," Kraken said as he headed toward the doorway. Flinging Orin's flask to the ground, Kraken leaned toward the burly mercenary and said in a low growl, "watch him close, will yah?" Kraken walked through the doorway as Liam followed. The massive man in the doorway sneered at Orin while looking over the dead Outlaws. The men left Orin in silence within the dusty room, leaving the door cracked. Orin could see the mercenary's shadow as he propped himself up on the exterior wall next to the doorway.

Sitting in the darkness, Orin listened to White Feather's steady blood drip until it stopped. He heard laughter outside, and occasional horns as the Righteous Warheads celebrated their victory. He reflected on the events of this day and how he was led to join with these mercenaries. Kraken referred to the Outlaws of the Forest as savages. Still, the way Orin saw it, the Righteous Warheads were the savages. Orin could not understand why his brother would lead him to become captured and enlisted into this group of barbarians. And the fact that Liam would remain with them all this time willingly was odd enough. His comrades who fought bravely earlier now decayed silently beside him as the Righteous Warheads festivities continued outside.

Orin reasoned he had to get out of these bindings and find his brother before it was too late. He didn't want to sit in this musky room next to his dead former comrades while contemplating his fate. Orin wasn't sure if he would receive another isolated opportunity. So, he slowly sat, pulling the plastic bindings against the chair until his wrists burned. Once he could take the pain, he tried to pull his wrists apart to wear on the material. Orin would then bring his body weight forward in the chair to place strain on the bindings. Repeating this motion, Orin remained as quiet as possible so as not to alert the mercenary outside near the door.

CHAPTER 18: ESCAPE

Orin broke free of the bindings around his wrists sometime later after a slow and laborious process. Cheers, laughter, and horn blasts, which resonated around the camp earlier, were now non-existent. Orin believed most of the Righteous Warheads retired for the evening.

The guard outside the door looked inside on occasion, but Orin could see his umbra move across the light on the floor, providing him with a cue. Whenever the mercenary would poke his head through the slit in the doorway, Orin would stop moving and appear to look down as if he were in a deep sleep. In this manner, Orin was able to snap the bindings and loosen the ropes wrapped around his torso.

Orin waited until the guard finished checking in on him again as he knew the next check wouldn't be for several minutes. He silently used his hands to pull the rope up and over him while slipping out from the bindings. As he crouched low, he heard his knees pop from being seated for an extended period. Orin waited and breathed slowly to see if the mercenary outside would check to see the sound source.

Convinced he was in the clear, he continued to crawl toward Ta-Tu in the corner. Ta-Tu kept a knife on the inside of his deerskin pants. Orin felt the dead man's clothing and touched the metal underneath the leather. His heartbeat quickened as he reached across the man and dislodged the knife by the handle, barely poking from the pants' waistline. Orin whispered a quick thanks to the dead man and proceeded to crawl toward the entryway.

Orin crept along the wall gradually to avoid alerting the man standing inches away on the other side of the wooden barrier. He peered through the small slit in the crack of the door at the mercenary on the other side. The man propped himself with one leg on the building and the other firmly planted on the ground. Orin could not fully see the man's body but saw his hands in a crossed position.

If I act quickly, I can kill him before he can draw his weapon or alert the others, Orin considered as he held the handle of Ta-Tu's blade firmly in the palm of his hand. Orin took hold of the edge and pulled the door open while moving outside. Orin looked around and saw the campfire turned into glowing charcoals. He noticed a few men sleeping on the ground near the smoldering flames and turned his attention toward the mercenary.

Upon noticing Orin's escape, the mercenary stood up and reached for his bat leaning against the wall. Orin plunged forward with the sharp of his knife, pointed toward the man's head. He felt a slightly hollowed thud as he sunk the blade deep into the man's neck. The mercenary's eyes widen as a gurgle escaped his opened mouth. His tongue dangled toward his chin as the burly man sank to his knees. Orin removed the blade and drove it again deep into the man's eye socket. The man let out a few final croaks as he fell backward and rested leaning against the exterior wall of the clapboard shack.

Orin removed the blade from the eye and wiped it off on the pants of the dead man. He quickly searched his pockets for anything of value. The rugged mercenary had a switchblade and a silver pocket watch. Orin pocketed both before reaching back into the tent and retrieving the flask Kraken threw on the ground earlier. Although it was emptied, Orin stuffed the container into his back pocket for use later. His mouth watered at the prospect of tasting sweet whiskey.

Orin moved toward the back end of a neighboring wooden structure remaining in the shade of the evening. The moon was concealed by heavy blankets of clouds. Orin kept his head low as he crept behind several of the surrounding buildings. He tried to peek over the various crates and barrels toward the center of the camp to gather intel on the layout.

After scanning from his secluded location, he spotted Liam talking to another mercenary while posted outside a large oval-shaped canvas tent. Lit torches surrounded the tent, indicating it belonged to someone of importance among the Righteous Warheads. *Kraken!* Orin felt a wave of relief wash over him at the sight of his brother in the late night. *Now to figure out a way to get over to him without drawing attention.*

Most of the Righteous Warhead members were lying on the ground or against various structures within the camp. Orin heard the occasional snores and grunts coming from inside the structures he crouched behind. Orin deliberately made his way across the rocky ground to avoid making too much noise. He ducked behind various crates and wagons while also using multiple pockets of the prickly brush to his advantage. Orin was thankful for the overcast sky producing limited visibility across the camp, which made his journey uneventful toward Kraken's tent.

Upon reaching the back of the canvas tent, Orin listened for any sounds. He heard mumbling coming from the front of the tent where he last saw his brother. Crickets played their melancholy melodies off into the distance, and Orin listened to the occasional laughter from across the camp. He kept his head low as he peered around the side of the tent toward the entrance. To his right were wagons, which were empty and thus not a threat.

The leader's tent was positioned in a manner overlooking the camp toward Orin's left. So, he decided stealth was the better option. *The last thing I need is to alert these mercenaries about my whereabouts. They would salivate at a chance to torture a captive from the battle,* Orin considered. He focused his attention on his brother and the other mercenary guarding Kraken's quarters.

The men stood on both sides of the door, facing out toward the camp in the darkness. They ceased talking as Orin held his knife at the ready in his hand. Liam stood closer to Orin with the other mercenary on the opposite side of the entryway. Orin could not approach the other side of this tent because it would expose him to the camp. If a mercenary looks in the tent's direction, they'd see Orin even in the cover of darkness.

Orin said a quick prayer under his breath. He tried to work up the courage to silence these men to avoid alerting the others without hurting his brother. As he peeked from around the tent's corner, he decided he would quickly dispatch the mercenary while trying to convince his brother to follow him.

Orin deeply exhaled as he scanned his eyes across the camp to ensure he was clear to advance. Crouching low, Orin scurried toward Liam and pushed his head against the wall while cupping his mouth. Liam looked at Orin with a wide-eyed expression and tried to struggle against his older brother's grip. Orin knew he had to knock his brother out; otherwise, he would alert others to his position. Orin quickly took the handle of his knife and hit Liam's head twice with great force. Liam's eyes rolled up into his skull, and he slumped down toward the ground.

The other mercenary shouted in surprise as he saw Liam fall and began to ready his rifle toward Orin. Orin promptly moved in and tackled the man to the soil, placing his hand tightly over his mouth while pinching his nose. The man tried to breathe and started to turn a deep shade of purple as he squirmed underneath Orin. Orin lifted his arm with the knife closer to the man's face as he fended off the assault by frantically swinging his hands. The man kicked a couple of rocks down the small rise alongside the camp, which sent them skittering down toward the central campfire.

Orin jabbed his knee into the man's groin, which sent him gasping for breath. The man's arm went limp for a moment. This brief lapse allowed Orin to bring the knife stabbing toward the man's shoulder and upper chest near his heart. The man fought against Orin's blows for a few seconds before slackening his limbs and resting facing toward the cloudy sky.

Convinced the man was dead after stabbing him twice more, Orin looked toward his brother, who was knocked out and placed limply against the canvas tent. Orin diverted over to his brother to ensure he still had a pulse. He felt a light rhythmic beating on the side of his neck with his fingers.

Orin arose to hear a shuffling sound from within the tent, followed by a few snorts. Orin knew he did not have time to cover his tracks if Kraken were to step outside. He decided to try and silence Kraken. Kraken was the one who initially brought the brothers into this situation by decimating the Squad of Liberty. And now, the Righteous Warheads had decimated yet another group, the Outlaws of the Forest. He wanted nothing more than to bring his fury and revenge upon Kraken. Orin began to shake as he thought about how many innocent lives and those dearest to him were lost because of this man sleeping yards away.

As he crouched near the door listening for signs Kraken heading toward the entryway, Orin thought about obtaining the rifle from the dead mercenary near his feet. After a brief moment, he thought better of it. Alerting others to his location, even if it meant certain death for Kraken, would hinder his chance of getting Liam out of camp safely. Orin continued to hear various noises and shuffling coming from within the tent and figured Kraken was moving around.

Orin reasoned it was only a matter of time before Kraken walked out of his tent and saw his guards disabled on the ground. Orin knew he had to promptly act if he were going to get out of this campsite alive with his brother. He drew the flap to the side and stepped into the entryway of Kraken's tent.

A bed was located at the far end of the tent from the entryway. Orin noticed a table with a torn geographical map sprawled out held down with multiple metallic objects. Candles casually bounced their light in every edge of the room. Orin could see from the candlelight that Kraken laid on his back, actively rubbing his brow with his fingers. Orin firmly held his knife with the blade toward his target as he crept across the tent to the bed.

As Orin made his way toward Kraken, he saw his wineskin and bag against an end table near the bed. The wineskin appeared nearly as full as when Orin last saw it. His heart began to beat faster in anticipation as he closed in on Kraken. He could almost taste the delicious booze now and wanted to hurry and kill this man so he could have his alcohol.

Kraken continued rubbing his forehead with an index finger and thumb in slow motions. Kraken laid still on the bed with his eyes closed. Orin approached carefully to reduce the noise his boots made on the rocky surface. As he continued to take each step, his thoughts turned toward Atticus and his fellow members of the Squad. Killing Kraken would mean revenging his friends and mentor. Orin's palms and neck began to emanate perspiration as he edged closer to the bed.

Orin could smell the musk of Kraken while drawing closer. As he closed in on the Kraken, Orin lifted his blade and held his arm in a position with the sharp edge aimed toward Kraken's neck. Orin drew a deep breath when he was a few feet away.

As he worked up the resolution, he lunged forward toward Kraken. Kraken opened his eyes and caught Orin's arm as the blade stopped inches from his jugular vein. Kraken deeply growled while spittle flew from his gritted teeth as he held Orin's wrist at a distance. Orin felt a dull pain in his right side as he was met with Kraken's knee to his ribs. He broke from Kraken's hold and fell back a couple feet before recomposing himself.

Orin was surprised at the man's sudden strength when he appeared to be nursing a head injury seconds earlier. Orin's heart pounded through his chest as he thought about his next move. Kraken stood up from the bed and bounded through the air toward Orin. Orin slashed with the knife and stopped the assault momentarily as Kraken received a gashing wound across his forearm.

Kraken stumbled back and held his arm while grinning at Orin. "You little shit. The audacity, you must attack me in my own tent! After I provided you with a chance? With hospitality? Surely Ruth wasn't all that bad of company, was he?"

"Ruth, your mercenary?" Orin questioned between heaving breaths while holding the sharp end of his knife toward his enemy, "he's dead. Killed him with this blade, like I'll do you," Orin growled as he lurched toward Kraken with all his might.

The men fell back onto the bed, and Orin heard a snap as Kraken's back hit the mattress's side. Orin twisted his body to avoid Kraken's grasp as he tried stabbing the man below him. Kraken turned his body, and the blade poked him repeatedly, making little cuts along his arms. Orin seized the opportunity to grab Kraken's face with his other hand and start gouging his eye. Kraken howled as he sent a foot flying toward Orin's groin.

Orin gasped for air as the wind rushed from his lungs. He felt a sharp pain as his arm was ripped back by Kraken's firm grasp. Kraken sent another heel kick with his barefoot toward Orin's chest, which propelled him stumbling backward toward the ground. In the struggle, he lost his grip on the knife, which was sent clanging against the rocky surface. Kraken let out a shrill shriek as he scrambled around Orin to find a weapon of his own.

Orin took this moment to try and crawl across the stones toward his knife. He felt an intoxicating punch to the side of his face, and he was sent off his balance, crashing toward the ground. Orin was dazed, and the room started to tilt and spin in all directions while maintaining focus on Kraken. A foot connected with Orin's jaw, and he rolled a few feet to try and avoid the incoming blows. Spitting on the ground, Orin felt two teeth fall from his mouth. A string of saliva stretched from a swollen lip and puddled near a rock crevice. Orin spat again, wiping his mouth and scrambled to his knees as Kraken bounded on him and began punching him with closed fists.

Orin brought his arms closer to his torso to protect himself as Kraken frantically swung his fists from left and right. Orin heard him yelling something but couldn't make out what he said above the ringing in his ears. Orin felt light-headed, and the room spun as he received blows from Kraken's pounding fists. A fist connected with Orin's eye, and he was sent sprawling toward the end-table near his backpack. As he fell, his cherrywood revolver sitting on the end-table caught his eye.

Kraken noticed this gaze and quickly reached for the weapon. Orin kicked Kraken's knee, and he heard a loud crack as the man was sent in two directions toward the Earth. The joint in his knee popped, and Kraken's bone snapped through the skin of his thigh. He screamed in agony, and Orin's heart pounded as he reached for his knife on the ground. Orin picked up the blade and sent the point straight down toward Kraken's chest as the man laid nursing his jutting leg bone. Kraken let out a silent gasp of air as the knife crunched into his chest.

Orin watched as Kraken slunk back toward the ground, and his breathing relaxed. Orin figured this was his chance to get out of camp as he began to gather his backpack and tied the wineskin to his belt. After tucking the revolver into his pants, he crawled out of the entryway and turned toward his brother.

The camp was mostly silent, with a few low voices and snoring heard in several tents. Orin turned toward Liam and tapped him on the face with an open palm. Liam breathed deeply but remained motionless. Orin moved quickly to wrap his brother's arms around his body as he hoisted him over his shoulder.

Orin headed southwest in the direction of a significant gap in the wooden post parameter. He remembered seeing some of the Outlaws in Himlick's group, making their way through the opening during the battle. Orin deliberated each step in his passage toward the gap in the fence. Whenever possible, he chose to keep low behind crates, barrels, and structures.

Once safe near a small lake on the far side of the campsite, Orin deeply sighed while dropping Liam on the rocks next to the water. Orin began slapping his hand hard across his brother's face to awaken him. Liam did not respond, and so Orin scooped up water in the cup of his hand and splashed it across Liam. His brother awoke to sputter as the chilly ridge flurry hammered down from the neighboring peaks.

They were safe now as Orin couldn't hear even the faintest snore or voice in the distance. He held a hand firmly under Liam's chin to steady his face as he regained consciousness. Liam studied his brother's face while his eyes and mouth widened. Orin quickly placed a hand over Liam's mouth and tried quieting him.

"Liam, it's me! Your brother!"

Liam squirmed from Orin's grasp as he regained his awareness. Orin held his brother firmly against the rocks and again pleaded with his brother. Liam gasped and sputtered water from his lips as he twisted his body.

"Liam! Listen! It's me, Orin! What has gotten into you?" Orin questioned crying as he struggled with his brother. He slapped Liam again on the side of the face in frustration as he said, "snap out of it! You're better than this!"

"Krak-!" Liam began shouting as he arched his back to break Orin's grasp.

"No, Liam! Kraken is dead!" Orin hissed as he held his palm over his brother's mouth, "Kraken is dead, and you are not a Righteous Warhead." Orin slapped his brother again, "you are a member of the Squad. Wake up, Liam!"

Liam laid on the ground and stared up at Orin while panting for breath. "Orin?" Liam mumbled through Orin's hand, covering his face.

Orin smiled and shook his head as he released his clutch on his brother. "Yes, Liam. It's me. You're safe now, buddy." He gave Liam a long grasping hug as they lay on the far end of the shallow lake near the camp's outskirts.

As the brothers enjoyed their reuniting embrace, they heard voices began to shout in the distance toward the center of the camp. Orin grabbed his brother by the arm and pulled him to his feet, "can you walk?"

"Yes, I can manage," Liam replied.

"Let's get the hell out of here and find your utopia!" Orin smiled as he held his brother by the arm and led him through the wooden posts' opening. The men crawled up the southwestern slope overlooking the campsite. Orin kept glancing back into the camp as they climbed. He heard periodic shouting rise above the howling mountain wind that sailed down the ridge. The men continued at a steady pace, stumbling every so often while holding onto one another for support.

Orin shifted the rifle's weight and backpack as the men made their way up the slope's steep section. Orin found the rocky precipice easier to traverse when he wasn't getting shot at by rifles and mortars. Still, the men stumbled periodically in the cloudy night as there was minimal visibility. As Orin looked back toward the camp, he could see torchlight flickering and movement about the grounds. He had no doubt they would know of his crimes and come looking for him quickly.

"Let's go, Liam," Orin encouraging said. He nudged his brother's shoulder, progressing up the slope. He said, "we're almost to the ridge," Orin pointed toward the ridgeline above them. They were making steady progress, and each step brought the dark horizontal silhouette of a line closer.

When they reached the ridgeline without being spotted by the Righteous Warheads, the brothers took a moment to rest. Orin stared back down at the camp. Torchlight bounced near the structure where Orin was initially being held with Ta-Tu and White Feather. He could see the light flickering near Kraken's tent and figured they must now realize what has happened. Occasional shouts were heard above the wind. Orin sat against a nearby boulder and took a long drink from his wineskin.

"It's good to see you again, Liam," he said as he offered the wineskin.

Liam took the wineskin and drank deep gulps from the pouch. Liam squeezed the bag encouraging the honeyed whiskey to pour down his throat.

"Easy on that brother, or you'll end up like me," Orin joked as he took the wineskin back and drank. His head began to feel dizzy again, but the pounding headache subsided as he swallowed the booze.

"Where should we go now?" Liam inquired as he giggled from the alcohol spell. He swirled his hands across the horizon, indicating he was open to an adventure.

"I have an idea."

"You mean?" Liam asked.

Orin nodded his head. "I've been thinking we take a trip deeper into the mountains and try to find this utopia."

A broad smile flashed across Liam's face as Orin mentioned utopia. "Let's do it. We need to get out of here while we still can."

"Agreed," Orin said as he stood up and gave Liam another embracing hug. "It's good to see you again, brother."

"You too, Orin," Liam answered.

CHAPTER 19: UTOPIA

The brothers wandered through the night westbound to create distance between themselves and the Righteous Warheads. They traversed ridges and hiked down rocky precipice pathways leading through clearings and valleys beyond. As the sun broke the eastern horizon, the men stopped for a short rest near the edge of a forest.

Lush green pine needles provided a thick canopy from the sun rays piercing over the ridgelines. Brown dead needles littered the forest floor. Orin squinted through his swollen eye and saw several rodents running among the brush, between the trees. A few birds chirped as the sun continued to rise in the east.

A flurry pushed the men to continue hiking through the night, but could not cut through the dense forest of pine trees. Orin stirred a meager fire as the men ate from a can of string beans and pickled potatoes. They both sat on the same rotting log next to the campfire and warmed their numbed limbs. The men endured relentless bone piercing winds throughout the twilight hours.

"So, what happened back at the Squad camp before it was attacked?" Orin asked as he gulped down a potato ball. The saltiness of the potato made Orin's face cringe as he chewed through the mushy texture.

Liam hesitated before responding, and Orin could see his brother staring at a twig on the ground. Orin knew this look; it was the look Liam wore while spiraling down a vortex of thought and memory.

Orin chewed softly as each bite sent a dull pain along his bruised cheek before sipping from his wineskin. As the bitter liquid flowed down his throat, Orin flashed a grin toward his brother and smacked his lips.

"Here, by the looks of it, you could use another drink," Orin said as he tossed the wineskin toward his brother.

A muffled thud was heard as the container hit Liam in the thigh and fell toward the ground. The flask made clunking noises as the whiskey spilled onto the pine needles. Liam stumbled, trying to reach the container and shaking, struggled to lift it to his lips.

"Are you okay?" Orin asked with his eyebrows furrowed in a concerned expression as he tilted his head, "do you need help?"

"I'm fine, I'm fine." Liam softly repeated as he held his palm toward Orin to fend off any inquiry. Orin watched his brother fumble for a moment with the wineskin's lip before taking several long sips of the alcohol. Using his fingers, he wiped off the dripping liquid from the corners of his mouth and handed the whiskey back to Orin.

"Liam, I know what they did was messed up. What I had to go through..." Orin took a swig from the booze as Liam shifted his gaze. He was starting to feel a buzz from the liquor, and his thoughts became cloudy. Orin's throbbing eye where Kraken had smashed him hours before was subsiding with every drop of drink.

"It was a mess, Orin." Liam's eyes teared up as his body shivered while sitting on the log. Orin placed his hand on Liam's faded jeans and noticed his brother's eyes looked different. They appeared hardened and tiny cracks formed in the corners when he spoke. Liam's tattered brown shirt collected booze dripping from his thick mangy beard.

"I remember standing in the field, and I saw Kraken riding over the plains toward the east. He wore that awful black trench coat towering down from his black steed. The smoke made it difficult to see much of anything. Still, I do remember seeing him as clear as day," Liam paused as a shiver ran across his shoulders, "aside from the burning in my shoulder, that's the last thing I remember before the blast."

Orin gave an understanding look toward his brother as he said, "that's what knocked me out. I remember seeing you in the field and then darkness. I woke up in the rain after the battle." He drank from the wineskin feeling the warm buzz wash over his body, temporarily removing any concerns he had with the world. His pain and headache had nearly subsided as he sat on the log next to his brother.

"So, you were there. I figured you missed the battle as you were out hunting," Liam paused for a moment, "I was isolated from the group for a long time. They forced me to march chained to the back of the caravan as they raided ruins and settlements along and through the foothills."

"What happened when they took you?"

"I was brought to the camp we escaped within a week or so, the days seem to blend together. I was kept with a couple other Squad members who were eventually shot for insubordination or some sort." Liam began to slowly breathe as he reflected on his memories with the Righteous Warheads. Orin handed him the wineskin, and he took a swig before continuing, "I saw them hurt innocent people, Orin. Including women and children without regard. They are bad, bad people only out for themselves. And those horns, Orin. Always with those damn horns!"

"What's the deal with the horns, anyways? Intimidation?"

Liam shook his head and shrugged his shoulders. "I don't really know why they blow the horns. I do recall they only use them when an attack is imminent, though. Probably a form of intimidation, and those mercenaries get off on scaring the living shit out of settlers."

"I know," Orin said as a shiver coursed through his spine, "Kraken is dead, though. I stuck the knife right through his chest." Orin paused for a moment to reflect on his last encounter with Kraken. He hadn't confirmed if Kraken was deceased or not. *I stabbed him in his chest, so he must be dead, right? Either way doesn't matter. We're safe and peaks away from their camp,* Orin reflected on the fight while looking through the trees toward the east.

"What did they have you do?" Orin inquired as branches rustled overhead in the wind. Birds in the trees grew louder in their chatter as their homes were shaken in the soft breeze. A sickly chipmunk with greenish-grey patchy fur darted out and hissed in the direction of the men before chittering as it skipped away.

Liam stared in the direction of the creature and took another swig of spirits before responding, "Odd jobs here and there. Once my arm was healed from the gunshot wound, I was promoted quickly through their ranks, and eventually, Kraken trusted me with his post. He thought I was one of the 'righteous ones' as he liked to call his most devout followers."

"Why did you join Kraken's ranks if you couldn't stand his cause?" Orin asked in a suspicious tone.

Liam shot Orin a stern look and furrowed his eyebrows while saying, "what choice did I have in the matter? Was I alone? You weren't there. The Squad members I was with were annihilated. What choice did I have in the matter," Liam repeated as his face became beet red, "they would have killed me, too." Liam softly whispered as tears began to fall on his frayed jeans.

Orin winced through the pain in his ribs as he squeezed his hand over Liam's knee and brought him closer for an embracing hug. He smelled his brother's smoke-scented locks and felt tiny twigs stuck in his hair, scraping his face as he held Liam on the log. They sat for several moments as Liam quietly cried and drank more of the booze.

Something was bothering Orin since he found his brother inside the camp. "Liam," he started, "why did you turn me into Kraken when we found each other behind the wagon?" Orin pulled away from his brother and held his shoulders at a distance to see Liam's face for a response.

Liam's frown and droopy eyes turned straight and neutral as he looked back at Orin. His green eyes reflected sunlight from the teardrops clinging in the corners. Orin felt sorry for his brother at that moment while he awaited his response.

"I didn't want to," Liam began with a quivering voice, "believe me. I didn't want to." Liam started to slowly shake his head as he looked toward the fire. "I was surprised to see you. And to be honest, I wasn't sure if it was you," Liam took another swig, "but I saw Kraken on his steed heading in our direction while you were standing there. I had to do something, or he would have shot us both."

Orin frowned as he heard his brother's reasoning before snatching the wineskin from his hand and taking several gulps of the drink. His brother's reason was sensible. If

Kraken knew they were brothers reuniting to flee, he would have killed them both on the spot.

"But when I was tied in the room…" Orin trailed off as he took another sip while looking at his brother from the corner of his eye.

"I didn't want to see you like that, but there was nothing I could do. The mercenary guarding you was a mean bastard. I once saw him smash a man's skull flat with the end of that bat. Once I saw you, I knew you would get out alive. You have that tenacity about you," Liam smirked as he continued, "when I saw you again last night outside Kraken's tent, I didn't think that'd be you, and I was surprised. I thought some more of those Outlaws snuck up on the camp. We were taking potshots at all hours from the ridgeline for a week from those forest dwellers."

Orin was content with Liam's explanation and didn't think his brother had any malicious intentions. Orin patted Liam on his back as he took another drink from the leather bag. The sun leisurely crept its way toward the center of the sky as the men rested on the log, stoking the fire with a small stick.

"It's all good, Liam."

"You know, you better lay off that stuff," Liam said with a short chuckle as he pointed a feeble finger toward the wineskin.

"Says you," Orin gruffly replied, taking another swig from the wineskin. He was thankful for the pristine *Turnerburg's Distilled Whiskey* bottle, which still remained within his bag. Orin planned to share it with his brother once they found utopia or even if they didn't as he still had his doubts. The men silently sat as Orin reflected on White Feather, claiming supply runners spoke of a strange city where crops grow lush, and the rains do not produce boils on the skin to the west. *It was worth checking out*, Orin assured himself as he sat on the log beside his brother deep in the woods nestled between two grandiose peaks.

"What happened to you between the first battle and your heroic rescue of me?" Liam asked, rubbing the last of the tears from his eyes.

"That, my brother is a very long story," Orin said, smiling, "come on, we better get a move on. We don't want anybody tracking us down." The men stood up and began packing their items for their journey west. They planned to climb the next ridge and scout their surroundings for signs of the utopia and potential threats.

* * *

The brothers looked toward the ridgeline towering above them toward the west. Behind them, they left the wooded thickets tucked in a valley between two towering peaks. They were walking for nearly an entire day as twilight began to settle across the land.

A brisk wind wafted down from the northern ridges, sweeping through the valley. The pine trees rustled in the breeze, and various birds engaged in their mating calls. Orin's hair floated high in the wind above his shoulders as he faced toward the ridge above them.

After a moment of reprieve and another drink, they continued climbing over the numerous stones and slabs. Slow but steady progress was made on that slope as the brothers scrambled toward the top of a ridge.

"You know the Outlaws weren't bad people," Orin said between heaving breaths and continued climbing, "at least they weren't like the freak cultists I met."

"Oh yeah?" Liam questioned.

"Yeah. The cultists worshiped their psyche or some type of mental energy. They thought by recognizing and encouraging their dark tendencies, they were brought closer to a higher form of being. Something about transcending consciousness through their shadow tendencies."

"Sounds interesting."

"I'd figured you might like that weird shit. But you wouldn't like it so much if you knew those cultists wanted to forcibly enlist me in their cause to capture settlers for their entertainment."

"What did they do with them?"

"They sacrificed them, I believe. I saw a strange ritual room covered in blood." Orin shivered as he climbed over a large boulder in their path. "What did they call themselves...?" Orin thought for a moment as he slid a few feet down the slope on skittering pebbles. "Ah, Penumbra, it was," Orin shouted in excitement upon his sudden recollection.

"Penumbra?" Liam questioned as he stumbled over a smaller boulder.

"Yes, Penumbra. A strange bunch."

"What else did you do on your adventure?"

The air gradually became thinner as the men climbed, and talking was sapping more energy. Orin took a swig from his wineskin as they stopped for a moment to catch their breath. The wind whistled in from the north ridges down upon the brothers standing on the steep slope.

"I met this quack of a freak show operator," Orin bluntly stated as he swallowed another drink.

Liam lifted his eyebrows curiously in anticipation of his brother's story. "Do tell," he encouraged Orin.

"He had a chicken, which was a sight to see. He also had these twin girls who could contort themselves into unbelievable positions with their bodies. It was all good until he confessed one drunken evening at a tavern in Ádyto that he stole those girls from their parents."

"You've been to Ádyto?" Liam asked in a high-pitched tone.

"Yes, I've been there on a couple of occasions. Jerry, the bartender, interesting fellow," Orin chuckled, "I caught up with the freak show merchant who still had the twins while traveling with the Outlaws. I beat him to a bloody pulp, and I don't know what of the twins." Orin frowned as he stared at a nearby rock, slowly sipping from the wineskin.

"I'm afraid I made a bad decision in beating that man. I am not sure if those twins were better off for it. Especially now that the Outlaws are gone." Orin's voice trailed off in the wind as he stared into the trees below them.

"Were you drunk at the time?"

"No, I wasn't," Orin replied curtly and took a slight offense at the assumption. He drank often, but he wasn't drunk every time he made a poor decision either. Besides, he didn't see how his drinking was affecting anything involving beating Two-Bit for forcing Mao and Tao into his freak show.

The men finished their snacks and set their sights on the ridge overhead. Orin's legs ached from walking in the last week. Still, he knew that setting distance between themselves and the Righteous Warheads was the best decision. If they found a utopia in the process, even better.

The ridge loomed a hundred paces overhead as the moon crept over the eastern horizon. An eerie reddish-yellow haze radiated from its surface and splashed onto the landscape below. Orin noticed the pine tree tops emanating a touch of orange as they soaked in the moonlight.

As the men reached the upper ridgeline, Liam gasped and stood in his tracks. He looked back at Orin and eagerly motioned to climb the remaining few paces toward his position. Liam heaved with every breath, and his eyes widened while standing on the ridge. Orin complied as he placed his step to climb over the remaining boulders onto the ridgeline. Orin looked toward the west, and his breath rushed from his lungs as he beheld the sights below.

A soft orange glow radiated from a geodesic dome-like shield. Its spherical shape was luminously transparent. It allowed Orin to see buildings made from granite and quartz with towering columns raised tens of feet from the surface. Hovering electronic boxes floated in the air between the buildings, scanning with a beam toward the ground. These buildings covered the entire expanse reaching miles toward the other side of the valley.

Liam rapidly tapped Orin on the shoulder as he pointed down toward a path, which leads to a box structure with double doors. The doors appeared to lead to a vestibule entrance before allowing entry into the central city. Liam excitedly bounced as he stood on the ridge facing the city.

A bird flew into the transparent shield, and Orin heard a thud before watching it fall hundreds of feet back to the Earth. *Whatever covered this city was not letting anything in through the air*, Orin sighed as he scanned the vast parameter.

"You think they will allow us entry?" Orin inquired with a heavy skepticism in his tone.

"I don't see why they wouldn't. We're two strong, capable men, well, after you get healed, that is," Liam laughed as he slapped his hand against Orin's back, "don't be so afraid, brother. We found it!"

"Yeah, you found it," Orin said in bewilderment. Along with the buildings, he could see intricate carvings and golden engravements spiraling down the various columns. From this distance, Orin saw small figures milling about among the buildings as if they were ants. The wind rushed around the men in heavy gusts that caused Orin to stumble a couple steps from where he stood.

Standing on the mountainside, the men embraced as they looked down toward the glorious city below them. Orin removed the bottle of *Turnerburg's Distilled Whiskey* from his backpack and held it up for his brother to inspect.

"Where'd you get that?"

"A gift from the freak show merchant I told you about."

"You didn't steal it from him, did you?"

"No! Certainly not. I earned this for guarding his wagon and ensuring he received payment one evening for a show." Orin retorted as he cracked open the shining bottle.

The moonlight bounced elegantly from the caramel liquid inside the clear glass bottle. Orin drank two long swallows before handing the bottle to his brother.

The men drank in celebration of their escaping the clutches of Kraken and his Righteous Warheads. They drank to the adventures they had and being reunited. The brothers swallowed down whiskey for those who hadn't made it on the journey.

Orin looked down toward the tree-line in the direction they came. The moonlight cast its ocherous glow across the tops of the pines. An obscuration of a man darted among the trees a couple hundred measures away. Orin squinted his eyes and rubbed them with his hands. *Was I hallucinating from the drink? Maybe it was the lack of sleep?* Orin saw another outline of a figure passing among the trees near the same position. His heart began to speed up, and his knees started to quiver as he stood looking into those trees, afraid of what he might see. *We are so close to utopia!*

A loud horn blast emanated from the tree-line to the east. Birds scattered into the midnight sky. Orin looked over to Liam, who was staring down into the trees wide-eyed and pale. He looked like he wet himself as he stood shaking on the ridge.

After a brief pause, another shrill blast from a horn echoed through the night.

* * *

www.ingramcontent.com/pod-product-compliance
Lightning Source LLC
Chambersburg PA
CBHW030655260626
47157CB00007B/2668